THE PRISONER'S KEY

GLASS AND STEELE, #8

C.J. ARCHER

CHAPTER 1

LONDON, AUTUMN 1890

"Tell her she can't have it, India," Miss Glass said from the sideboard where she poured tea. No, not Miss Glass. She was Aunt Letitia to me now that I was Matt's wife.

Matt's wife, Aunt Letitia…I still wasn't used to it after two weeks, but at least I no longer giggled when someone referred to me as Mrs. Glass.

I didn't have time to answer Aunt Letitia before Willie snapped, "Tell Letty it ain't up to her. Your old bedroom should go to me, India."

Aunt Letitia set the teapot down on the sideboard with a thud. She rarely joined us for breakfast, but today was a special occasion, the first day Matt and I were back. However, I was beginning to think she hadn't joined us to talk about our honeymoon but rather to ensure Willie didn't get in first with her request.

Aunt Letitia rounded on Willie with a ferocious glare that lost much of its effect in the dainty way she held the teacup and the frailty of the woman herself. "It *should* go to you? I disagree, as does India. Do not appeal to Matthew," she added when Willie turned to him.

Matt picked up the newspaper that Bristow had set beside his place. He smirked at me before hiding his face behind it.

"Why me and not Matt?" I asked.

"You're the mistress of the house," Aunt Letitia said as she sat with her teacup. "The allocation of rooms is up to you, now."

"Is this why you didn't sort it out while we were away? Because you couldn't agree?"

Aunt Letitia sipped her tea. Willie stabbed a sausage with her fork and pointed it at the elderly woman opposite. "I moved my things in, then not a minute later, she got Fossett to move 'em back. He refused to move 'em again, so I slept in there anyway so *she* can't get her way."

"I outrank you," Aunt Letitia said simply. "Of course the staff listen to me."

"Pig swill! You're Matt's aunt, and I'm his cousin. We're equal."

Aunt Letitia clicked her tongue then muttered, "Americans," into her teacup.

Matt flipped the top of the newspaper down and glared at his aunt then at Willie. "May India and I eat our first breakfast at home together without listening to you two squabbling?"

"This ain't your first breakfast as man and wife here," Willie said. "Just the first after your honeymoon."

His glare darkened, and I thought it best to step in before he was forced to choose between his aunt and cousin. Besides, Aunt Letitia was right, and it was now my duty as mistress of the house to make decisions about room allocations. Matt had to pay for the roof over our head, and every piece of furniture in it, as well as the servants' salaries. Frankly, he had the easier job.

"Why do you want my old room anyway?" I asked his aunt. "Yours is larger."

"I don't want it for me," she said with a sanctimonious air. "It's for Cyclops. He's been sharing with Duke, but now that your old room has become free, India, they no longer have to."

Cyclops and Duke arrived at that precise moment. They must have heard their names, because they both sighed and headed for the covered platters of food at the sideboard with stooped shoulders. This was a disagreement that had been going on for a while then, perhaps the entire two weeks of our absence.

"Why can't Willie move into my old room and Cyclops move into hers?" I asked. "Then all three can have their own space. There, problem solved."

"Nope," Willie said around her mouthful of toast. "Letty says Cyclops should have the bigger room. He's her favorite."

Cyclops gave her a smug look.

"He is not," Aunt Letitia said. "I like Duke equally well."

Duke gave Willie a smug look too. She rolled her eyes at both men.

"Cyclops is the biggest," Aunt Letitia went on. "He ought to have the bigger room."

Willie wiped bacon grease off her lower lip with the back of her hand. "She's calling you fat, Cyclops."

Cyclops merely grunted a laugh but ever-so-slightly sucked in his stomach as he pulled out a chair at the table.

Aunt Letitia turned to me. "Well? What have you decided?"

"I...I need more time." I bit into my slice of toast and chewed slowly.

Matt folded the newspaper and set it down. His lips were flat but his eyes twinkled. "More coffee, India, or would you rather escape?"

I narrowed my gaze. "You find this amusing."

"Infinitely."

"You're supposed to be on my side now that we're husband and wife."

"I am on your side," he said as he refilled our coffee cups

at the sideboard. "I support whatever choice you make in this regard, and all others."

The sickening thought that was never far away these past few weeks resurfaced. Would he support my decision to use Lord Coyle's information to blackmail Lord Cox into marrying Patience Glass, thereby freeing Matt to marry me? He knew Lord Coyle could help us, yet he'd refused the offered information, knowing it would put me in his lordship's debt. He didn't know I'd done precisely that. He'd be hurt if he found out. Hurt and furious.

I tried to push the memory of my betrayal aside, only to fail. I attempted a smile instead.

Matt tilted his head to the side as he handed me back the cup. "You look pale. Are you all right?"

I didn't have a chance to tell him I was fine, because Aunt Letitia gasped loudly and almost dropped her teacup. "She's with child!"

Everyone stared at me. Matt blinked rapidly, his aunt clapped her hands in delight, and Willie looked horrified.

"I'm not," I said with certainty. It was one rumor I wanted to suppress before it grew legs.

"It's too soon to know for sure," Aunt Letitia said, picking up her teacup.

Willie shoved an entire rasher of bacon into her mouth. "Leave her be, Letty," she managed to say.

"How many times have I asked you to chew with your mouth closed? You weren't brought up by animals."

"You haven't met my ma."

Cyclops chuckled, only to stop suddenly upon a stern look from Aunt Letitia.

Duke leaned forward and lowered his voice. "They've spent too long together. But you're back now, India, and we can fix up the shop. That'll give everyone something to do."

I'd told Catherine and Ronnie Mason to move into my father's old shop while I was away, but they insisted on waiting until the paperwork was complete. The leasing agreement had been finalized during our absence by our lawyer, and Cyclops had informed me that Catherine and Ronnie were ready to start cleaning the shop today. Everything had an inch of dust covering it, and we also had to remove any watch and clock pieces from the premises into storage. The Watchmaker's Guild had changed their rules to ensure no member could use parts handled by a magician. It was a clause written specifically to prevent Ronnie, their newest member, from purchasing parts cheaply from me. The guild's master, Mr. Abercrombie, had hoped it would prevent them from setting up shop altogether, as a way of getting back at me, but Matt had extended the Mason siblings a loan instead. The look on Abercrombie's face when we'd told him at our wedding had made the day even more memorable.

Matt rested his hand on my shoulder. I gave it a reassuring squeeze that must have satisfied him because he sat again.

"I have to meet Fabian Charbonneau this afternoon," I said. "But I'd like to stop by and see Catherine this morning. Let me know when you leave."

"You're still going to meet that Frenchman?" Cyclops asked, his one eye drilling into me. "Is that wise?"

"He answered my questions to my satisfaction. I'll get to control any spells I create, if I can create spells at all. We don't yet know. I trust him."

"I reckon it ain't him you got to worry about," Duke said. "It's your grandfather. Don't let Chronos take your spells from you, even if he says it's to save lives."

"I can handle Chronos," I assured him.

"He's her family," Willie said. "He ain't going to betray her. I ain't saying the Frenchman will betray her, but be careful around him, India."

Aunt Letitia nodded. "Willie's right. Mr. Charbonneau *is* French, after all. Remember the war."

"Which one?" Matt asked.

Aunt Letitia's fingers fluttered at the gray curls artfully arranged at her temple. "I can't recall, but I'm sure they betrayed us in one of them."

Betray. That word was like a hammer in my head, tapping out an incessant rhythm. I swallowed my coffee and avoided Matt's gaze.

Duke raised his cup in salute. "Seems like Miss Glass and Willie can agree on something after all."

Reminded of their squabble, Willie and Aunt Letitia both turned to me and began talking over the top of each other. They didn't stop until I tapped my butter knife against the plate.

"Enough," I bit off. "Honestly, who needs children when we have you two? Cyclops, do you mind which room you occupy?"

"I don't care where I sleep." He gave Aunt Letitia an apologetic shrug.

"Then you may have Willie's room and she may have my old one."

Aunt Letitia glared at him.

He rose quickly and grabbed a slice of toast off his plate. "We have to go. The Masons will be at the shop soon."

It was the signal for the rest of us to disperse too. Matt, Willie and I met up again in the carriage and drove to St. Martin's Lane, while Cyclops and Duke followed in a cart. We arrived to see Ronnie Mason on a ladder, scraping paint off the façade. Catherine stood nearby, a bucket filled with cleaning cloths at her feet.

She threw her arms around me before I set foot on the pavement. "Welcome back, Mr. and Mrs. Glass. How was the honeymoon?"

"Wonderful," I told her. "The weather was warm and the seaside perfect."

I could still feel the sun on my face and Matt's hand in

mine as we walked along Brighton Pier. It had been two weeks of uncomplicated bliss. We hadn't wanted to go far from London and Gabe Seaford, the magician doctor who'd helped me save Matt's life, so we'd chosen Brighton with its short rail journey back to the city.

"I hope you don't mind," Ronnie said as he descended the ladder. "But I thought I'd get started while we waited for you."

We all looked up at the remaining letters of the previous sign. Only the word WATCHMAKER was left. The name E. HARDACRE had been obliterated. A weight lifted from my chest and brought tears to my eyes. Tears of happiness.

Matt pressed his hand to my lower back and stood very close. I lifted my gaze to find him staring at me with that familiar intensity. He loved me. It was there in his eyes, the reassuring touch, the concerned downturn of his mouth.

And I loved him. He was everything I ever wanted or needed in a husband, friend and lover. He was my future, and I was his. Eddie Hardacre was a distant memory. Matt had helped me erase him from my life as thoroughly as the sign above my family shop had been erased.

I smiled and took Matt's other hand in mine.

He winked. "Are you going to give them the key?"

"Of course! I almost forgot." I fished the key out of my reticule and pressed it into Catherine's palm. "It's yours now."

She bounced on her toes and grinned. "Come on, Ronnie, let's do it together."

They both held the key and inserted it into the lock. A stale smell wafted out as Ronnie pushed open the door. Catherine opened the shutters and windows before my eyes had time to adjust to the dimness. The brighter light revealed dust covering the counter, display cases, and clocks. We'd boxed most of the time pieces up and stored them in a warehouse, but the heavier ones remained where they'd stood. Some hadn't been moved in months, and one large long-case clock had occupied the same corner for years.

I pressed my palms to its case and caressed the warm mahogany. Magic warmth. I recognized it now. My pulse quickened in response and my blood heated in my veins.

The pendulum in the housing throbbed.

I snatched my hands back and stared, wide-eyed, at the clock face. Its elegant brass hands held correct time but it was otherwise unremarkable. My old watch used to chime when I was in danger and had even saved my life. It had done those things independently of me. My new watch did not. Nor did it throb like this clock.

I pressed my hands to the wood paneling again and felt another deep throb that echoed within me. I'd worked on this clock often when I lived here, sometimes out of sheer boredom when I had little else to do. Just like I'd worked on the watch my parents had given me. I'd only tinkered with my new watch a few times. I'd begun to doubt my magic was as powerful as everyone thought and that my old watch had a special magic, put there by my father or grandmother. But now... Perhaps if I handled my new watch more, it would one day respond to me as this clock did. It might even save my life.

"India?" came Matt's quiet voice in my ear. "Everything all right?"

I turned to him with a smile. "May we take this one home with us?"

"I don't see why not. It looks heavy, but Duke and Cyclops will manage."

"They're still working," Catherine said as she admired a simple mantel clock on a shelf. "They're all running on time."

"Except this one." Ronnie lifted a black marble clock off the far end of the counter only to immediately set it down again. "It's heavy."

"We always had trouble with that one," I said. "It never kept correct time."

Willie opened the glass case and twiddled the hands. "Ha! The great magician ain't so great after all."

I nudged her aside and fixed the hands to the correct time, even though I knew it would lose an entire minute before dusk. "We'll take it home with us too. The rest can go into storage with the others until we think of something to do with them."

"Damn guild rule," Duke muttered. "All these clocks and watches will go to waste, and all the spare parts too."

"Damn Abercrombie," Cyclops said.

"Speaking of Abercrombie." Ronnie's blue eyes lit up, making him seem more like his spirited sister. Both siblings were slender and fair haired, and some would call them silly, although I knew better. Neither were silly, merely full of youthful exuberance. This new venture would see them mature quickly, but I hoped the burdens of business didn't erode their enthusiastic nature. "Abercrombie is no longer master of The Watchmaker's Guild," he went on. "They forced him to step down."

"Good," I said. "He didn't deserve to remain as master after he tried to stop you joining. I'm glad the Court of Assistants saw reason and ousted him."

"It's not just what he did to Ronnie," Matt said. "He tried to block you at every turn too."

"Nothing has changed there," Catherine said. "The guild still won't allow magicians in."

"And never will," I added. "None of the guilds will. It'll be the beginning of the end for their artless members if they give out memberships and licenses to magicians. It's understandable. Anyway, it doesn't matter to me. I'm not going to sell timepieces. But you two are, and if you stand about talking all day, this place won't be in a fit state for customers next week."

It was more satisfying than I cared to admit to learn that

Abercrombie had lost his position as guild master. He'd worn the title like a crown and wielded his power like a club. Hopefully the new regime would be less biased toward Ronnie. It wasn't fair that he should be tainted because of his association with me.

By late morning, we'd made considerable progress, and I'd learned two things. Firstly, that I'd become too comfortable living in Mayfair with servants at my beck and call. My back ached from scrubbing floors and I couldn't lift heavy objects. Secondly, Cyclops and Catherine were still avoiding one another yet couldn't stop stealing glances either.

I finally caught Catherine alone in the workshop where she was wiping down boxes of parts before packing them in a crate. "Has he spoken to you since the kiss?" I asked.

"Barely a word. Last time we spoke, we argued. He said the kiss meant nothing. I told him it meant something to me."

I clasped her hand. "I'm sorry."

"It's all right, India. Don't be sorry. I don't believe him. It *did* mean something to both of us. I may be younger than you, but I'm quite experienced in the ways of men. More than you were before you met Matt."

"Much more," I said then realized how that sounded. "I didn't mean you are a hellion. It's just that I was very naive, hence my mistake with Eddie."

She pulled a face. "Weasel. At least he's out of your life now."

I took in the clean bench and floor, the boxed up parts and empty spaces where clocks and watches had cluttered the surfaces for years. It was so bare, and yet the barrenness didn't upset me as much as it had to see Eddie working at the very same bench my father had occupied for years. "What are you going to do about Cyclops?"

She sighed. "I don't know. Give him time, I suppose, while I settle in to things here."

"It'll be good to be busy, and for him not to be."

"What do you mean?"

"You'll have work to occupy your mind, but after he's finished helping here, he'll have little to do. It'll give him time to think about you and come to the conclusion that he misses you and wants you in his life."

She sighed again. "I hope so." With a customary toss of her blonde curls, she shrugged off her melancholia and smiled. "Tell me more about your honeymoon. What was it like?"

"Lovely. The air was fresh, the hotel was—"

"That's not what I meant, India." She glanced at the door then leaned closer to me. "What was *it* like? Being with a man?"

"If you're trying to shock me, you failed. I'm used to Willie and her crassness. As to your question, I'll say that waking up in Matt's arms was delightful."

She made a sound of disappointment. "You can do better than that. I need more details." She slowly wiped over an already sparkling cog before repeating the action. "Without being too specific, of course. Just generalizations about the…" She searched for the right word before holding up the cog. "The mechanics."

I took the cog from her and placed it with the others in the box. "I'm sure your mother will discuss it with you when the time comes."

"Lord, I hope not. Besides, she won't tell me until the day before my wedding."

"So?"

She clutched the box of parts to her chest and leveled her gaze with mine. "What if I never marry? I don't want to die a spinster whose castle has never been conquered, India."

I stared at her, not quite sure which was worse—that she was talking about her death, or that she was considering losing her virginity to a man who was not her husband. I wasn't a prude, but Catherine was not the sort of girl to disregard societal norms. Then again, she had teamed up with her brother to manage their own shop against their parents' wishes, and she wanted to have a relationship with a man they disapproved of. It was time I admitted that. Catherine had a rebellious streak. I just wasn't sure how far that streak stretched.

"Cyclops won't agree to...conquer your castle unless he marries you," I said. "He's far too honorable."

She thrust out her chin. "If you won't tell me, I'll ask Willie."

"You'll do no such thing! Willie will teach you—"

The door to the shop opened and Matt strolled in. "What's Willie teaching?"

"Nothing," I said quickly, my cheeks heating.

Catherine suppressed a smile, and I realized I'd walked right into her trap. If I didn't tell her something, she'd go to Willie, and Willie would tell her more than a respectable woman needed to know.

"Keeping secrets from me already, Mrs. Glass?" Matt might have said it lightly, but the heat suddenly drained from my face. I felt ill again.

This secret wasn't going to hurt us, but my other secret would. Every time I thought about it, my insides tied into a knot. Now it felt like someone was pulling the ends of the knot, tightening it.

"I ought to return home and freshen up before my meeting with Fabian," I said. "Matt, will you accompany me?"

"Of course." He smiled effortlessly, but I detected uncertainty. We both knew I didn't need an escort, and he'd planned to remain there while I met with Fabian.

He helped me into the carriage and shut the door. "If you don't want to go to the meeting, you don't have to."

"It's not that." I blew out a breath, but failed to steady my jangling nerves.

Matt's frown deepened. "What's wrong?"

"I have something to tell you and..." I swallowed. "And you're not going to like it."

He sat back, his shoulders stiff, his sharp eyes focused on me as if that could gouge the words out of me. But the words had become stuck. I didn't know how to say what I needed to say. I didn't know if I should say it, I just knew that I wanted to end the wretched feeling that came over me every time I thought about the agreement I'd made with Lord Coyle.

Would telling Matt make me feel better? Or would it only make things worse?

CHAPTER 2

"Go on," Matt said. "You've come this far, you have to tell me now."

"Yes. Right. Of course." I swallowed again. It was now or not at all. "The thing is…you see…I was the one who convinced Lord Cox to marry Patience."

"How?" he asked, his voice threaded with steel.

"You know how."

He let the silence stretch as that gaze continued to spear into me. I held it, even though it took all of my willpower to do so. I couldn't look away now and let him think I was ashamed of my actions.

"It was the only way," I finally said. "If I didn't use Lord Coyle's information to blackmail Lord Cox, he would never have agreed to marry Patience. You would have remained betrothed to her. Indeed, you'd be married by now."

He broke the connection and turned to look out the window. A pulse throbbed in his throat above his neck cloth. "I asked you not to go to Coyle."

I took a leaf out of his book and let the silence go on.

It worked, and he continued talking, albeit in that tight, dark tone that worried me. "Now you owe him, India."

"I made it clear that I won't extend someone's life with Gabe. He knows I won't do something I don't want to do."

He slowly turned to face me. His features softened and he looked weary rather than angry. It didn't ease my anxiety or my conscience. "Do you think it matters what promises he made to you? If you refuse to do as he asks, he'll force you."

"He can't force me to do something I don't want to do."

He turned back to the window, his elbow resting on the sill. The edge of his finger skimmed over his top lip, a slow deliberate motion that would have been alluring if not for the tension between us.

"I suppose you're wondering why I waited until after we married before telling you." When he didn't speak, I went on anyway. "I waited because I thought if I told you beforehand, you would have ended our engagement and informed Patience that Lord Cox was being blackmailed into marrying her then married her yourself. I thought you would do it to save me from owing Coyle. And I didn't want you to save me."

He continued to stare out the window.

I clutched my reticule tighter. I'd known I'd receive either shouted fury or cold silence, so his reaction wasn't unexpected, but I preferred shouting. At least he would get it out of his system.

"I wanted you to marry *me*, Matt, and the only way to do that was to wait until after the wedding to inform you. I couldn't risk you backing out."

"We married two weeks ago."

"I enjoyed our honeymoon too much to ruin it." Tears stung my eyes and clogged my throat. Our happiness had come to an abrupt end and all because he hated that I'd betrayed him. How long would it take for him to forgive me? Would he ever completely forgive me or trust me again?

Neither of us spoke for the remainder of the journey. When we reached number sixteen Park Street, Matt alighted first and held the door open for me, then climbed back inside. I fought back my disappointment but the tears rose again. Not that Matt saw. He seemed to be taking great pains not to look at me.

Neither of us spoke. He probably couldn't bear to talk to me at that moment, just like he couldn't bear to look at me. For my part, I thought it best not to tell him that I would go against his wishes again if the alternative was to lose him.

* * *

FABIAN HAD TAKEN a house not far from where we lived. His family was wealthy, having used their iron magic to create marvels of industrial engineering, but he wasn't involved in the family business. Like my grandfather, Fabian was passionate about the possibilities of magic. He wanted to create magical wonders, the likes of which hadn't been seen for centuries, and to do that, he needed to expand his knowledge of the language of magic. But he wasn't powerful enough to do it on his own. According to him, I might possess the necessary power. I wasn't so certain, but I wanted to try. He'd agreed to let me decide what happened to any spells I created. He would not use them against my wishes.

The only one who knew about Fabian's promise and didn't like it was my grandfather. Chronos had been excited to learn that I might be a powerful magician and he begged me to work with Fabian, but that was before he realized he wouldn't get access to our new spells. I was relieved to see he wasn't at Fabian's house when I arrived.

But Lady Louisa Hollingbroke was.

"How lovely to see you again, India." She kissed my cheek as if we were old friends and invited me to sit and have tea, as if she were mistress of the house.

I glanced at Fabian but he merely watched on with a

serious set to his mouth and a small frown connecting his brows. He was a fine looking gentleman, with slicked back hair and a strong jaw, but it was his confidence that set him apart from most men. He seemed sure of himself without being arrogant and equally assured that he would get what he requested. I suspected it was the result of being born into a wealthy family and having an abundance of natural charm. Much like Matt.

"I wasn't expecting to see you here," I said as I sat.

"Fabian and I are old friends." Not only were they friends, but she had been the one to tell Fabian about me. It was the first time I'd seen them together, however, and I was struck by how alike they were. Not in looks—he had dark hair where hers was light, and he was considerably taller—but in character. They both exuded easy confidence.

"Why are you here today?" I pressed. "I thought we'd be alone."

"That's precisely why I came," she said. "You need a chaperone."

"I'm a married woman."

"Married women shouldn't be seen alone with a gentleman any more than unmarried ones. Tongues will wag."

"My husband isn't worried or he would be here."

"Perhaps it's not *your* reputation I'm worried about." She cast a small smile at Fabian, who'd yet to speak more than a greeting.

His gaze fixed hard on me. Was he avoiding looking at her? It was impossible to tell, although something troubled him. The small crease between his brows hadn't cleared.

"Louisa will not interrupt us," he said in a lilting French accent. "Please sit. I will bring my papers."

He left and Louisa poured tea. "Thank you," she said softly.

"For what?" I asked.

"For not objecting to me staying. Fabian said he would allow me to remain only if you didn't object."

I wanted to ask if she and Fabian were courting, but it wasn't my place and it wasn't relevant to my being there. She had no cause for jealousy, and nor did Matt. He knew it, but I wasn't quite sure Louisa did.

"Am I allowed to object?" I asked, rather snippily. "I didn't think you would care for my opinion."

She lifted the teacup to her lips. "Fabian cares."

"And you care about him."

She sipped.

I sipped too, and the moment for her to respond passed without a word.

"The last time we saw one another, we argued," I reminded her.

"My dear India, that wasn't an argument. Merely a minor differing of opinions. As I recall, you thought Mr. Hendry should be brought to justice for murdering that American cowboy, and I thought he could still make a valuable contribution to society without hurting anyone else."

"I still think Hendry should be brought to justice, but I know there isn't enough evidence to convict him. I also know Lord Coyle paid for lawyers to help Hendry because he is a magician."

"Not just any magician. He's the last of his line. If he dies without issue, paper magic dies with him." She set her teacup on the table, her movements dainty and graceful in a way mine would never be. "I have news of Mr. Hendry, as it happens. He married last week."

I almost spat out my tea. She'd warned me that Lord Coyle would find Hendry a wife, but I hadn't expected it to be so soon. Indeed, I hadn't been entirely sure Hendry would agree to it. He wasn't interested in women, let alone marriage, not even to appease society rules. He had no family to pressure him, and as long as his liaisons were conducted in secret, he wouldn't run afoul of the law.

"Coyle gave him no choice," she said, as if reading my mind. "He would have miraculously found some incriminating evidence and informed Scotland Yard if Mr. Hendry didn't agree to the marriage. As it happens, Hendry understood the importance of continuing his very special lineage."

"His bride is a magician?"

"Yes, but I don't know what type. Coyle wouldn't tell us."

"Us?"

"The other members of the Collector's Club. The Delanceys, Sir Charles Whittaker, among others."

Louisa had joined the club only recently, but I wasn't entirely sure if she was the sort of person they were looking for. While they wanted to collect and trade magical objects for personal enjoyment and profit, she wanted to bring magic into the public consciousness. I was still mystified that Lord Coyle had accepted her into their inner circle. On the other hand, their interests aligned with regard to Mr. Hendry. Neither wanted to see the paper magic lineage end.

Fabian returned clutching a large leather wallet. "Are you ready, Mrs. Glass?" he asked with a warm smile. "We shall work here, where there is tea and comfortable chairs."

"Here is fine, but if Louisa is to stay, I'd like to set some rules."

Louisa swiveled in the chair to face me fully. "There's no need for rules. I won't divulge anything to anyone."

I settled my gaze on Fabian, who frowned again, this time with curiosity. "She may sit somewhere she can see us but not hear us," I said. "She is not allowed to look at our notes or ask questions about our work."

"Come now, India," Louisa said with a delicate laugh. "You can trust me."

"If you are truly here merely as a chaperone, then these rules will not be unwelcome."

"Fabian—"

"Agreed." Fabian tugged on the bell pull to summon a servant. "Louisa, if you will be so good as to move to the landing. Sharp will make the area comfortable for you."

"The landing!" she cried.

"No rooms adjoin this one." He shrugged an apology as the footman entered. Fabian gave him instructions to set up a table and armchair outside the drawing room and to see that Lady Louisa's needs were met.

Louisa watched the proceedings in silence, her displeasure at being banished barely disguised. She did not object, however, and when the landing was set up with the chair angled so that she could see into the drawing room, she left with dignity.

"You can trust her," Fabian said to me as we settled on the sofa.

I glanced through the doorway to see Louisa watching me coolly. "I don't think *she* trusts *me* with you."

He grunted softly. "It is not what you think between us. We are simply friends."

I suspected she wished they were more. Whether Fabian wanted that too, I couldn't tell.

He opened the leather wallet and pulled out several pages with two neat columns of writing. The left column contained one word to a line in a language I didn't recognize, while the right column gave what appeared to be a definition of the corresponding word. That part was in English.

"Is this it?" I asked on a breath. "The language of magic?"

He nodded, smiling at my reaction.

I read down the left column, sounding out the words. When I reached the end, I asked, "Did I pronounce any of them correctly?"

"Some."

"How do you know? Are these words from your iron spell?"

"These four are." He pointed to the top four lines. "The others have been told to me by other magicians. They are simple words for simple spells." He removed the top sheet of paper to reveal more sheets beneath, all packed with handwritten words and descriptions. "These are more complicated ones. Some I learned from magicians, but most are from books I found in private libraries in Europe. I am not sure how to say some."

"The accent matters."

He nodded, and I suspected he already knew.

By the end of our two-hour meeting, I had an aching head, but Fabian no longer needed to correct my pronunciations. I'd also memorized some of the meanings. We'd progressed through a mere three pages. There were a dozen more.

"You are tired," Fabian said.

I rubbed my temples. "A little."

He handed me the three pages. "Take these. They are your copies. I will test you tomorrow."

I groaned, and he laughed.

The butler entered with a purposeful stride and a worried look. Louisa followed him, glancing over her shoulder toward the landing where she'd been sitting. I'd forgotten she was there, she'd been so quiet.

"Mr. Charbonneau, sir." The butler swallowed heavily. "There are three men here."

"Who?" Fabian asked.

"They wouldn't give their names, sir. They claim to work for your…" He glanced at me then Louisa.

"My what?" Fabian prompted. "You may speak in front of my friends. I have nothing to hide."

The butler leaned forward and whispered, "Your creditor."

Fabian stiffened. "I will speak with them."

The butler's cheeks flushed, and he wouldn't meet Fabian's gaze. "They don't want to speak to you, sir. They want to repossess the furniture."

Fabian shook his head and muttered something under his breath in French.

"There's been a mistake," Louisa snapped at the hapless butler. "Send the incompetent fools away. If they refuse, use force."

The butler hesitated, clearly wanting directions from his employer but reluctant to ignore the lady's instructions outright. The result was inactivity and a series of rapid blinks.

Louisa clicked her tongue and marched off. "I'll do it myself."

"Louisa, no," Fabian barked. To the butler, he said, "Let the men take what they must."

"Fabian!" Louisa all but stamped her foot. "You can't give in to thuggery. If this isn't sorted out now, you'll have a devil of a time getting your furniture back."

"I do not think there has been a mistake," Fabian said heavily.

Louisa's sharp intake of breath punctured the silence but she had the presence of mind not to question him further. She glanced at the butler. Fabian nodded at him to go.

The butler still hesitated. "Sir, if I may be so bold…will the staff be paid?"

Fabian squared his shoulders. "I will pay you what you are owed, but it is best to let go of unnecessary staff."

The butler balked. "We're all necessary."

Fabian swallowed. He looked like he was struggling to maintain his composure, but whether he was suppressing anger or distress, I couldn't be sure.

"Keep the cook, one maid and yourself," Louisa instructed the butler. "Inform the others they will receive their wages before they leave. That will be all."

The butler exited to the sound of furniture being moved downstairs.

"I'll see myself out," I said, gathering the papers Fabian had given me.

"That is not allowed." Fabian crooked his arm for me to take and gave me a smile. "I will escort you and ensure your safe departure."

I took his arm and we walked out of the drawing room together. Louisa followed.

"Do not be alarmed, India," Fabian said, patting my hand as we descended the stairs. "It is a financial problem, that is all. I must learn to live more...how do you say? Frugal?"

"Frugally."

"Financial problem?" Louisa asked from close behind. She sounded quite upset, more so than Fabian. "How can that be?"

Another elegant wave of his hand dismissed her question. "Do not trouble yourself, dear ladies."

Louisa huffed but didn't ask any more questions. I wished she'd persisted. I wanted to know how a member of one of the wealthiest families in France didn't have enough money to pay for furniture and a full staff. And how he could be so accepting when his belongings were being removed as he escorted his guests out.

Fabian greeted the tall, gangly man overseeing his two thick-necked colleagues as they carried out the marble-topped hall table. "Please, will you allow my friends to pass," he said.

The man stepped aside and touched the brim of his hat as Fabian escorted me through the doorway. Louisa did not follow, and Fabian didn't ask her to leave.

He assisted me down the front steps. "Do not worry, India. I am not leaving London."

Was that the intention of the person or people behind the repossession? To cut off Fabian's supply of credit and force him to leave London and end our association? It was a delicate topic and impolite to ask, so I merely smiled and nodded before walking off in the direction of home.

* * *

"IT WAS QUITE STRANGE," I told Aunt Letitia as we sat in the drawing room, waiting for the others to return from the shop. "He didn't seem shocked. He must have expected it. Although I think he was embarrassed to have his furniture repossessed in front of his guests." I studied the shirt I was mending yet hardly noticed the stitches. My mind was still on the scene that had transpired at Fabian's. "Louisa was more put out. She seemed to think it an impossibility that such a thing could happen to him."

"Isn't his family wealthy?" Aunt Letitia asked.

"Very. So why can't he pay his creditors?"

She took the shirt from me and plucked the needle out of my fingers. "You're going to prick your thumb if you don't concentrate."

"Oh. Thank you."

"His family must have cut off his allowance," she went on.

"But surely he has an income from other sources," I said. "He must have investments, like Matt."

She peered at me over the rim of her spectacles. "If he has devoted his adult life to learning about magic then he may not have an income other than what his family gives him. I doubt he has ever had to worry about where his next meal comes from or who pays his staff's wages."

Willie breezed in, followed by Cyclops and Duke. But not Matt. "Who're you talking about?" she asked as she threw herself into an armchair.

"Get up!" Miss Glass cried. "You're filthy."

"I washed." Willie stretched out her hands, palms up. Her shirtsleeves had been rolled to her elbows and she wore no jacket, only a waistcoat. "We all did."

Matt finally entered and went straight to the sideboard to pour a drink from the decanter. His aunt frowned her disapproval at him drinking liquor before dinner, but she didn't say anything. He downed the contents in one gulp and went to pour another, but stopped.

"Anyone else?" he asked.

Willie put up a finger but the others declined with sheepish glances at Aunt Letitia. She continued sewing.

Matt handed the glass to Willie and sat without pouring himself another. I was more relieved than I cared to admit. By his own admission, Matt used to drink too much. I didn't want to cause him to return to old habits. The tension in the air was awful, however, and I almost reached for the decanter myself just to do something.

I gathered my nerves and faced him instead. As if he felt my gaze, he finally looked up. His eyes were shadowed, his lids heavy, but I was relieved he could at least look at me.

"How was your afternoon with Charbonneau?" he asked.

"Fine, for the most part," I said. "I learned some new words. But just before I left, his furniture was repossessed."

His brows arched, a silent request for more information. I told them what I'd told Aunt Letitia.

"Serves him right," Willie said when I finished.

"How?" Duke asked.

"He shouldn't be relying on his pa's money. He should get his own."

Cyclops nodded agreement, but Duke didn't look convinced. "His parents are still alive, aren't they? He won't inherit anything until his father dies, is my guess. It ain't easy to get your own money when you got nothing to invest in the first place."

"He could work," Willie shot back. "Like the rest of us."

"*You* don't work."

Willie sank into the chair. "That's different."

"I don't work," Matt pointed out. "Not in the traditional sense. I inherited everything I have."

"You worked for the law back home," she pointed out. "We all did."

"You can't compare the small amount we earned to what my father's estate gives me. *He* amassed a fortune. Not me."

"Why're you brooding?"

Matt fell into silence.

Willie frowned and turned to me. "India?"

"Fabian's family must have cut him off," I said quickly. "Unless Fabian finds another line of credit, he can't stay in London much longer."

Thankfully Willie didn't ask me again why Matt was unhappy, but I suspected the conversation would arise again later.

Duke snapped his fingers. "Coyle!"

I gasped then pressed my fingers to my lips.

"What about him?" Matt asked, sitting forward.

"Coyle will lend him money if Charbonneau asks," Duke said. "He's interested in magic and wants India to learn more about it."

Matt sat back again, shaking his head. "Charbonneau wants to expand the use of magic whereas Coyle wants to keep it private and exclusive. If India and Fabian manage to create more spells, it might devalue his collection."

"Or it might give him something new to collect," Cyclops said.

Nobody spoke and the silence blanketed us, hot and smothering. Matt's gaze wandered to the sideboard where his glass sat empty. Then it drifted to me.

I swallowed heavily. "Coyle's motives are not yet clear," I said.

"He's only interested in helping people if he can get something in return," Matt said.

"True, but if the alternative is to fail or lose something precious, Fabian might deem the risk worth it."

Matt looked away.

Willie screwed up her nose. "Charbonneau will only have to return to France and beg his family to give him his allowance. That ain't so bad."

"Isn't it?" I snapped.

Willie cocked her head to the side. "What's wrong?"

Neither Matt nor I said a word.

Aunt Letitia lowered the shirt to her lap. "Are you cross with him because of afternoon tea next week?" she asked me.

I blinked. "Pardon?"

"That's not Matthew's fault. I organized it."

"What afternoon tea?"

"The one with Beatrice and the girls. I just told you about it. Honestly, India, you're so forgetful sometimes."

"They haven't returned to London yet," I said.

She picked up the letter she'd been reading upon my entry an hour earlier. "They arrive back in two days. It is early to be returning to the city but my sister-in-law loathes the country-side, as do the two girls. Patience won't be coming of course, just the two unmarried ones."

"Aunt Beatrice agreed to have afternoon tea with you?" Matt asked.

"She did. I'm sure it's to bury the hatchet with India and start afresh. Now that you are married, she'll want to make her peace with the future Lady Rycroft. Her own future depends on it."

"Huh?" Willie asked. "What's India got to do with her future?"

"She doesn't want me to send her away if her husband dies before her," I said. "After Matt inherits the title and estate, he could ask her to leave."

"But I won't," he said.

Aunt Letitia passed the shirt back to me, her eyes clear and bright. "But Beatrice doesn't know that, and I see no reason to reassure her. So you see, India, you shouldn't worry about the afternoon tea. You have the advantage over her." She rose. "Now, stop snapping at Matthew so I can change for dinner with a clear conscience. I suggest you all change, too. You can't dine dressed like you've spent the day at the docks."

Willie watched her leave, leaning forward until she was

out of sight. Then she slapped her hands down on the chair arms. "What's really wrong between you two?"

Matt merely shook his head so I did too.

"You're both as tense as bow strings," she went on. "Go on, tell me."

Cyclops shushed her. "Leave 'em be."

"Nope. I can't stand it no more." She shot to her feet and stamped her hands on her hips. "If you two don't fix it soon, it'll tear you apart. I've seen it happen to good people."

Matt rose. "Nothing's wrong, Willie." He held out his hand to me. "Shall I help you dress for dinner?"

I placed my hand in his and smiled as he closed his fingers. "Thank you."

We left, the picture of a perfect couple.

He let go of my hand as soon as the bedroom door closed behind us and headed for the dressing room, tugging on his neckerchief. I followed.

"We should talk about this," I said.

"There's nothing more to say. You told me your motives for going to Coyle, and I told you why I objected. Neither of us will agree the other was right." He removed the neckerchief and started on his shirt buttons.

I crossed my arms. "You can't be angry at me forever."

He clicked his tongue as a button gave him trouble. "Damn it," he muttered.

I stepped closer and took his hands, drawing them away. I undid the button, slowly. He fixed his gaze on a point above my head, as if my nearness didn't affect him. But the throb of the vein at his throat and the sudden intake of breath gave him away.

"You're wrong if you think Coyle would leave me alone if I hadn't gone to him about Cox," I said softly. I finished with the top button and moved down to the next. "He would have found something else to trap me, or made something up."

"You don't know that."

Another button released, I parted his shirt to reveal the patch of smooth skin above the smattering of dark hair on his chest. I leaned closer so that he would feel the heat of my breath and the pillow of my breasts. His Adam's apple jumped. I resisted the urge to kiss him there and continued to the next button.

"At least this way we can face him together," I murmured. "If I'd never gone to him, and you married Patience, I would be on my own against him."

"I wouldn't allow it."

I pressed my palm against his chest to capture the vibrations of his voice. "You wouldn't have a choice. Your conscience wouldn't let us be together, even in a platonic way."

He closed his eyes and breathed deeply. "India..." he murmured.

I stared at the vein in his throat until my vision blurred from my tears, then I pressed my lips to it. The rhythm of my blood synchronized with his.

He circled his arms around me and held me tightly, tucking my head beneath his chin. "Together," he said. "Forever."

I CONTINUED to meet with Fabian over the next week. Each time I went, something was different. First, it was the absence of a footman. The parlor was almost bare and the drawing room rug had disappeared. Finally, the tea service came in an ordinary set that was most likely the one used by the servants.

One thing remained the same, however: Louisa. She sat on the landing during each of my visits, watching us. She always arrived before me and welcomed me cheerfully, inviting me to sit and have tea. Fabian's smile tightened at the edges but he never asked her to leave.

He looked weary, which was understandable considering his worsening finances. I never commented on the missing furniture or staff, not even when the slice of cake he served tasted salty. The butler must be trying his hand at baking.

The only time I commented on the situation was when Fabian seemed unfocused toward the end of the week. I'd already repeated myself three times and not received an answer, so I tapped his arm.

"Are you all right, Fabian?" I asked when he blinked at me.

"*Bien sur*." He shook his head when he realized he'd responded in French. "My apologies. Yes, I'm fine."

"You look exhausted."

"I am not sleeping well." He attempted a smile, but I wasn't reassured. "Please, sit, and we will begin."

Louisa had been about to leave us to sit on the landing, but she stopped. "My poor Fabian." She looped her arm around his and hugged it. "Do take care of yourself, darling. I would be most upset if you fell ill."

My poor Fabian? Darling? Had their relationship changed from one of friendship to something more? Or had I been blind to it all along? If so, Fabian had lied.

He extricated himself from her grasp. "Thank you, Louisa. Please, if you would leave us to work in peace."

"Of course." She touched his cheek in a sweet, intimate gesture.

He flinched. "Please, Louisa." The hint of steel was light but I heard it, as did she.

Her nostrils flared, but she moved away as asked.

The following day, I received a message from Fabian in the morning asking me to meet him at his new address in Chelsea. Because of the extra distance, and the drizzling rain, I took the carriage and asked the coachman to return in two hours. I regretted sending him away when no one answered my knock.

I was about to go in search of a hack when I thought I heard a shout from inside. I tried the door and, finding it unlocked, opened it. Louisa's voice carried down the stairs but I couldn't see her.

"Stop being so stubborn!" she all but shouted. "Let me help you. I can pay for the other house. This one is not worthy of you."

"No, Louisa." Fabian's voice wasn't as loud but I heard it clearly.

"Listen to me, darling."

I shouldn't be eavesdropping on their private conversation, and backed up toward the front door again to leave. Then Fabian scolded Louisa, and I found my feet wouldn't move. I had to hear more.

"Do not call me that," he said. "I am not your darling. I am not your anything."

"You should be," she snapped.

"Stop this. You are going mad."

"You are the mad one, Fabian. Think about what I'm proposing."

"I have. The answer is no. I told you that when you asked me the first time."

"You haven't considered it properly. Listen, Fabian. I have more money than I know what to do with. I can support us in a Mayfair house with dozens of servants. You'll never have to crawl back to your family and beg them to reinstate your allowance. You can rub their noses in your good fortune."

"No, Louisa. Marrying you will mean I can never go back to France."

Marry her? Good lord, *she* had proposed to *him* and he'd rejected her! Poor Louisa.

"So?" she pressed. "What's in France for you?"

"My family," he bit off.

"The family that wants to control and manipulate you. The family that cut off your allowance and are forcing you to live like this!"

"This is not a terrible place." He sounded amused. "There are artists and writers nearby, and my landlady is a good woman."

"Don't pretend with me. You and I are alike, and I know that living like this—"

"We are *not* alike." He growled something in French and footsteps stomped overhead.

I retreated outside and was about to knock, pretending I'd just arrived, when a woman dressed in widow's black approached from the street. She introduced herself as the landlady.

"I'm here to visit Mr. Charbonneau," I told her. "He's expecting me."

She invited me inside and closed the door behind us, loudly. Fabian appeared a moment later on the stairs.

Louisa didn't stay for our meeting. She smiled tightly at me then went on her way, ignoring the landlady who opened the door for her.

It took a full thirty minutes before Fabian relaxed, but once he did, he was the most cheerful he'd been in the past week. He didn't mention Louisa, and I didn't ask about her.

I couldn't stop thinking about her, however. She was right, and marrying her would solve Fabian's financial problems. She was a wealthy woman with her own fortune that would become his if they wed. Why would his family reject her if their fathers had been friends? Why would Fabian reject her?

The answer to that was quite clear—he didn't love her. Perhaps he didn't even like her.

She, however, seemed very keen to have him. Because she loved him? Or was there another reason that had more to do with his magic?

CHAPTER 3

Afternoon tea with Lady Rycroft and her two younger daughters was changed to dinner at their London address, gentlemen included. I was glad to have Matt there, although I would have been happier without the presence of Lord Rycroft. Matt's uncle was a bully and a snob. He didn't like his own sister, let alone me. He couldn't even look at me as he greeted me. Thankfully, we didn't sit together at the table.

With an intimate family dinner, it didn't matter that the women outnumbered the men, but Lady Rycroft insisted married couples couldn't sit together. I found myself with Aunt Letitia on one side and Lady Rycroft on my other while Matt was wedged between his two cousins opposite.

Hope Glass, the youngest of the three sisters, sat with demure dignity, the perfect young lady. As a beauty and only recently turned twenty-one, she had the better opportunity to marry well out of all three sisters. If Lord Cox hadn't fallen in love with Patience, and I hadn't forced him to marry her after he learned of her indiscretion, Hope probably would have married first. She could be amiable and good company—

when she wasn't being cruel and trying to destroy my relationship with Matt.

The middle sister, Charity, was quite the odd creature. Like Hope, she could be agreeable when she needed to be. But once she tired of the performance, she revealed a rebellious side that needed to be fed with thrills and danger.

Dinner was a trial. A person could only endure so much polite conversation. We discussed our honeymoon, Patience's honeymoon, the estate, farming, London, and that most reliable of English conversation starters, the weather. Matt didn't look as bored as I felt, but that could have been because he was better at hiding it. Like his two cousins, he was capable of performing when necessary. I did notice that he hardly said a word to his uncle except when directly addressed.

Seated at the head of the table, Lord Rycroft spoke barely a word to anyone. He contributed to the conversation only when prompted by his wife. It was Lady Rycroft who carried the evening, with help from Aunt Letitia. It would seem both women wanted this meeting to go ahead. I knew Aunt Letitia's reason, but I didn't know Lady Rycroft's. Perhaps she had no ulterior motive and her reason for inviting us to dine was exactly the reason she gave—she wanted to get to know me better now that we were related.

She certainly asked me a lot of questions. Few were actually about me, however. Most were about the acquaintances in our "circle." She wasn't talking about Willie, Duke or Cyclops.

"The Delanceys aren't our sort of people, of course," she said as she cut off a corner of beef from the single, small slice on her plate. "What are they like, India?"

"I hardly know them," I said.

Matt arched a brow at me from across the table. I shrugged. He opened his mouth to speak but was cut off by Charity, who fell into a quiet conversation with him that I couldn't hear. It was so quiet that Matt had to tilt his head toward her, and Hope leaned closer to him too. I wondered if that had been Charity's intention, but Hope suddenly hissed at her sister and gave a hurried shake of her head. Eyes wide, Matt reached for his wine glass.

"I hear you've also been seeing much of Lady Louisa Hollingbroke," Lady Rycroft said to me. "I don't like to speak ill of other members of my sex, but I do think I should warn you, India. We are family, after all."

"Warn me about what?" I asked.

"Louisa is quite the vixen. Did you know she's wealthy in her own right? Extraordinary, at such a young age. Why it wasn't put in trust for her until she married, I'll never know. Girls like her, with everything at their fingertips, know how to use their good fortune to their advantage."

"Does she lord it over everyone?" Aunt Letitia asked.

"She manipulates people." Lady Rycroft cut off another small corner of her beef but did not eat it. "Tell me about the Frenchman, India."

I stared at her. How did she know about Fabian? Had she been spying on me? Matt frowned, proving he had been listening.

"His name is Charbonneau," Aunt Letitia told her sister-in-law. She had already finished her meal, having eaten her customary minute quantity. "He is a friend of Lady Louisa's, so India tells me. There's nothing untoward in India visiting him. Matthew allows it, and Lady Louisa is always present."

I concentrated on my food.

"Wealthy?" Lady Rycroft asked.

"Don't be so vulgar," Aunt Letitia scolded.

Lady Rycroft set down her knife and fork, having eaten little of her beef. "If family can't have a frank discussion about such things, then how are we supposed to judge a character?"

"But at the dinner table?"

"Very well. We won't discuss the particulars. I already

know that the Charbonneau family are industrialists, and there is only one kind of industrialist."

"Oh? What kind is that?"

"The wealthy kind." She flashed a small smile at her daughters. Charity didn't appear to be listening, but Hope probably was. Her attention certainly wasn't on Charity as she spoke about bullfighting in Spain. Nor was Matt's attention.

"And is he the eldest son?" Lady Rycroft asked me.

Aunt Letitia clicked her tongue.

"It's not a question about money," Lady Rycroft shot back. "India?"

"He has an older brother," I said.

Lady Rycroft's gaze met her husband's at the other end of the table. He saluted her with his wine glass. "Ha! Your plan is scuttled, my dear."

"What a shame," she said softly. "I heard your Mr. Charbonneau was quite charming."

"He's *French*," her husband said, as if Fabian had a disease.

"He is," I said lightly. "And every bit the gentleman. It's a wonder he's unmarried with so many fine qualities. Perhaps he's looking for a love match."

Lord Rycroft snorted.

"I think India's right," Aunt Letitia said. "I believe Lady Louisa has been to his Mayfair house many times. Hopefully someone tells him about her true nature before he makes a mistake."

Good lord, she was wicked. She knew Fabian had moved out of his Mayfair house and into a more modest residence due to his financial woes. She was baiting her sister-in-law, trying to encourage her to push one of the girls into Fabian's path, only for them to find out his financial predicament. It would result in embarrassment for all concerned, and Fabian didn't deserve that.

"Actually, he's in Chelsea now," I said.

"Chelsea?" Lady Rycroft spat out the word as if it were bitter.

Out of the corner of my eye, I saw Hope wrinkle her nose. Matt saw it too and smiled into his wine glass. He winked at me over the rim.

Dinner finally came to an end after a dessert of soufflé and marbled jelly, but the torture continued in the drawing room. Matt and Lord Rycroft peeled away to smoke cigars and drink whiskey in another room, while we ladies waited for them. Both Matt and his uncle looked as if the last thing they wanted was to be alone together, but it would seem convention was too strong, and neither made an excuse.

I stood by the door, waiting for the others to take their seats so I could position myself at a distance, but unfortunately Charity accosted me. She dragged me to the corner of the drawing room, much to her mother's annoyance.

"Come back here, India," Lady Rycroft called from the sofa. "Sit with me."

"In a moment, Mama," Charity said. "Let me talk to my cousin first."

"What could you possibly have to discuss over there?"

"It's private." Charity angled me so that I was facing the room and she had her back to her family. Her fingers dug into my bare arms until I wrenched free.

"What's this about?" I asked.

"You know." She nibbled her lower lip and took me by the arms again. She gave me a little shake. "Cyclops."

"What about him?"

"Hasn't he told you?" She giggled. "We kissed."

"What?"

"Shhh." She glanced over her shoulder. Seeing no one but her sister scowling at her, she turned back to me.

"When?"

"While you were away. We had a liaison in Matt's stables."

She pulled me closer with a jerk and whispered, "It was wonderful."

"I don't believe it." I'd been about to say he wouldn't do such a thing, but he *had* kissed Catherine. "He wouldn't do such a thing with you," I said instead.

"He did. Ask him."

"I will."

She licked her lower lip and her grip tightened. "Don't let him tell you he didn't like it. He did. I know he did. Do you want to know how I know?"

"No."

"I'm in love with him," she went on without missing a beat. "I love everything about him. His shoulders, his hands, his skin and fingernails."

"Fingernails?"

"They're lovely. You've never noticed?"

"No."

"You ought not to ignore him, India. It's not very nice."

Either this had gone too far or she was making it all up. Neither would surprise me, where Charity was concerned.

Hope came up behind her sister and slapped her arm. Charity released me. "Stop this at once," Hope hissed. "You're embarrassing yourself."

Charity sniffed. "You're just jealous because you couldn't get the man you wanted but I got the one I wanted."

"You haven't got anyone!"

"Haven't I?" She pushed past Hope and flopped into a chair near the window.

"Ignore her," Hope said. "The infatuation with Matt's coachman won't last."

"Cyclops isn't the coachman," I bit off. "They're friends. Perhaps your failure to recognize that is part of the reason you failed to get the man you wanted."

Charity giggled into her hand only to stop suddenly when her sister's freezing glare bored into her.

I was about to move off when Hope caught my arm. Her grip was no less bruising than her sister's.

"How did you do it?" she whispered.

"Do what?"

"How did you get Cox to marry Patience?"

I snatched my arm away. "Patience is a lovely person. She's warm and kind, and Lord Cox is a good man. He wanted to marry her. I just reminded him of that."

Her mouth twisted into an ugly sneer. "Bollocks. When he found out she'd already been with a man, he was horrified. Sickened. He wouldn't have changed his mind, certainly not so quickly. You convinced him to marry her, and I'm not referring to extolling her many dull virtues. You forced him. I want to know how."

"Your sister isn't dull, Hope. Quiet and cautious, but not dull. That's why it was easy to convince him that she made a mistake and regretted it. Men like Lord Cox look beyond the obvious and search for real beauty and truth."

"Nonsense." She'd never looked more like her father than in that moment, all derisive and arrogant.

"Did they look happy on their wedding day? Did he look like a man sickened by the woman he'd married?"

Her silence was the answer I needed. Both Matt and Aunt Letitia had said Lord Cox looked happy that day. He hadn't seemed like a man backed into a corner or regretting marrying his bride. His happiness soothed my guilty conscience somewhat, although not completely.

I marched off. I wanted to leave but Matt hadn't made an appearance. If he failed to show up in the next two minutes, I was going to feign illness.

Lady Rycroft patted the sofa cushion beside her. "Come and sit by me, India. I want to ask you something."

"If it's about Fabian Charbonneau, I have nothing more to say."

"Forget him. He's not important now." She touched the

amethyst jewel pin attached to the white turban wound tightly around her head. She always wore turbans that covered most, but not all, of her hair. From what I could see of it, her tresses were steely gray and pulled back tightly, exaggerating the slant of her eyes and smoothing out the fine lines on her forehead.

I sat between her and Aunt Letitia. Did I want to pretend to faint or feign a stomach complaint? Both would have them thinking I was with child, and I wasn't sure I wanted to endure that conversation now.

"Tell me about Lord Coyle," Lady Rycroft said.

"Coyle!" I blurted out. "Why?"

"Yes, Beatrice, why?" Aunt Letitia asked. "Surely you're not considering *him* as a marriage prospect?"

Charity's head turned, suddenly interested in our conversation.

"Who's Lord Coyle?" Hope asked.

"Why wouldn't we consider him?" Lady Rycroft asked her sister-in-law. "I believe he has many fine qualities. I've never met him myself, but—"

"He's positively ancient!" Aunt Letitia cried.

"He's younger than you."

Charity made a sound of disgust in her throat and turned back to the window.

"How old *is* he?" Hope asked.

"Enough of your pestering, child! It's giving me a headache." Lady Rycroft self-consciously touched the amethyst on her turban again. "The stink surrounding Patience's back and forth with Lord Cox won't dissipate unless we do something. Their marriage was conducted in haste after being called off, and everyone wants to know why. They'll continue to overturn stones until they uncover her grubby little secret."

"Surely it won't matter now that they're married," I said.

Lady Rycroft made a miffed sound through her nose. "You

wouldn't understand. Your world is different to ours, India. Let me explain it in simpler terms. A man's status is like a shield. Marrying a powerful man will send a message that there are no secrets worth uncovering. So the better marriage that Hope can make, the sooner people will forget about the circumstances leading up to Patience's wedding."

"You mean, the better *Charity's* marriage, not mine. Don't you?" Hope asked, voice thin. "She's the eldest unmarried daughter."

"Hope, dearest, Lord Coyle has never married. In all his years, he has not been tempted. If one of you is to tempt him now, who do you think has the greatest chance of success?"

Poor Charity, to be compared unfavorably to her sister by her own mother, and within her hearing, too.

Instead of looking offended, Charity's lips curled into a smile and her eyes flashed in the lamplight. "You *are* the beauty of the family, Hope. Witty and intelligent too, so they say, and good company. Not to mention your figure is the sort that men desire."

"Enough, Charity," her mother scolded. "Hope is a good girl who puts her family's needs first. She's not selfish, and she's never done anything that could cause offence."

Charity rolled her eyes. "I see you told her," she said to her sister. Was she referring to her kissing Cyclops? I still doubted it had happened, but the truth didn't seem to matter to Charity.

"If you are quite serious about this," Aunt Letitia said, "then I'm sure Matthew will set up an introduction with Lord Coyle. India, perhaps you could invite him to dine with the family. Charity may come too, of course, in case his tastes are...unconventional."

"You agree with this?" I asked.

She stared innocently back at me. "Why not? He's wealthy and titled. The Glass family would benefit from the connection."

"Setting aside the large age difference, there's the matter of his deviousness. I don't trust him." I couldn't go into the particulars of why, but I had to warn them.

"Hope's devious too," Charity piped up.

Her sister gave her a withering glare.

"I don't think he's someone you want to be associated with," I went on. "I urge you to look elsewhere. There must be dozens of other eligible gentlemen who would gladly court Hope—and Charity too. Indeed, I'm sure there are several already in love with them."

"Not of Coyle's ilk," Lady Rycroft said.

"Begin at the top, I always say," Aunt Letitia declared. "If he doesn't agree then we work our way down."

"He won't reject her." Lady Rycroft appraised Hope with a critical eye, as if she were a horse she was considering purchasing. "When she tries, Hope is the most desirable girl at the ball."

Hope sat quite still, her hands folded in her lap. She looked demure and agreeable, and quite immune to her mother's backhanded praise. I couldn't tell if she wanted to marry Lord Coyle or not.

"So it's settled," Lady Rycroft said. "India will organize the dinner party."

"Yes, do hurry," Charity teased. "Lord Coyle must be secured before my sister comes to her senses."

Lady Rycroft clicked her tongue. "If only we'd had sons."

Matt and Lord Rycroft entered, bringing the faint scent of cigars with them. Rycroft arched his brows at his wife and she gave a smile. He nodded and headed for a drinks trolley the butler had pushed in earlier.

"Sherry, ladies?" he asked.

We all declined, but he poured a glass and gave it to Hope before resting a hand on her shoulder. She took a long sip.

I caught Matt's attention and he made our excuses to leave. Not even Aunt Letitia protested that it was too early.

She might be in agreement with her sister-in-law on the matter of Lord Coyle, but she didn't want to spend any more time with her than necessary.

"Did Beatrice talk to you about Coyle?" he asked as soon as the carriage jerked forward.

"She did," I said. "Lord Rycroft also spoke to you about it?"

He took my hand and rested it on his thigh before folding his own hand over it. "I told him it was a bad idea. It didn't change his mind."

"Why are you both against it?" Aunt Letitia asked. She sat opposite, bundled up in a fur coat despite the mildness of the evening. "Setting aside the age difference, I think they're well suited."

"It's not a matter of ten years," Matt said. "More like forty."

"Closer to thirty, I think."

"Lord Coyle is not a nice man," I told her.

"And Hope isn't a nice girl," she shot back.

"She's young and naive," Matt said.

"She's manipulative and nasty. If anything, we should warn Lord Coyle away from her. If she decides she wants to become Lady Coyle, nothing will stop her. As you've pointed out, he's old, and old men die suddenly, leaving behind widows. Imagine the havoc Hope could wreak on London if she were a wealthy, merry widow. I shudder to think."

I stared at her, open-mouthed. I wasn't quite sure if she was implying Hope might murder him or if she was simply being off-handed.

"I told my uncle I won't invite Coyle to dinner," Matt said. "That decision is final."

"Then why did he look so satisfied just now?" I asked.

He squeezed my hand. "Because I didn't say I wouldn't introduce them."

"Matt!"

"I told him it was up to Hope. If she wanted to meet him

then I'd see if Coyle was amenable. She won't be, so there's no need to worry."

"She *is* amenable," I said. "Matt, we don't want him in the family."

"No," he said darkly. "We don't. I won't mention Hope to him. Or Charity."

"And go back on your word?" his aunt said. "No, Matthew, you must keep it. You have to introduce them now."

She was right. A gentleman's word was an unbreakable bond, particularly to an honorable man like Matt. But I comforted myself with the knowledge that Hope would change her mind once she saw Coyle. His age might not be a problem, but the man was as ugly on the outside as he was within. Besides, Coyle couldn't be interested in marriage or he would have wed. He was unlikely to end his bachelorhood now.

* * *

"Do I ignore you, Cyclops?" I asked as we sat at the breakfast table the following morning.

He paused as he buttered his toast. "No. Why?"

"It recently came to my attention that I might not take as much notice of you as I should."

He frowned. "How much should you notice me?"

"Yes, India," Matt bit off, stabbing his knife into a small tomato. "I'd like to know the answer to that too."

Cyclops eyed the tomato and put up his hands in surrender. "Don't involve me in your squabble."

"We're not squabbling," I said. "Matt, use your fork. Just because Aunt Letitia isn't here doesn't mean you can resort to your cowboy ways." The three of us were alone, the others not yet having risen. After a later than usual night, Aunt Letitia might not join us at all.

Matt suddenly grinned, putting Cyclops at ease again. He picked up his knife and continued spreading butter.

"Charity thinks I don't pay you enough attention," I said.

His hand stilled. "Ah."

"May I see your fingernails? Charity says they're lovely."

He looked as if he wanted to run out of the room.

"She also said you two kissed."

Matt choked on his tomato and coughed until his throat cleared. Cyclops poured him a cup of tea.

"When were you going to tell me?" Matt asked after taking a sip.

"Who?" Cyclops said. "Me or India?"

"Both of you. Why am I the last to know something like that about my best friend?"

"Last to know what?" Willie said, swaggering in with Duke at her heels. "And he ain't your *best* friend."

"I'm going to finish breakfast in my room." Cyclops went to take his plate but Duke caught his wrist.

"You've got to tell us now," Duke said.

"I don't."

Willie clapped her hands on my shoulders and massaged. "You have to or we'll force India. You know she'll crack like a walnut."

"I will not!" I cried. "I'm sorry, Cyclops. I didn't mean for them to find out. I hoped we could discuss it privately."

"This about Catherine?" Willie asked.

"No," Cyclops said morosely.

"But it is about a girl or you wouldn't be looking all coy."

Cyclops gave her his fiercest glare. A stranger would have run off, terrified they'd woken his angry side. But we knew better.

Willie wasn't giving up so easily. She sauntered to the sideboard and picked up a plate. "If it ain't about Catherine then it must be about another girl who buzzes around you like a fly."

Willie and Duke exchanged smiles. "Charity," they both said.

"So what did you two do?" Duke asked, joining Willie at the sideboard.

"Nothing!" Cyclops wiped his hand over his face. "She's a dime short of a dollar. I want nothing to do with her."

"More like a dollar short of a dollar." Willie set her plate next to Cyclops and threw her arm around his shoulders. "She might be mad but that don't mean you didn't kiss her."

I gasped. "How do you know they kissed?"

Willie chuckled and sat.

"*She* kissed *me*!" Cyclops blurted out. "You've got to believe that."

"I do," I assured him, and not even Willie disagreed with me.

"She found me in the stables," he went on. "It was just a couple of days before you two got back from your honeymoon."

"You're rarely alone in the stables," Duke said doubtfully.

"She was lucky you were, or her reputation could have been ruined if someone saw," I said.

"I think she was watching and waited for the others to leave." Cyclops pushed his plate away and rested his elbows on the table. He lowered his head to his hands. "I asked her if she was looking for Miss Glass, and she said she wanted to see me. She backed me into one of the vacant stalls—"

"*She* backed *you* up?" Willie hooted. "She ain't a big girl."

"She was relentless. She kept coming at me, telling me…" He cleared his throat. "Telling me things a lady shouldn't. Don't make me repeat it in front of India, Willie."

"Tell me later," she said, eyes gleaming.

Duke sat at the table, not bothering to hide his grin. "You could have told her no."

"I did." Cyclops looked down at his hands. "But not until it was too late. She's like a...a cat, all friendly at first, then next thing you know, it's sunk its teeth into you."

"She bit you?" Willie burst out laughing.

"No!" Cyclops groaned. "Christ, Willie, it was bad enough without you making it worse. She kissed me, and I pushed her away. End of story." He pointed his fork at her. "And if you breathe a word of this to...to anyone, I'll tell Brockwell that you like women."

Willie's laughter died. "You wouldn't."

"I will if you speak of this ever again."

She pouted. "Can't I even tease you about it?"

"No."

"Come on, Cyclops, let me tease you. I won't mention it to Catherine, I swear, but I got to make a joke of it in private every now and then. That's what friends do. It means I care about you."

He continued to glare at her.

"Spoil sport," she muttered, cracking the shell of her boiled egg with a violent whack of the spoon.

"What did you say to her afterward?" I asked.

"Everything I could think of to discourage her," Cyclops said. "Honest, India, I didn't invite it. I'm just glad no one saw. Does anyone else in her family know?"

"I think Hope might."

"I think so too," Matt said. "Last night at dinner, Charity said she wanted to tell me something important about one of my staff. Hope cut her off before she could speak, and the conversation moved on."

"Cyclops ain't staff," Duke said.

"Charity thinks I am." Cyclops sighed. "She was trying to get me into trouble with you so you'd send me packing. Wasn't she?"

"But why?" I asked.

"She's not all there." Willie tapped her forehead. "Who knows why she does anything?"

I looked to Matt, and he had the same grim look on his face that I suspected I wore. It was more than likely that Charity knew exactly what she was doing, and by getting Cyclops dismissed, she hoped he would go to her and beg for her assistance. It would give her power over him.

But she didn't know that Cyclops meant more to Matt than a mere employee.

"You don't have to worry about her," Matt assured him. "If she approaches you again, tell her you've informed me and that she can expect a visit from me."

"I ain't hiding behind you, Matt."

"I got a suggestion," Willie said, wiping her mouth with the back of her hand. "Tell her you like men."

"No," Cyclops said.

"Fine. Tell her your old cowboy's got a disease."

I was about to ask what she meant when I realized cowboy was a euphemism.

"That won't stop her." Cyclops sighed. "I'll just keep ignoring her. She'll give up eventually."

Bristow entered carrying a piece of paper on the silver salver. A small newspaper article was pinned to the back. "A message has arrived from Detective Inspector Brockwell of Scotland Yard."

Willie put out her hand to accept it.

"It's for Mr. Glass."

Matt took the letter. "'This might be of interest to you,'" he read. He unpinned the article, skimmed it, and glanced at me. "It's about Charbonneau. He's in prison."

CHAPTER 4

I read the article, twice, before passing it on to Cyclops. "Poor Fabian," I said, shaking my head. "We must help him."

Matt nodded.

"What'd he do?" Willie asked.

"He's been declared bankrupt," Matt said.

"The English still have debtors' prisons?" Duke asked. "Most of our states outlawed them, but some still have 'em."

"Bankruptcy no longer incurs a prison sentence here, either," I said. "Except when the debtor is deemed able to pay the debt off but doesn't. Under that circumstance, he can still go to jail."

"He'll be in a debtor's prison, won't he?" Cyclops asked. "They ain't too bad."

I shook my head. "We don't have debtor's prisons anymore. If the court thinks he has the means to repay his debt but refuses to do so, then it's essentially theft. He'll be put with regular prisoners."

"That ain't right."

"None of this is right," I said heavily. "I remember a neighbor of ours fell ill once and couldn't keep his shop open. He couldn't pay the rent so the landlord took him to court. He was sent to prison where he was expected to miraculously find the money to repay the debt. Some of us gave him what we could afford, but it wasn't enough. His health was already poor, and the prison conditions exacerbated his illness. It was a bitterly cold winter that year, and he wasn't strong enough to get through it. His jailors found him dead one morning."

Matt closed his hand over mine. "I'll pay off his debts."

"Thank you, Matt." I stroked his cheek and kissed him. "But hopefully it won't come to that."

* * *

NEWGATE PRISON WAS as imposing as I expected it to be. The brick walls, filthy with soot and suffering, seemed to extend forever and must give the prisoners no sense of hope. The warden allowed us through after checking our belongings for weapons. Unlike a regular prisoner, debtors could have visitors come and go throughout the day.

Another guard led us to Fabian's cell down a bland corridor punctuated by cell door after cell door. Our echoing footsteps were a beacon to the prisoners. I could hear them through the walls, begging for food, but it was the request for company and conversation that filled me with despair. What a lonely existence.

I knew from the spacing of the doors along the corridor that the cells would be small, but I wasn't prepared for how small. Fabian's cell fit only a bed, washbasin, stool and small table. His personal effects of plate, mug and bible sat on a shelf wedged into one corner. The narrow rectangle of spring sunshine tried valiantly to cheer up the cramped cell, with its ubiquitous whitewashed walls, but the high, barred window simply wasn't big enough for it to succeed.

The quip I'd been preparing on our journey died on my

lips, and instead I simply greeted Fabian with a flat, "Good morning."

He shot to his feet upon our entry and went to readjust his tie. Finding it gone, he fidgeted with his cuffs instead. He wore his own clothes, not a prison uniform, but whether that was because he hadn't been issued with one yet or because debtors didn't wear them, I wasn't sure.

"We came as soon as we heard," Matt said.

"We thought we'd see you at court this morning, but it was all over by the time we arrived," I added.

The color rose to Fabian's cheeks. "Thank you, but you should not have come. I will not be in here long."

"Of course," Matt said. "The situation will be sorted out soon."

"You are good friends." He offered us a smile but it was weak. He looked tired and not at all like his well-groomed self. His hair was unruly and his jaw shadowed with stubble. "Please, India, sit." He indicated the wooden stool. "I would offer you tea but I do not yet know how things work here. I could ask the guard—"

"We're not here for tea," I said. "We're here to make you an offer."

He shook his head. "I know what you will say and I cannot accept your loan."

"Why not?" I asked.

"Because a gentleman does not ask his friends for money."

"You didn't ask, we offered."

"And a gentleman *should* ask his friends for help," Matt said. "His friends *want* to help. Take the loan, Charbonneau, and pay us back when you can. I know this is merely a temporary problem."

Fabian looked away.

"What happened?" I asked gently.

"I failed to meet the first repayment two weeks ago, so the man I borrowed from began proceedings. I told him, under oath and in front of witnesses, including the press, that I did not have the means to repay yet and that I needed time."

"They didn't give you time, did they?" I asked.

"They did not. And they know my family is wealthy, so they claim I could pay." He shook his head sadly. "I was assigned a court date of today, cross-examined, then deemed bankrupt but with means to pay off my debts. And here I am."

"What were the terms of your original agreement?" Matt asked.

"A modest interest and regular payments. It is true that I could not pay him yet, but I did not think he would act so quickly." He clicked his tongue and muttered something in French. "I did not expect to be without income for so long here. Every day was another expense, another day I could not repay."

"How were you planning to repay?" Matt asked.

Fabian hesitated for so long, I thought he wouldn't answer. He seemed to be cut from the same cloth as Aunt Letitia, and considered money a vulgar topic. But it only took a little more coaxing on my part before he finally spoke.

"You were relying on your allowance," I said. "But your family withdrew their support, didn't they?"

He nodded. "My father cut off my allowance when I left France. I refused to do as my parents wished, and my father became angry."

A weight settled in my chest. "Because you wanted to come here and work with me."

"No! No, India, it is nothing to do with you." He dragged his hand through his hair, ruffling it more. "It is because I left, yes, but not because of my study of magic. They wanted me to marry a woman of their choice. An American woman from a rich industrialist family. I have never met her."

"Both families wanted a strategic alliance to shore up their business interests on two continents," Matt said with a knowing nod. "It's not uncommon."

"It is very common for two families to want to increase their power," Fabian said matter-of-factly. "I do not blame my parents for wanting it. But I could not do it. Even if she is beautiful, and would make a wonderful wife, I cannot do it. I vowed many years ago to marry a woman of my choosing."

Tears sprang to my eyes and the weight in my chest lifted. "It's so romantic that you want to marry for love."

Fabian shook his head. "You do not understand. I do not care to marry for love either, unless the woman I love is a magician."

I blinked, hard. "A magician?"

"You want to continue with the magical lineage," Matt said. "Don't your family want that too? So that the future of the company is in safe, *magical* hands?"

"The company *is* in safe magical hands," Fabian said. "My brother married a girl from a magical family to keep the line strong. His wife was chosen by our parents to give the business the best chance of continuing into the future, of...how do you say it? Best chance of flourishing? My brother has children, so it was deemed unnecessary for me to also marry a magician. That's why my parents chose an American heiress. Our marriage would one day mean I inherit her father's company, providing an alliance between my future father-in-law's company and my brother's. It would mean expansion across the world."

"But you don't care about the business," I said. "Magic is your passion, not commerce. That's why you came to see me and risked your parents' ire."

Fabian nodded.

"That's why you want to marry a magician, not an artless. You don't want to dilute the magic in your blood." It sounded calculating, but it was no different to what his parents strove for, or indeed what many families in high society wanted. The

Rycrofts wanted their girls to secure husbands that could improve their situation, even if that meant choosing a husband like Lord Coyle. Fabian had merely swapped a financial alliance for a magical one.

"Have you found a suitable bride yet?" Matt asked.

"I have not searched since..." Fabian cleared his throat. "Since arriving in London."

I suspected he'd been going to say since finding out I was engaged to Matt. It wasn't polite to discuss financial matters, but it was even more uncouth to tell a man that he'd coveted his wife. To Fabian's credit, he hadn't once tried to separate me from Matt before we married. And to Matt's credit, he'd allowed me to visit Fabian every afternoon for a week without chaperoning me.

Fabian smiled. "I am young. I have time."

"I feel a little responsible for you being here, away from your home where you could at least talk to your parents," I said. "Please allow us to pay off your debts until your family reinstates your allowance."

"They will not reinstate it, but I do not care. Coming to England is worth it. This..." He indicated the cell. "This is an inconvenience, but it will not be for long."

"If your parents won't change their minds, how do you expect to pay off your debt and be released?"

He smiled, but it vanished as his gaze flew to the doorway behind me. "Louisa!"

"Fabian, you poor thing!" Louisa swept into the room and grasped his elbows. "Are you all right? I came as soon as I heard."

He kissed both of her cheeks in familiar greeting. "I am well. Do not worry about me."

"I do worry. This place is awful. Simply awful. India, Mr. Glass, thank goodness you're friends to Fabian too. Now, let's get to work and set you free." She removed a rolled up document from her large reticule and looked around the room. "Is there no pen and ink?" With a huff, she turned to the guard at the door. "Fetch writing implements." When he didn't move, she made a shooing motion. "Off you go."

"You have to pay him," Fabian said, sounding amused.

"Oh." She opened the drawstring of her reticule but Fabian closed his hand over it.

"I know what this is." He took the document from her. "It is not necessary." He unrolled the document, read it, then handed it back to her.

She pushed it against his chest. "Set aside your masculine pride and fill in the details of your creditor and the amount owed. I'll have the money sent to him immediately."

"I do not need your money."

Louisa's gaze shifted to Matt. "I'm too late?" Did I detect a hint of disappointment in her voice?

"I am not accepting a loan from Mr. Glass either," Fabian said.

"Then how will you pay back your creditor? How will you get out of this Godforsaken place?"

"That is not something I can tell you."

"Your father has reinstated your allowance?"

"*Non*."

"Has someone else offered to pay off your debt?"

"Louisa," he chided. "Do not worry." He took her hands and smiled gently. "I know you care for me as a friend but your help is not necessary."

Her eyes pooled with tears and she blinked rapidly. She did care for Fabian, but I was certain it was as more than a friend. She loved him.

And he had rejected her because she wasn't a magician.

He let her go and stepped away, rejecting her once more.

"How did you know I was here?" Fabian asked us.

"A friend of ours read it in the newspaper this morning," Matt said. "He recognized your name."

I hadn't told Brockwell about Fabian, but Willie admitted that she had mentioned him in passing.

"And you, Louisa?" Fabian asked.

"Unhappy news travels fast in our circle," she said.

He frowned. "I do not belong to a circle, here in England."

"You do, you just don't know it." At his blank look, she added, "There is a community of powerful people with an interest in magic."

"Magicians?"

"I don't know. Some might be."

It was his turn to look disappointed. "You are part of this community, India?"

"No," I said.

"She could be," Louisa said. "If she wanted."

Fabian seemed satisfied with that answer, but I couldn't think why. If I were in his shoes, I'd want to know who belonged to this community and what their purpose was. Perhaps he didn't want to get involved since he didn't plan on staying in London for a long time.

Matt and I made our excuses, leaving Fabian with Louisa. He didn't look entirely unhappy about it, but nor did he seem completely enamored by her presence.

"I feel sorry for her," I said as we followed the guard along the corridor. "That's not something I thought I'd say about a woman who has everything."

"You think she loves him?" Matt asked skeptically.

"Yes, don't you?"

"I'm not sure it's love or a need to control him."

"Perhaps those are one and the same thing to her, as impossible to separate as a pendulum from an escapement."

His lips tilted with his smile.

"Thank you, Matt," I said as we approached the exit. "It was good of you to offer him a loan. It's a pity he didn't accept it, or Louisa's."

"Why?"

"I'm worried his masculine pride has got the better of him, as Louisa seems to think, and he intends to work off his debt in prison." I stopped. "We ought to tell him that could take years, not days. He might not be familiar with how the system works here."

"The system is probably the same in France. But I don't think that's what he intends to do, either. He seems convinced he won't be in here long, however." He put out his arm for me and I took it.

"Which means he has accepted a loan from someone else," I said.

Matt seemed unsurprised by my reasoning which meant he'd already come to the same conclusion. The guard opened the door for us but before stepping outside, Matt asked him if Fabian had received any visitors other than us or Lady Louisa. The guard confirmed that he hadn't.

"Then how does he intend to get out?" I asked as we climbed into the carriage.

"He must have another source of income," Matt said. "One he couldn't access immediately. Whatever it is, it's none of our business. If Charbonneau's not worried then I don't think we should be either.

* * *

TINKERING with my watch usually soothed my nerves but not after the visit to Newgate, nor the following morning. Fabian had spent a night in that cell. I couldn't begin to imagine what it must have been like for him inside those walls, surrounded by real criminals. We had to free him, but unless he accepted Matt's loan, I couldn't see how.

I set aside my watch and opened the housing of the black marble clock from my father's shop. After almost thirty minutes, I realized there was no way I could fix it in my present state of mind. I opened the notebook I used in my studies with Fabian instead. There would be no meeting today; no opportunity to work with him on improving my knowledge of the known magic words. I had memorized almost all of the ones he knew how to pronounce, and we were about to move on to experimenting with others he'd uncovered through his years of research. He hoped that, between the two of us, we could string them together to form new spells.

I closed the book again, however. I had no aptitude for learning today.

"Can I help?" Matt asked, entering the sitting room. He joined me at the desk and peered over my shoulder. "Are you trying to study or fix the clock?"

"Both. Neither." I sighed. "I can't concentrate on anything this afternoon. What about you?"

"Instructions have been sent to my bank, but without knowing how much Charbonneau is in debt for, I don't know how much to set aside."

"He might not change his mind."

He rested his hands on my shoulders. "The money will be available if he does."

I tilted my head back to see him better. He leaned down and kissed me on the mouth.

"There's nothing more we can do," he said. "Why don't you visit Catherine and Ronnie? Take Cyclops with you. He could use the distraction too."

Cyclops refused to go with me, but the arrival of Lady Rycroft and her daughters made him change his mind.

"We were just on our way out," I told them. "Bristow will inform Aunt Letitia and show you to the drawing room."

Lady Rycroft looked affronted. "It's not her we came to see. I wanted to ask you if you've spoken to Lord Coyle."

"Not yet." I drew on my gloves. "If you'll excuse us, we have to go."

"Us?"

I indicated Cyclops, trying and failing to look inconspicuous in the shadowy recesses of the entrance hall.

Charity's eyes narrowed. "Didn't my cousin dismiss him?"

"One doesn't dismiss a friend." I signaled for him to step up alongside me but he hung back.

The grooves around Charity's mouth deepened with her frown.

"Didn't you hear India refer to him as a friend at dinner?" Hope asked.

"I thought she was joking."

"Why were you discussing him at all?" Lady Rycroft asked her daughters.

"Charity mentioned him to India," Hope said, all sweetness. "Didn't you, Sister? Why was that again? I've forgotten."

Lady Rycroft's severe brows plunged. "Charity?"

"I... He..." Color drained from her face.

"Did he speak to you?"

Charity was trapped and she knew it. The only way out was to deny they'd met at all. Or embrace it. She chose the latter, but embellished it with a lie. "Yes," Charity blurted out. "And he was very...forward."

Lady Rycroft clutched at her throat and gasped and gasped again, as if she couldn't draw breath. "I feel faint," she said, voice trembling.

Hope grabbed her mother's reticule and wrenched open the drawstring. "Here," she said, waving a blue ceramic bottle beneath her mother's nose. "Try and breathe, Mama."

Lady Rycroft breathed deeply and flapped her hand at her chest. Charity took her arm to help steady her while Hope continued with the bottle of smelling salts.

Cyclops sank further into the shadows.

"My poor girl," Lady Rycroft muttered.

Charity's tale was quickly spinning out of control, and she didn't look as though she would change it. She didn't care what her lie meant to Cyclops, only that it made her look innocent. I couldn't allow her to continue with it.

"The only forward one was you," I snapped.

"Me!" Charity scoffed. "I'm just a girl."

"You're a nasty little wasp who likes to sting. It was you who came in search of Cyclops and waited until he was alone in the stables. It was you who backed him into a stall."

Lady Rycroft shoved Hope's hand and the bottle away. "I beg your pardon! How dare you say such slanderous things about one of my girls!"

"It's true," I said simply.

She stepped toward me and bared her teeth. She looked every bit the tigress defending her cubs, all signs of a fainting spell gone. "You may be Matthew's wife now, but you cannot speak to my girls like that. They are *born* Glasses. Before you damage the reputation of a young lady, remember that *you* lived under Matthew's roof for months before you married."

I stiffened. "I have no wish to damage Charity's reputation, but she called into question the honor of a dear friend, and I have a right to defend him in my own home. Cyclops has more honor than your entire family, and I will not hear otherwise."

"How dare you!" Lady Rycroft spat, spraying me with saliva. She looked as though she would say more, but Bristow returned.

"Miss Glass will see you in the drawing room now, my lady," he said, as if he'd not just overheard us arguing.

Cyclops grabbed my arm and steered me toward the door. "Let's go, India."

I stopped at the door, however, and glanced over my shoulder. Lady Rycroft was flanked by her two daughters, her chin out and back ramrod straight. She was the eponymous noblewoman, born to order people like me about.

But I held the upper hand.

"If you wish me to invite Lord Coyle to dine with Hope,

you'll cease your accusations." I marched out, clutching Cyclops's arm, my blood thrumming through my veins.

Neither of us spoke until we were in the carriage and well away from the house.

"That horrible, nasty woman," I hissed. "And her daughter's no better. I'm beginning to think Charity's not mad at all. She seemed to know what she was doing when she implicated you."

"Thanks for defending me, India, but it wasn't necessary," Cyclops said.

"Lady Rycroft wouldn't have given up until she'd run you out of London."

He leaned forward, resting his elbows on his knees, and sighed. "Why does it matter? I ain't going to tell anyone what Charity did."

"She thinks the only way to ensure the truth about Charity remains hidden is to get on the front foot and paint you as a reprobate. If the gossips hear something that contradicts her story, it'll be too late, and they'll be disinclined to believe the truth." I crossed my arms over my chest. "She has quite a nerve, accusing you of being at fault. She ought to hope Matt doesn't hear about it."

"Don't tell him." He sat up and settled those liquid brown eyes on me.

"I don't like keeping secrets from him," I said.

He crossed his arms too. "Tell him if you have to, but it'll put him in an awkward position."

He was right. Matt's relationship with his family was precarious enough without adding this to the mix. Besides, the last thing I wanted was to run to him every time I had a problem. "If Lady Rycroft stops accusing you, I won't tell him."

"Then let's hope she really wants Hope to marry Coyle."

* * *

Cyclops hadn't made me promise not to tell anyone else, only Matt. While I wouldn't tell Willie or Duke, because their outrage might see them do something foolish, I could talk to Catherine about it. I wouldn't have brought it up, however, if she hadn't noticed that something was wrong.

"Those springs don't deserve it, India," she said with a crooked smile.

I looked down at the springs I'd been removing from the box and was placing in the drawer in the workroom. Perhaps placing wasn't the right word. I'd been throwing them, and when the springs did what springs do and jumped out of the drawer because I'd thrown them too hard, I called them all sorts of names.

"Sorry," I said. "I'm angry."

"At Nate?"

"No, of course not."

She eyed the door to the shop where Cyclops and Ronnie were rearranging the clocks. "It's just that he seems unhappy. I thought perhaps you two argued."

"Nothing like that. Very well, I'll tell you."

The crooked smile returned. "I'd like it noted I didn't pressure you."

I told her about our encounter with Lady Rycroft, which of course meant I had to tell her about Charity's encounter with Cyclops. She stood there, riveted to the spot, her face growing darker with each tick of the gilt and porcelain mantel clock.

"The nerve of her!" she cried when I finished. "Horrid, spiteful, vindictive creature!" She slammed down a box of parts on the bench, knocking a watch Ronnie had been working on and sending it skittering across the smooth bench surface.

I caught it before it fell off. "Lady Rycroft is all of those things, but she's not worth breaking a watch over."

"I'm not talking about Lady Rycroft. I don't blame her for

protecting her daughter's reputation. But Charity thinks she can do as she pleases with a man's life, without thought to his reputation and without consequence to herself. I am so relieved you were there to defend him, India. Imagine if you weren't."

Cyclops and Ronnie entered, carrying boxes. Ronnie set his box down on the bench, but Cyclops hesitated. He eyed me then Catherine. We both resumed unpacking.

"New delivery," Ronnie said, tapping the box with his finger. "Put the other one over there, Cyclops. My sister will help you unpack it. India, will you help me out in the shop? I've got some questions about a certain clock."

I peeked through the gap in the door as it closed behind us, and I saw Catherine and Cyclops standing exactly where we'd left them, neither looking at the other.

"They're in love," Ronnie said, voice low. "Don't look so shocked, India. I've known for some time that my sister had feelings for him, but I wasn't sure how he felt until now."

"You asked him?"

"I did." He shifted a shiny brass carriage clock along the shelf behind the counter only to move it back again. "He couldn't deny it, although he tried. It was obvious he was lying, and I told him so. He told me he wouldn't act on his feelings, that it would pass." He shrugged. "And I said it wouldn't pass for Catherine. I've never seen her like this before, all forlorn yet determined to make a go of the shop too."

"And what did he say?"

"Nothing. He hardly spoke after that." He jerked his thumb at the door to the workshop. "They just need time to talk alone, without anyone watching. Did you notice how charged the air was in there?"

"Er, yes."

"It's a good sign, if you ask me."

The front door opened, ringing the little bell positioned

above it. Matt strode in, followed by Willie and Duke. I knew from their grim faces that something was wrong.

My heart leapt into my throat. Surely Lady Rycroft hadn't appealed to Matt. She must know he'd take Cyclops's side.

"You need to hear the full story," I said, rounding the counter to meet them. "Charity lied to her mother and claimed Cyclops accosted her in the stables."

"I don't doubt it," Matt said.

"Letty told us what happened," Willie said. "She overheard the whole exchange. This ain't about the little Glass witch, this is something else."

"It's Charbonneau." Matt took me by the elbows and dipped his head to meet my gaze. "Brockwell sent a message. Charbonneau escaped from prison last night."

I gasped. "Escaped! How?"

"The police don't know. But that's not all. There's a bigger problem. The man he owes money to was found dead this morning. Stabbed."

My stomach plunged and the blood rushed between my ears. I could hardly hear my own voice as I said, "And the police think Fabian did it."

CHAPTER 5

"He didn't do it," I said for what felt like the thousandth time. "Fabian is no murderer. He's a good, kind man."

Brockwell clasped his hands over the paperwork on his desk only to unclasp them and scratch his sideburns. Both of them. The deliberate delaying tactic wouldn't work on me this time, and I managed to neither tap my foot nor prompt him. It took a great deal of effort, however.

"If he is a good man, why was he in prison for theft?" Brockwell asked.

"It wasn't theft, and you know it. He couldn't repay his debts."

"According to court documents, his family is extremely wealthy."

"His family, not him. They cut off his allowance."

"Which the court documents also mentioned," Matt said. He sounded far calmer than I felt. That was his tactic when dealing with the unflappable detective inspector, and I wished I could emulate it.

"If the court believed him, he would not have gone to prison." Brockwell put up his hands to ward off further protests. "I admire your loyalty, but I think you should reconsider. Mr. Fabian Charbonneau is a suspect in the murder of Douglas McGuire." He smoothed a palm over the file on the desk. "He is our only suspect."

"May I see the report?" Matt asked.

"No."

"Then why are we here, if not to help you?"

"To answer my questions about Fabian Charbonneau." Brockwell indicated the chairs opposite his desk. Neither Matt nor I had sat yet. "I'll do it in here, in deference to your considerable help to me in the past. Sit, Mrs. Glass." His mouth inched up at the corners. "I'm not yet used to calling you that."

I sat. "We'd be happy to answer your questions, Inspector. Anything to clear Fabian's name. What do you want to know?"

"Why do you meet with him every afternoon?"

"I can't tell you that."

Brockwell's lips pursed. "Is it to do with magic?"

"Yes," Matt said. "There's no need to hide it," he said to me. "He won't tell anyone."

I sighed. "Fabian is a magician and we—"

Brockwell groaned. "Another one," he muttered. "No offence, Mrs. Glass, but your kind have caused me no end of headaches these last months." He flipped the papers on his desk until he found the one he wanted. "According to witnesses, Charbonneau visited McGuire the day before he was incarcerated."

"Perhaps he was making an arrangement to repay the debt," Matt said.

"A monogrammed handkerchief was also found at the scene of the murder with the initials F.C. embroidered in blue thread. Those are Fabian Charbonneau's initials."

"And if I were going to set someone up for murder, the

first thing I'd do is place something at the crime scene that belonged to that person. Is that all you have, Brockwell?"

"There is, of course, the matter of Charbonneau's escape from prison on the very night his creditor is murdered."

Neither Matt nor I responded.

"On the very night after you two visited him."

"Are you accusing us of helping Fabian escape?" I snapped.

Matt leaned forward, his earlier amiability replaced by a scowl. "Let me be clear, Inspector. Neither India nor I had anything to do with Charbonneau's escape or the murder of his creditor."

"Forgive me, but I must be impartial."

"Be impartial, but use your instincts."

"No, Mr. Glass, I must look only at the evidence."

"But that's the thing, you don't have evidence linking India or myself to his escape."

He cleared his throat but did not relax his shoulders until Matt sat back. "You weren't the only ones who visited him that day."

"Would you accuse Lady Louisa to her face?" I asked.

"If I have sufficient evidence."

"Did he have any other visitors?" Matt asked.

Brockwell shook his head. "I'll be speaking to Lady Louisa Hollingbroke today."

"There's another explanation behind his escape," I said.

"India," Matt warned. It would seem he'd come to the same conclusion as me, but wasn't sure whether we should divulge it to the police. I saw no choice. Brockwell would keep pressing until he found an answer, and I didn't want him pressing on me.

"You know who helped him?" Brockwell asked, reaching for his pencil.

"Nobody helped him," I said. "He did it on his own."

He set down the pencil. "No one escapes from Newgate,

Mrs. Glass. Not these days. It's a very secure facility. He must have had help, either from a corrupt guard, or a friend who smuggled in a lock picking device."

"Or he made a key from something readily at hand," I pointed out.

Brockwell cocked his head, frowning, but it quickly cleared. "Ah. What is his magic craft? Keys?"

"Metal," I said. "Specifically iron. He can shape it with a spell. All he needs is a small piece to insert into the lock."

"Diabolical," Brockwell said on a breath. He sounded impressed, however. His skepticism of months ago was nowhere in sight. He accepted my explanation without question.

"Can you think of something in the cell that he could use?" I asked. "The tine of a fork?"

"Prisoners aren't allowed forks or knives. Wooden spoons only."

I tried to think of the items I'd seen in Fabian's cell, but none had been metal in nature. "What about bed springs?"

Brockwell shook his head. "Slats."

Matt clicked his fingers. "The bars across the window. Were any missing?"

"I don't think so but I'll send a constable to check."

"It might not be missing," I said. "Fabian might have shaved off just enough to fashion a key that fits in the lock. The bars are high up and a missing sliver would go unnoticed."

Matt nodded, but Brockwell sighed. "The commissioner won't like that explanation. They won't want it presented in court."

"Then you'd better set about proving Charbonneau *didn't* commit the murder, or it will come out."

"And how do I do that?"

"Find out who did murder McGuire. Don't worry, Inspector," Matt said breezily. "We'll help you."

Brockwell sighed again. "I knew you'd say that." He gathered up the papers on his desk and handed them to Matt. "I had these copies made for you."

I blinked at him. "You intended to involve us all along?"

"It depended on your answers." Brockwell clasped his hands on the desk again. "Please inform Miss Johnson that I can't see her tonight as arranged. I have a lot of work to do."

"She'll be disappointed," I said, teasing.

"As am I, but murder comes before pleasure."

I suppressed a laugh. "How committed you are, Inspector. No wonder Willie speaks so highly of you."

A smile flirted with his lips. "She does? Well, thank you, Mrs. Glass. Kind of you to say. I'll be thinking of that as I sift through evidence gathered at the crime scene."

"Nicely done," Matt said, offering me his arm as we exited Scotland Yard.

"Which part? Telling him Willie likes him or telling him how Fabian escaped?"

"Both."

He assisted me into our waiting carriage and gave the coachman instructions to return to number sixteen Park Street. "We're going home?" I asked.

"I am." He held up the paperwork. "I want to read through this. I thought you might like to question Lady Louisa Hollingbroke."

"I suppose Brockwell didn't say I couldn't. Indeed, Louisa might say more to me than to the police. An excellent notion, Matt, and I'll go just as soon as I learn where she lives. Mrs. Delancey will know. What a mess Fabian has landed in. I wonder if he knows Mr. McGuire is dead."

"I wonder where he is," Matt said.

"Hopefully Louisa knows. Who else would he turn to but an old family friend?"

Matt rubbed his finger along his lower lip. He was

working up to saying something. Something he thought I wouldn't like to hear.

"Go on, Matt. Out with it."

He paused then said, "You know that Charbonneau never intended to pay off his debt, don't you?"

I sighed. "I know. He practically told us that yesterday. But murder? Do you think him capable?"

"You know him better than me. Do *you* think him capable?"

"No, I don't."

"Then we'll help clear his name."

He pressed my hand to his lips, and I settled into his side, not wanting him to see me, lest he notice my doubt. I didn't think Fabian was a murderer, but I'd been wrong about people before.

* * *

MR. DELANCEY'S position at Rotherby's bank meant he kept long hours at the office, so I was surprised to see Sir Charles Whittaker leaving the Delanceys' home. I was even more surprised when I saw him climb onto a small private brougham pulled by a handsome black horse. He drove it himself. Keeping a horse and carriage in London was a luxury few could afford.

"India, what an unexpected pleasure." Mrs. Delancey embraced me with more enthusiasm than even Catherine. She ushered me into the drawing room and insisted the butler bring tea, despite my refusal. "You *must* stay and have tea with me. I'm starved for decent company."

"Oh? But isn't your husband at home?"

"My dear, you are a newlywed, so your mistake is understandable, but when you've been married as long as Mr. Delancey and me, you'll come to realize that decent company is found outside the home. Anyway, he's been at the bank all day."

Perhaps she'd sent Whittaker away after telling him the same thing. But wouldn't Sir Charles have gone to the bank first, it being a weekday?

My mind raced with the possibilities behind his visit, none of which were very honorable. But I pushed them aside. Sir Charles's visit couldn't have been for any reason other than a simple social call on a friend. Servants talked, particularly to masters who paid their wages, and Mrs. Delancey wouldn't be so foolish to conduct anything untoward right under their noses.

She asked me about the wedding and holiday, and I gave her brief answers. I was very much aware that the last time we'd spoken, I'd been cross with her over her support of Mr. Hendry. It made for an uncomfortable meeting, and I was glad when the tea arrived. Sipping gave us both something to do.

"I know about Mr. Charbonneau," she said after a particularly long pause in the conversation.

"What do you know about him?" I asked.

"That he is a magician from France, that he wants to work with you to expand his understanding of magic, and that he was imprisoned for debt." The lines around her mouth pinched. "Tell me, India, how does a man from a family as wealthy as his is purported to be find himself in such a predicament?"

"I'm not here to spread gossip," I said.

Did all the other members of the collector's club know about Fabian's imprisonment or just a select few of the inner circle? And had she heard it from Louisa or Coyle, because surely it had to be one of the two. Coyle might not be a friend to Fabian, like Louisa, but he had his spies.

"But you *are* here for a reason," she said. "You want something from me, and I'll give it to you when you've answered my questions." She smiled sweetly. "Now, why did Mr. Charbonneau's family cut off his allowance?"

"Why do you think he had an allowance?"

She cocked her head to the side and gave me a knowing look. "India, my dear, I am surrounded by England's wealthiest. I know how families like the Charbonneaus treat their children and ensure their loyalty. I know when loyalty is broken, there are consequences, usually of a financial nature such as the one your friend has found himself in. So what did he do?"

I set down my teacup and rose. "I won't be discussing his private affairs with you. Good day, Mrs. Delancey."

"Mr. Delancey would have loaned him the money, you know."

I stopped and allowed her to talk. Perhaps I could turn this situation to my advantage after all.

"But Mr. Charbonneau never came to him," she went on. "Now it's too late. He's in prison, and it's only a matter of time before his family find out. His poor mother. She'll be terribly ashamed, and worried too, naturally. If it were my child, I'd do anything in my power to free him. Anything at all."

So she didn't know he had escaped. That meant she didn't know he was a suspect in his creditor's murder.

"Perhaps I can convince him to ask Mr. Delancey for a loan," I said.

"An excellent notion! Yes, do tell him my husband is willing to help magicians in every way he can."

I nibbled my lower lip. "But we're new friends, and he won't like discussing financial matters with me."

"You're quite right, but there is someone he might listen to. His old friend, Louisa." She winked, as if she'd divulged a secret. I wondered if she knew about Louisa's romantic interest in Fabian.

"Yes, of course." I smiled. "What a good idea. I'll speak to her immediately. Where can I find her?"

She gave me the address quite happily and thanked me for doing everything in my power to bring Fabian and Mr. Delancey together.

* * *

THE DOOR WAS ANSWERED by a butler as ancient as Louisa's great-aunt was purported to be. The aunt was Louisa's only living relative, and by all accounts, she let her great-niece rule the household. I gave the stooped butler my name then repeated it when he asked again, cupping his ear.

"Lady Louisa is not in," he said in a plummier accent than the aristocracy used. "You may leave your card." He picked up the salver from the hall table and waited for me to deposit my card. I had none. Now that I was married, I ought to have some made up.

I carried a few of Matt's cards with me and placed one on the tray beside two envelopes, one other card, and a small parcel wrapped in brown paper and tied with a blue ribbon. Magic warmth washed over my hand. It must have been strong magic because I felt it through my glove. I pulled my hand back and eyed the items. They were all made of paper.

Mr. Hendry was communicating with Louisa! But why?

"I'd like to speak to Louisa's aunt, if I may," I said, hoping my plan proved to be not as mad as I thought. "It's important. Can you see if she's at home?"

The butler hesitated then bowed. I worried he wouldn't be able to right himself, but he managed it with only a slight wobble. He set the salver down then walked steadily and quite slowly away, but not in the direction of the stairs. He was making his way to the bell pull to summon a footman.

I had very little time, even though he was as slow as a snail. I skimmed my fingers over the letters and card on the tray. None sported direct heat, only the residual warmth I'd felt moments ago. I touched the paper wrapped around the parcel and heat flared.

I hesitated then dismissed all doubts about my actions. If Mr. Hendry was communicating with Louisa, we needed to know why, even if it meant peeking at someone's mail.

The butler reached for the bell pull and gave it a hard jerk. He turned, hands at his back, and approached me once more at his slow, unsteady pace. I slipped the parcel behind my back and untied the ribbon by touch alone.

A door hidden in the paneling of the far wall opened and a footman appeared. The butler gave him instructions to see if Louisa's aunt was up to receiving callers.

By the time the footman disappeared up the stairs, I had the ribbon untied and the paper unwrapped. The object inside was hard and long, but as warm as slippers placed before a fire. *It* held the magic, not the paper. I'd wager it was iron magic, but without seeing the object, I couldn't tell. With the butler now addressing me again, I couldn't even return the object to the tray.

"Pleasant weather, isn't it?" I cringed. If I were to successfully return the object, I needed to distract him, not engage him.

"Yes, ma'am. Very pleasant." He glanced at the stairs. The footman, a younger and more sprightly version of the butler, would be back soon, with or without Louisa's aunt. I had to think of something quickly.

In the end, I didn't have to do anything. The butler became distracted by the rattle of wheels on the street outside, proving his hearing was selective. He squared his shoulders and opened the door. To my utmost surprise, Louisa stepped out of a gleaming back carriage, assisted by Lord Coyle.

I dashed away from the doorway before they saw me. With my back to the door, I studied the object in my hands. It was a silver letter opener with the word Claridge's engraved on one side of the handle in elegant script. On the other side, the number 24 had been etched. The numbers were small and untidy, as if they'd been hastily placed there. They were also the warmest part of the letter opener. The magician had written that number.

It had to be Fabian. He wasn't a silver magician, but the opener wouldn't be solid silver, merely silver plated. He'd manipulated the metal beneath.

"I'm telling the truth," came Louisa's voice from the other side of the door. "And I do not like the implication that I'm lying."

"You must see it from my point of view," Lord Coyle intoned. "You are his only friend in London, the only one he would turn to, so of course I naturally assume you know his whereabouts. You would conclude the same thing if you were in my position."

They must have stopped at the top of the steps, and they didn't seem to mind that the butler overheard them.

"You're mistaken," Louisa countered. "He is not without friends here. There are people in London who would go to great lengths to protect him."

Coyle grunted. "I know who you mean, and I disagree. Her husband wouldn't allow it."

"He would give his wife anything if she asked for it."

Were they talking about Matt and me?

"Not if it endangered her life," Coyle said. "Listen to me. The fact is, he escaped and the police want him. If you do know where he is, be careful. That is my advice."

"Thank you. It's very kind of you to worry about me, but I can assure you, I don't know where he is."

"Then I'll bid you good day." There was a pause, long enough for him to kiss her hand. The butler cleared his throat, but to no avail. No one paid him any attention.

I checked to see that he wasn't looking my way, then with my heart in my throat, I hid the hastily rewrapped letter opener between the folds of my skirt. I couldn't allow Louisa to see it. Not before I'd had a chance to speak to Fabian first. If she helped him, he might be beholden to her, and I doubted he wanted that.

"You have a visitor, madam," the butler said to his mistress. "Mrs. Glass."

Louisa poked her head around the door. "India! How delightful." She led the way inside, followed by Lord Coyle.

He bowed over my hand. I kept my other tucked into my skirts, my fingers gripping the opener tightly in case it should slip.

"I suspect you came here to ask Louisa the same thing I did," Coyle said. "The whereabouts of Fabian Charbonneau."

"Yes," I said on a rush of breath.

"I'll tell you what I told Lord Coyle," she said. "I am not aware of his whereabouts. I wish I was. I want to help him. His lordship has just informed me of his escape and the murder of his creditor. It's a most worrying time and I'm terribly anxious."

"As am I," I assured her. "If you do learn of his whereabouts, please send a message to us immediately. We have a strong interest in clearing his name."

"We all do," Lord Coyle said. He bowed to each of us in turn. "I will leave you two ladies to your tea and gossip."

"Actually," I said, following him out. "I'd like to speak to you."

We both said our goodbyes to Louisa. She watched us leave with a curious frown connecting her brows and a tight smile on her lips.

"Is this about Charbonneau?" Coyle asked. "Or our arrangement?"

"It's about dinner." I stopped at his carriage. My own was parked down the street. They must not have noticed it upon their arrival. Had they been out together or had he met her on his way here? "Matt and I would like to extend an invitation to you to dine with us. Shall we say Thursday?"

His fluffy white eyebrows arched. "This is most unexpected."

"I suspect it is. Is eight o'clock suitable?"

His tuberous lips pursed as he searched my gaze. Looking for my motive? After a moment, he grunted. "Eight o'clock on Thursday." He touched the brim of his hat and nodded at his hovering footman to open the door of the carriage.

I walked off to my own conveyance, my hand and the letter opener buried in my skirts. "Home, ma'am?" the coachman asked.

"No," I said. "Claridge's hotel."

I didn't remove the opener until I was safely inside the cabin then I unwrapped it again. The warmth infused me immediately. It definitely came from the numbers, not the letters. The exclusive hotel must have engraved its name on all its letter openers, but Fabian had added the room number. *His* room number. It had to be. He wanted Louisa's help and this was his way of sending for her without risking putting his name to a message. Nosy staff or a great-aunt wouldn't know the meaning behind it.

A nosy magician would, however.

I was a little put out that he'd sent the message to her and not me, but perhaps it was understandable. They were old friends and we were acquainted only a few weeks.

I tucked the letter opener into my reticule but it was too long, and the end poked through the drawstring opening. If I held the reticule just so, I could enclose the silver handle in my palm so that it wasn't visible.

Claridge's Hotel was still the grand dame of hotels, despite lacking modern amenities like ensuite bathrooms and elevators that newer luxury hotels boasted. A handful of guests mingled beneath the enormous chandelier in the foyer, their wealth on display in their jewels, fine clothes, and air of self-assurance. I wasn't made to feel out of place, however. The footman greeted me with a welcoming smile and directed me to the counter. Another footman offered me refreshments, and a porter bowed as I passed him. I was no different to their other guests, I realized.

Several months ago, before meeting Matt, I'd worn functional cotton or woolen dresses. Now I wore the latest fashions made by one of London's most popular *modistes,* soft leather boots and fine gloves. A maid arranged my hair in a style that suited me, whereas I used to pull it back tightly for the simple reason that loose hair got in the way of my work. I had changed so much that sometimes I didn't recognize myself in the mirror in the morning. The fact was neither good nor bad; it simply *was.*

"I'm here to meet Mr. Fabian Charbonneau," I told the staff member at the reception counter. "Could you send a porter to his room to announce me? He's my cousin," I added, lest he think there something untoward in a woman asking after a man at a hotel.

The receptionist inspected his ledger, running his gloved finger down the neatly written names. He shook his head. "There is no one by that name here, Madam."

It made sense that Fabian would register under another name to avoid notice. "Room twenty-four, I believe," I said.

He checked the register again. "No, Madam. There is no Charbonneau in room twenty-four."

"Sometimes he goes by another name," I said with a smile.

"I can't divulge the names of guests, madam." He looked worried that I might create a scene. "I'm sorry."

"It's quite all right. Tell me, is the man in room twenty-four French?"

"I don't know. He is foreign, but so are most of our guests."

"Thank you. I'll come back later."

"If you'd like to leave a card, I can see that he gets it."

I declined. Fabian didn't seem to want me to know his

whereabouts. If I was going to convince him that I could help, he had to listen to me and not avoid me.

I sat in one of the armchairs for an hour, but Fabian didn't return. The receptionist was replaced by another staff member, and the porters gave up asking me if I required assistance. Indeed, they stopped looking at me altogether. When a group of four women entered the hotel and headed straight for the staircase, I fell into step behind them. None of the staff stopped me.

I peeled away from the group on the second floor and quickly located room number twenty-four. I knocked but there was no answer. I moved down the corridor so that Fabian wouldn't see me until I chose to reveal myself.

It was another eighteen minutes before he finally appeared.

"Fabian," I said, rushing toward him.

His head jerked toward me, but I couldn't make out his expression thanks to the angle of his hat and raised collar of his coat. He turned his back to me and fumbled with the key in the lock.

"Fabian, stop a moment. I can help." I caught his arm but he shoved me off so violently that I lost my balance and fell back against the wall opposite.

"Apologies," he muttered before letting himself into the room. He slammed the door behind him and the lock tumbled on the other side.

Why would he do that without listening to me? The Fabian Charbonneau I knew was a gentleman and my friend. He wouldn't push me. Had his experiences with our prison system changed him so dramatically?

Or had I got him so completely wrong?

CHAPTER 6

"You should have used this on him," Willie said, inspecting the letter opener. "That would have stopped him in his tracks." She tossed it in the air and caught it by its handle.

Duke snatched it off her. "I better take this before you cut yourself."

Willie had spotted me upon my return to the house and knew immediately that something was amiss. I asked her to follow me to Matt's office, and she'd summoned Cyclops and Duke along the way. There I told them and Matt how I found the letter opener at Louisa's then went on to Claridge's in search of Fabian. Matt hadn't stopped scowling since I mentioned Fabian had pushed me away to escape.

"I'm not going to stab a friend," I told Willie.

"You sure he's your friend?" she shot back. "Seems to me he don't think much of you if he pushed you."

"Agreed," Matt said darkly. "When I get my hands on him—"

"He was desperate," I cut in. "He doesn't know what he's doing. He's confused and frightened, and I'm sure he was sorry as soon as he did it." I was rambling, something I did when I was worried. I was worried about Fabian's wellbeing, but I was worried about the change in his behavior, too.

Matt took my hand and directed me to sit. "I'll go to Claridge's and talk to him. Nothing more."

"You're not going without me."

"And me," Cyclops said, crossing his arms and looking as formidable as ever. "He can't treat you like that after everything you've done for him, India."

"We're going too," Willie said. "Me and Duke."

I took back the letter opener and ran my fingers over the numbers. "I can't believe he would send this to Louisa and not me. I can't believe he'd push me, either."

"Did he even look sorry?" Cyclops asked.

"He apologized, but I didn't see his face."

"Then how do you know it was Fabian?" Matt asked.

"Of course it was him." But even as I said it, I knew he might be right. I couldn't be completely sure if it had been Fabian. I'd seen his nose but not the rest of his face. He was the right size, but Fabian was average height and girth. "It might not have been him," I conceded.

"Then who was it?" Duke asked.

"That's what we'll find out," Matt said.

"I think I'll stay home, after all," I told them. I'd be unable to convince a stranger to trust me, and I was still a little shaken. Four of them would be quite enough to confront the fellow.

I walked with them down the stairs, still clutching the letter opener.

"I can't believe you stole it," Willie said. "Mrs. India Glass, thief."

"I am not," I bit back.

"Wait until Letty finds out."

"If you tell her, I'll have Mrs. Potter remove bacon from the menu for a month."

She huffed. "That ain't fighting fair."

* * *

MATT RETURNED HOME ALONE NOT long after he'd left with the others. "He checked out," he said. "He'd registered under the name Robert Smith."

"An alias," Aunt Letitia piped up from where she sat on the sofa. She peered at Matt over the rim of her glasses. "Don't look so surprised. India told me where you went and why, and I'm not at all surprised the fellow registered under a false name. He clearly doesn't want to announce his whereabouts to the world."

"Where are Willie and the men?" I asked.

"Checking other hotels," Matt said. "He has to have gone somewhere."

It was unlikely the man would choose the same alias, however, and we all knew it.

"What else can we do?" I said.

"I think we should pay a visit to the only other person in London who knows Fabian."

"Chronos."

* * *

MY GRANDFATHER RECEIVED us at home at his Crouch End lodgings with a wild look in his eyes and ink stains on his fingers. He ushered us inside and slammed the door.

"Come inside, quickly," he said. "Did anyone see you?"

"There were a few people wandering about," Matt said. "Chronos, are you all right?"

"What sort of people? Did they look suspicious? Were they on foot or in a conveyance?"

"Both. And no, none looked suspicious, but I wasn't taking any particular notice."

Chronos clicked his tongue. "I expected better from you,

Glass. You're used to clandestine adventures. India is as naive about these things as a child."

"What things?" I asked.

"Come with me." Chronos led the way up the stairs only to stop on the landing and glance back to the entrance hall. "Did I lock the door?"

"Yes," Matt said, taking my grandfather's elbow. "Come and sit down."

Chronos waved him off. "Stop treating me like I'm old."

He entered the parlor ahead of us. The curtains were drawn and the only light came from a gas lamp hissing in the corner. It was late afternoon and still light outside.

"Why hasn't your housekeeper opened the curtains?" I asked.

"I gave her the day off. No, India!" He caught my arm as I headed toward the curtains. "Don't open them."

"What's gotten into you?"

"Someone's watching me." He removed the newspaper from the sofa and indicated we should sit. "I don't want them to see what I'm doing."

"What are you doing?" Matt asked as he sat.

"Nothing."

"Then what does it matter if someone is watching you?" I asked.

"I don't know."

"Why do you think someone would want to watch you?"

"I don't know!" Chronos threw his hands in the air and let them fall on his knees as he sat in an armchair. "Stop being difficult."

"We're not being difficult," I said through a clenched jaw. "We're simply asking sensible questions. You are giving nonsensical answers."

Chronos appealed to Matt. "You have my sympathies, Glass."

I bit down on my lip to stop myself firing back a retort.

Matt cleared his throat. "What makes you think someone is watching you?" he asked.

"Sometimes I see a black carriage out there." Chronos waved a hand at the curtain. "I can't see the coachman's face."

"Perhaps he's waiting for his passenger," I said. "Perhaps the passenger is visiting one of your neighbors."

"Or perhaps he's inside the carriage, watching me."

"A hackney cab?" Matt asked.

"A brougham."

My heart leapt into my throat. "Whittaker," I said on a breath.

"He doesn't have a carriage," Matt said.

"He does now. I saw him leaving the Delanceys' in a brougham. He was driving. Was the horse black?" I asked Chronos.

He nodded. "It must be him! Who is he?"

"Sir Charles Whittaker is a member of Coyle's group. He was following me, for a while, until we warned him off."

"Good for you, Glass." Chronos gave Matt an approving nod. "So why is he following *me* now?"

"Most likely for the same reason we're here," Matt said. "Because he thinks you know the whereabouts of Fabian Charbonneau."

Chronos frowned. "Is he missing?"

We told him about Fabian's imprisonment for debt, his escape, and the death of his creditor. The sensational tale riveted him. Every twist saw his jaw drop a little more.

"Scotland Yard thinks Charbonneau murdered McGuire," Matt finished.

"He didn't!" Chronos declared. "He's no murderer. Tell your detective inspector friend that Fabian is innocent and he should look elsewhere for a killer."

"We have told him and he is," Matt said. "But Charbonneau still needs to be found. Escape from prison is a very serious offence."

"Not if his debts are paid. Can you pay them off, Glass?"

"Chronos!" I cried. "You can't ask that."

"Why not? I saved his life and let him marry my granddaughter. He owes me."

I gave him a withering glare.

Matt's eyes gleamed with humor, but he otherwise looked perfectly serious. "I've already offered to pay off the debt. Charbonneau declined. I may still pay the victim's widow if we don't hear from him soon."

"Yes, yes, do that." Chronos rubbed his head, making the white strands of hair stand on end. "Then find the real killer so Fabian can come out of hiding and you two can continue your work, India." He shifted forward and fixed his gaze on me. "It's very important you keep up your studies while he's away. You have enough to revise alone."

"How do you know?"

"You've been working together over a week. If you haven't learned some things in that time, I question your capacity for education."

"And I question your capacity for telling the truth."

His gaze narrowed. "Are you accusing me of harboring him?"

I shrugged, not quite willing to say it out loud.

"Well he's not here," he said hotly. "You can check, if you like."

"That won't be necessary," Matt said, rising. "I see no evidence of a second person staying here. We'll confront Whittaker now and warn him away."

"He'll deny it."

I wasn't quite as certain as Matt that Chronos wasn't harboring Fabian, and told him so as we drove off. "He can't be trusted. He pretended he was dead for decades."

"Not to your face," he said.

"And if I were hiding someone, I'd keep the curtains

closed and explain it by making up a story about someone watching me."

"My, my, Mrs. Glass, remind me never to do anything that will give you cause to mistrust me."

I huffed out a breath. "I'm sorry, Matt, but he vexes me without even trying."

"So I see." He put his arm around my shoulders and took advantage of a sharp corner to slide me along the seat, trapping me. "Will a kiss make you feel better?" he murmured in my ear.

I tried to keep a straight face, but gave up as he nuzzled the sensitive patch of skin beneath my ear. "It might, if it's a very, very good kiss."

He spent the rest of the journey making me feel better.

* * *

THE LAST TIME we'd spoken to Sir Charles Whittaker, we'd accused him of following me, so it was understandable that he greeted us with caution and an immediate defense before we'd even finished greeting him.

"I haven't been following you," he said, eyeing Matt cautiously. "I've been home almost half an hour. Ask my housekeeper if you don't believe me."

"And prior to that?" Matt asked.

"I told you, I haven't been following you. What is this about?"

"You have a new conveyance and a horse to pull it."

"So?"

"How does a bachelor of modest means afford a new brougham and horse?"

The usually cool, debonair gentleman adjusted the tie at his throat and stretched his neck out of the collar. "I came into an inheritance recently. What business is that of yours?"

"Your conveyance was seen outside a Crouch End house

with you in the driver's seat. It was parked for a long time, and neither collected nor deposited passengers."

Sir Charles gave Matt a blank look. "Crouch End? I don't know anyone there."

"You're lying." Matt's carelessly tossed accusation made me draw a sharp breath, but Sir Charles didn't blink.

"No, Mr. Glass. I have not been sitting in my conveyance watching anyone in Crouch End or otherwise. Broughams are common vehicles in the city. Now, if you've finished, my dinner will soon be ready."

He tried to shut the door, but Matt wedged himself into the gap and muscled it open again.

I angled myself so I could still see him over Matt's shoulder. "We haven't finished, as it happens," I said. "Tell me what you were doing at the Delancey residence this morning."

"Visiting my good friend, Ferdinand Delancey. Why?"

"He wasn't at home. You would have known he was at work by that time."

"I didn't," he said flatly. "Sometimes he leaves late. If you don't believe me, ask Mrs. Delancey. I saw her only briefly." He glared pointedly at Matt's arm, holding open the door.

"You know about Fabian Charbonneau going missing." Matt didn't state it as a question.

Sir Charles hesitated then nodded. "Yes, but I don't know where he is."

"Do you think anyone else among your collector's club circle knows his whereabouts?"

"If they do, they're very good liars. As far as I am aware, they all want to find him."

"Why?" I asked.

"To help him, of course. He's a magician, and our group has an interest in protecting those like him. Mrs. Glass, if you find him, I implore you not to hand him over to the police. Bring him to me, not the others. I'll help him."

"Help him fight the charges of murder?" I hedged.

"Help him leave the country. Do you understand what I'm saying?"

"That you will help a suspect in a murder escape justice?"

"That I will give a magician his freedom without conditions attached." He said nothing about whether he thought Fabian guilty or not. He probably didn't care.

"Are you implying that the others will only help him so that he'll owe them a favor?" Matt asked.

That familiar sick feeling settled in my stomach again. I knew all too well that Lord Coyle collected favors from people, as if they were objects to add to his magical collection.

"How far will some of the members go to have Charbonneau indebted to them?" Matt pressed.

"What do you mean?" Sir Charles said.

"Would someone kill for him?"

Sir Charles's chest expanded with his deep, measured breath. A thin line creased his brow, marring the smooth surface. "That doesn't make sense, Glass. Why would anyone kill his creditor when it would only implicate Charbonneau?"

"So that they can help Charbonneau and collect their favor."

"That is a very big leap you're making, and a nasty accusation. Be careful, Glass. You don't want to accuse the wrong person. There are some very powerful people in that club."

Matt moved out of the doorway, and Sir Charles slammed it in his face.

"He has a point," I said as we drove home in the murky light of dusk. "Why would anyone kill McGuire to free Fabian of his debt and prison when it would only implicate him in the murder?"

"Perhaps the killer didn't know Charbonneau had escaped."

"Then why place the handkerchief at the site to implicate him if he's supposed to be in jail?"

"That could have been someone else's doing, after learning

of Charbonneau's escape. Someone who *did* want to implicate him. That person would then offer to help Charbonneau leave the country, ensuring he owes them a favor." He looked through window back to Whittaker's house as we turned out of the street. "But first, Charbonneau needs to be found."

It seemed rather far-fetched to me, but I could see the sense in it if there were two guilty parties, a murderer and someone who later planted evidence at the crime scene.

Matt sat back with a sigh. "I know what you're thinking, and I agree," he said. "My theory is too convoluted."

"But not unsound."

"In my experience, never jump to complicated solutions if a simple one will do."

"The problem is, we don't have a simple theory."

* * *

WILLIE, Cyclops and Duke stayed out late so we didn't talk to them until the following morning after breakfast. They each reported a lack of success. No one under the names Robert Smith or Fabian Charbonneau was staying at any of the first or second class hotels in the city.

"Want us to try the low-down, meaner accommodations?" Willie asked, propping her booted feet on Matt's desk.

Duke pushed them off. "Where're your manners?"

"I think I left 'em in a pub somewhere." She grinned at him and he rolled his eyes. She kept her feet on the floor, however.

"We could go to the hotels further afield," Cyclops said.

"We'll abandon the search for now," Matt said. "Without knowing what name he registered under, we'll never find him."

"What about you two? Where did you go yesterday afternoon?"

"Chronos's house," I said. "It's possible he's harboring Fabian, but we can't be certain. He's acting rather suspiciously, but that could be because he's being followed by Sir Charles Whittaker."

"Whittaker?" Duke asked. "Why him?"

"For the same reason we went to see Chronos. He believes Fabian is there."

"I want the three of you to watch Chronos in shifts," Matt said. "Look for any suspicious behavior or any indication someone else is living there aside from him."

Willie put up her hand. "I'll take first shift."

"Try not to let him see you," I told her. "He knows you well."

"Want me to search the house if he goes out?"

Matt hesitated then shook his head. "He's family."

"You're far too kind," I said. "I wouldn't be."

We discussed our theories with them, but they agreed that while the suggestions for what might have happened were logical, they were not likely.

"I reckon we need to look closer to McGuire's home," Duke said. "Seems to me someone else has a better reason to murder him than Charbonneau or one of the collector's club."

"Agreed," Matt said. "But the problem is Charbonneau's handkerchief. If he didn't drop it there himself—"

"Which isn't likely," I cut in.

"Then someone planted it there to incriminate him."

"So the killer held a grudge against McGuire *and* Charbonneau," Willie said.

"I'd wager it's someone indebted to McGuire," Cyclops said. "Money lenders in England are probably as hated as money lenders in America. Find the person who owes him the most money and you've got your biggest suspect. Then you just need to find out why he holds a grudge against Charbonneau too."

We dispersed with that in mind. Matt and I planned to see Brockwell and ask him if he knew the names of McGuire's customers, but Brockwell called on us before we left. He removed his hat in the entrance hall and clutched it in both hands as he gazed up the stairs.

"She's not here," I said, biting back my smile. "We'll tell her you called."

"That's kind of you, but don't go to any trouble," he said.

"No trouble at all. I'm sure she'd be delighted to know you asked after her." In truth, I didn't know anything of the sort. Willie played her cards close to her chest when it came to her intimate relationships, and this one was no different. I didn't know if she was in love with him or he was merely someone to pass an evening with.

Brockwell scratched his sideburns. "The truth is, Mrs. Glass, I'd rather you didn't tell her I asked after her."

"You're avoiding her?"

"What's she done now?" Matt asked on a sigh.

"No, no, nothing like that." Brockwell gave a nervous little laugh. "I need to concentrate on my work, and she's a distraction."

We invited him into the library to discuss the case. He passed his hat to Bristow and removed his coat. "I'm glad I didn't catch you at breakfast," he said idly. "I know that your type sometimes start the day late."

Matt arched a brow at him. "My type?"

Brockwell scrubbed his sideburns. "Pardon me, it was just an expression. No offence meant."

"None taken," Matt muttered as he sat in one of the deep leather armchairs by the fireplace.

"Since breakfast is finished, would you like tea?" I asked. "And cake?"

Brockwell all but smacked his lips together in delight. "Tea and cake would be very fine. Very fine indeed. Your cook is a marvel, Mrs. Glass. I tell all my colleagues about how light and airy her sponge is."

"Mrs. Potter is excellent." I nodded at Bristow, hovering in the doorway. He bowed out of the library.

"Any luck finding Charbonneau?" Matt asked.

"None," Brockwell said. "Have you questioned your magical acquaintances, Mrs. Glass?"

"Yes, and we've also had no luck," I said. "He has thoroughly disappeared."

He clicked his tongue.

Neither Matt nor I brought up the letter opener I'd found at Louisa's house, nor our visit to Chronos.

"What about other suspects?" Matt asked. "Have you found any among McGuire's acquaintances?"

"We're still making inquiries, but..." He winced, as if he had some unpleasant news to impart. "I don't like to suggest it, but I must. I am suspicious of the widow."

"Why?" I asked.

"She has been most unforthcoming with information. She will not answer my questions nor allow me access to her husband's business papers. I explained to her that it is necessary to pry into his affairs if I am to catch his killer. At which point, she broke down in tears. I couldn't get another word out of her. I have tried three times now, and every time I have left empty handed. I am usually an excellent judge of character, if I do say so myself, but Mrs. McGuire is puzzling. I'm not sure if I have a manipulative murderer on my hands or a frightened woman."

"What would she be frightened of?" I asked. "The killer coming after her?"

"I am not entirely sure of that either." He didn't meet my gaze, however, and I suspected there was more.

We were interrupted by Bristow wheeling in the tea trolley. I poured the tea and held the sugar bowl while Brockwell dropped a cube into his cup and stirred. I took my time cutting the cake and placing slices on plates. Then I held out a plate to Brockwell, only to draw it back when he reached for it.

"If you want to hold things back from one another..." I

said with an arch of my brow. Out of the corner of my eye I saw Matt smirk into his teacup.

Brockwell gazed longingly at the cake then sighed. "Very well. It relates to my reason for coming anyway, and you need to know. The thing is, we had a complaint almost a year ago from the McGuires' neighbor about a disturbance at the McGuire household. She claimed to have heard Mr. McGuire shouting at his wife, and Mrs. McGuire screaming. The constabulary investigated at the time and the sergeant was told by Mr. McGuire that everything was well and that the neighbor mistook a simple marital disagreement for something more. When they insisted on speaking to Mrs. McGuire, she presented herself to them. She sported a bruised cheek and the sergeant suspected the husband had inflicted it. Mrs. McGuire denied he'd hit her, however, even when the sergeant spoke to her alone. She claimed she walked into a door."

"Did he take the husband to the station for further questioning?" Matt asked.

"No. Unless Mrs. McGuire accused Mr. McGuire, nothing could be done."

"So he just left her there with her violent husband?" I asked.

"He could do nothing more without her accusation."

"Did the sergeant tell her where to find help? Did he tell her the legal process that would follow if she did want to accuse her husband?"

"I am afraid not."

I handed him the cake, since he'd fulfilled his side of the bargain, but he set the plate down on the table without tasting the sponge. "I will have a word with the sergeant in question, and make recommendations to his superiors to educate their men on the best way to handle issues of a domestic nature when they arise. Unfortunately, they arise all too often."

"Thank you, Inspector. That's good of you to do something."

"I don't like suggesting this," Matt said darkly, "but Mrs. McGuire is even more of a suspect now. If her husband abused her again, she might have finally snapped."

"No one could blame her for killing him," I said.

"Agreed."

"It is certainly a possibility," Brockwell said. "But it doesn't explain why she'd refuse to hand over his paperwork. It wouldn't implicate her. In fact, it would expand our list of suspects beyond her."

"Unless there is something in that list that does implicate her," Matt said.

The poor woman. She must have been pushed to her limits if she had indeed killed him.

"Please, eat your cake, Inspector," I said. "Mrs. Potter wouldn't want it to go to waste."

He took a large bite. Cream spilled out of the layers and the corners of his mouth, plopping onto the plate. Brockwell's eyes fluttered closed in bliss.

Matt and I ate our slices with more dignity but no less enthusiasm. Mrs. Potter's cakes were worth savoring.

"That brings me to my reason for coming," Brockwell said after licking his fingers clean. "Mrs. Glass, I need your help with Mrs. McGuire. I think a woman's touch is required if she is to be convinced to hand over her husband's belongings. We could do it forcefully, of course, but I'd rather save that until we've exhausted all other options."

"I'll see what I can do," I said.

"Thank you." He rose to leave but remembered something. "We have a witness who saw a figure leaving Charbonneau's residence on the night of the murder, after midnight. He isn't a reliable witness, however." He made a drinking motion with his hand. "If he can be believed, I assume it was either Charbonneau returning to collect something before he disappeared, or someone collecting the handkerchief to place at the scene of the murder."

"Did the witness identify the figure as man or woman?" Matt asked.

"Male, but that doesn't mean it wasn't a woman dressed in male clothes." He chuckled. "Now that my eyes are open to such things, I see it more and more. Miss Johnson says she finds men's trousers comfortable. Having never worn women's clothing myself, I can't comment."

"Naturally," Matt said, sounding a little bewildered.

"Did anything else appear to be missing from Fabian's residence?" I asked.

"Hard to say without an inventory of his belongings," Brockwell said. "But nothing seemed out of place."

"Are your men watching it?" Matt asked.

Brockwell nodded. "Charbonneau may return."

I thought there was more likelihood of Willie wearing a corset.

* * *

WE WERE ABOUT to leave to visit the widow of Mr. McGuire when a letter arrived from Gabriel Seaford, the magician doctor who'd helped me save Matt's life. His magic flowed through Matt's veins, while my magic extended it beyond its short span through Matt's watch.

Matt brought the letter in to me in the sitting room where I was making sure Aunt Letitia had everything she needed while we were out. The grim look on his face had me worried.

"What is it?" I asked on a rush of breath.

While Matt's immediate future looked positive thanks to the combination of Gabe's and my own magic, there was always the danger that it wouldn't last and we would need to cast our spells into the watch again. It was that longer future I feared would be snatched from us if Gabe were no longer reachable.

"It's the most curious thing," Matt said. "Lady Louisa Hollingbroke called on him. She turned up on his doorstep yesterday after he'd finished at the hospital. She used your name as an introduction, India."

I sat heavily on the sofa beside Aunt Letitia. "She knows about his magic."

"She does," Matt said.

"Does it matter?" Aunt Letitia asked. "He doesn't have to donate anything to her collection if he doesn't wish to."

"She didn't ask him for a donation." Matt handed her the letter and she set aside her book. "She asked him if he has a fiancée."

"He told her he doesn't," Aunt Letitia read. "He goes on to say that she then asked him if he hopes to marry one day soon. She has all but proposed! What a forward little hoyden! If her family knew, they'd be extremely embarrassed. He's not even a baronet."

"He's a good man," I said defensively. "We owe him a lot."

"I like Mr. Seaford too, India. All I'm saying is that she ought to put that fortune to use and look higher. There must be an impoverished earl or marquis in need of a wife somewhere in the country."

I ignored her snobbery. It wasn't the time to point it out, and doing so would achieve nothing. Besides, there was something far more serious to worry about.

"She wants to marry a magician," I said to Matt. "Fabian wouldn't have her, so she's trying another bachelor magician. Gabe's magic is rare. That must appeal to her."

"She knew we wouldn't introduce her to Gabe, so she introduced herself," Matt said. "I don't like that she used your name."

"She's used to getting what she wants."

"I don't understand," Aunt Letitia said. "Does she wish to

have magic at her fingertips for her own private use? Like electric lighting or indoor plumbing?"

I smiled at her analogy, but it quickly faded. "Perhaps, but it's more likely she wants to marry a magician in the hope she will have magician children. I can think of no other reason."

"Nor I," Matt said.

Aunt Letitia folded the letter and thrust it back at Matt. "Then you must warn Mr. Seaford immediately, before he's seduced by her large fortune."

CHAPTER 7

I left Matt to write a letter of warning to Gabe and drove to Mrs. McGuire's home alone. I had pictured an abusive husband and money lender as living in a miserable area known for criminal activity, where the houses were crammed with poor families struggling to pay their rent and children begged on the streets. But the small terraced Chelsea house was well maintained, if unremarkable in appearance, and the neighborhood quiet.

I introduced myself to the housekeeper, who answered my knock, and requested to see Mrs. McGuire. She told me to wait on the doorstep.

A few minutes later, a small woman dressed all in black opened the door. A black veil covered her face, making it difficult to gauge her reaction when I asked if she'd answer my questions about her husband. The slamming of the door in my face left no room for misinterpretation, however.

"Mrs. McGuire," I called out. "I am not with the police."

No response.

"I'm an independent inquiry agent hired to find your husband's killer. Will you help me, please, one woman to another?"

The door reopened a mere crack. I could just make out the eye blinking at me behind the veil. "Go away," she said in a Scottish accent. "I have nothing to say to you."

"Then do not say anything. All you have to do is show me your husband's ledgers and contracts."

The eye narrowed. "You *are* with the police."

"I'm trying to help my friend, a suspect in your husband's murder. He didn't do it, and I have to prove it or..." I swallowed. "I'll admit that I've spoken to the police and they told me you wouldn't hand over Mr. McGuire's documents to them. I saw my opportunity to see the documents for myself and find evidence to clear my friend. Will you let me in? I'll be no trouble."

"How can I trust you?"

Her question caught me off guard. I had no way of proving I wasn't out to harm her, dupe her, or destroy vital clues. "I hope my word is enough. I am who I say I am, a concerned friend of a suspect. He didn't do it. You must believe me."

The veil billowed with her breath then flattened against her nostrils. "I... I can't," she whispered. "Please, don't ask me to betray him."

"Betray who? Mrs. McGuire, who are you protecting?"

She slammed the door again.

I huffed at it, not yet willing to give up. I'd hardly begun to tell her everything I'd planned to.

"Please, if you are still there," I said through the door, "I want you to know that I am aware of how he treated you. He was a monster and what he did was unthinkable. But I also know the police failed you when they investigated. They could have done more to help you. You must have felt abandoned and very much alone, so it's no wonder you don't want to help them now."

Nothing. Not even a squeak of a floorboard or receding

footsteps. It gave me hope that she was listening on the other side of the door.

"If you've done something wrong and are trying to cover it up now, I want you to know I'll do my best to help you. I can pay for a lawyer," I added lamely. I could make no other promises, not without lying, and I didn't want to do that. If she had killed her husband, I couldn't stop the police arresting her.

Still no answer from the other side of the door.

I sighed and returned to the carriage.

* * *

"SHE WAS VERY NERVOUS," I told Matt upon my return.

He and Aunt Letitia had been out walking in the park when I arrived, and I'd settled into an armchair in the library with a book. I'd read very little of it by the time they returned. My encounter with Mrs. McGuire troubled me too much to concentrate.

"When she realized why I was there, she completely closed up," I went on. "She wouldn't even let me in."

"That's odd." He moved his chair closer to mine and indicated I should put my foot on his lap. He then proceeded to remove my shoe and massage my toes.

I checked the door, worried that his aunt would walk in at any moment. "Not as odd as you might think," I said, frowning at an unpleasant memory. "It might be a reaction to her abusive husband."

"He can't hurt her now."

"I know, but her confidence has been shattered. If the abuse was sustained over a period of time and no one helped her, I can imagine it destroying what fight she had to begin with."

"I suppose," he said, nodding thoughtfully.

"A distant cousin of my mother's had a husband similar to

Mr. McGuire. She didn't tell anyone that he hit her until after he died, and then only her sister. My mother said her cousin had been a friendly girl before she married, but became introverted and anxious afterward. She lost all confidence."

"Why did she never tell anyone? Her sister would have helped her, surely—and your mother."

"My mother said her cousin was too afraid of him to speak up, but she was also ashamed. She blamed herself for inviting the abuse, thinking she'd done something to displease him."

"Did she regain her confidence after his death?"

"Not really. She remained anxious and unsettled until her own death almost two years later. I remember my mother telling me, after she learned of his abuse, and shaking her head in disbelief. She didn't understand why her cousin couldn't see she wasn't to blame and that his death freed her."

We fell into silence. Matt massaged my foot, but I could tell his mind wasn't on the task. He stared into the unlit fireplace, his brow furrowed. Like me, he was grappling with the information, and the similarity between Mrs. McGuire and my mother's cousin.

"I might be quite wrong," I said. "Mrs. McGuire might be trying to hide the documents from us because she knows they'll implicate her or someone she wants to protect. She mentioned not wanting to betray someone."

"There's only one way to know for certain. We have to get those documents before she destroys them."

"If she hasn't already. How will we get them?"

I knew from his face that I wouldn't like his answer. And that meant only one thing.

"No. No, Matt. I forbid it. We're not breaking into her house."

"*We* are not breaking in. I am, alone."

I crossed my arms and withdrew my foot. "No."

"Last time you entered a house with me, you almost got caught," he said. "I won't risk it a second time."

"That's not what I meant. I mean you cannot break into the home of a widow who is showing signs of nervousness. It could shatter her nerves completely if she came upon you."

"Then we'll just have to make sure she doesn't come upon me."

* * *

WITH CYCLOPS WATCHING CHRONOS, Matt took Duke with him to Mrs. McGuire's residence. Willie and I watched on from the carriage parked up the street as the two of them knocked on her door. Dressed in working clothes and armed with a copy of the *Public Health Act 1875* and a box full of tools, they eventually talked their way inside. No doubt Matt used his charm to full effect to explain to Mrs. McGuire that there'd been reports of a strange smell emanating from her house and she had to vacate while they investigated. I expected her to refuse, but she dutifully stood on the pavement while Matt and Duke entered.

Willie and I were present in case Mrs. McGuire got tired of waiting, but we weren't needed. Twelve minutes after talking their way in, they emerged and spoke to Mrs. McGuire. She returned inside, closed the door, and was none the wiser. We drove off and met them around the corner where they climbed in alongside us.

"I reckon I could be a real sanitary inspector," Duke said. "Ain't nothing to it. You don't even need to fix the problem, just report on it."

"What did you tell her before you left?" I asked.

"That it must have been a false report." Matt opened the tool box on his lap. "We gave her house a clean bill of health." He pulled out a ledger book and handed it to me. "Once we located McGuire's office, it was easy to find this. He kept everything in here, the names and addresses of the men who owed him money, the principal and interest, repayments, everything."

I flipped open the book and scanned the first few pages then flipped to the last entry. Fabian's name appeared in entries dated the previous three weeks, but not before. I didn't recognize any of the other names.

"Is he owed any unusually large amounts?" Matt asked.

I returned to the front of the book where each loan had been summarized. "Not particularly, although this entry has an asterisk next to the name and is for the largest amount."

"Maybe the asterisk is *because* it's a large amount," Willie said. "Let me see." She took the book and checked the details. "Mr. Hubert Stanhope, partner in the Ingles Vinegar Company, South Lambeth."

"That's an industrial area on the other side of the river," I said. "Ingles is a vinegar manufacturer."

"The vinegar business can't be good if Stanhope has to borrow money," Duke said.

"They manufacture cordials and wine too," I said. "I didn't realize the business was suffering, although they're certainly not the only vinegar manufacturer in London."

"I've seen Ingles' embossed bottles in the pub," Willie said.

Matt took the ledger back. "I assume that loan is a personal one to Mr. Hubert Stanhope. McGuire wasn't a big money lender and wouldn't be loaning funds to large scale manufacturers." He returned the ledger to the tool box. "Tomorrow we'll pay a visit to Mr. Stanhope at his place of business."

"What about Brockwell?" I asked.

"After our visit, we'll hand the ledger over to Scotland Yard with any other information we gather. I'm sure Mr. Stanhope will respond better to our questions than the inspector's."

* * *

We found Mr. Stanhope in the company's utilitarian brown brick building fronting South Lambeth Road. The staff working in the office wore suits and carried pencils. They studied ledgers or documents on the desks before them, and they peered at Matt and me above their spectacles as we passed. I caught a glimpse through the windows of a garden courtyard surrounded by more brown brick buildings, the tallest of which was topped by a water tank. Horses pulled carts laden with barrels or crates, and steam billowed from an engine used to pump water from a well. Out there was where the business of making vinegar, cordials and wine happened. This office building was for the managers and accountants, the sales representatives and myriad other staff needed to run a medium sized manufacturing business.

We were shown into a large room with an equally large desk and a tall bookshelf, neatly stacked with the ledgers to the left and other books to the right. A quick glance over the spines revealed they were mostly accounting books, and were organized alphabetically by author. Several paintings of the same set of buildings depicted from different angles hung on two of the walls, while a window on the third wall overlooked the courtyard.

The man behind the desk closed the enormous ledger he'd been inspecting, removed his spectacles, and rose. "My assistant tells me you're private inquiry agents," Mr. Stanhope said, "but he didn't say what you're inquiring about."

According to the assistant who'd escorted us, Mr. Stanhope was the company's chief accountant as well as business partner to Mr. Ingles. Like the office, he was neatly presented with just the right amount of cuff showing, a collar that was neither too high nor too pointed, and a gray tie of the same shade as his suit. He was balding, a little portly but not fat, and exactly how I expected a chief accountant to look.

"My name is Matthew Glass, and this is my wife, India,"

Matt said. "We're investigating the murder of Mr. Douglas McGuire. You knew him."

Mr. Stanhope's face froze, the welcoming smile still in place.

"Do you mind if we sit?" Matt asked. "We just have a few questions. It won't take long."

Mr. Stanhope's features thawed. He stroked his beard then his tie before sitting heavily. He nodded and indicated we should occupy the chairs opposite.

"I read about his death in the newspaper," he said. "His murder, I should say. I expected this call, although I thought the police would come. Who do you work for again?"

"We're assisting the police on a consultative basis," Matt said. "Scotland Yard employs us from time to time with particular cases."

"Particular cases?" he echoed.

"Cases requiring a certain line of inquiry."

"I don't understand."

It took me a moment to realize what Matt was trying to say. He wanted to lead Mr. Stanhope to the conclusion that we helped the police in cases involving magic, but he was being far too subtle. Mr. Stanhope merely looked confused. Unless we told him directly, he wouldn't grasp Matt's meaning, and I wasn't sure we should bring up the subject of magic with a man who may not believe in it.

"What my husband means to say is that the police call on us when a woman's touch is required," I said.

"And this case requires a woman's touch?" Mr. Stanhope asked.

"Yes."

"I see."

"I'm glad you do. Please tell us how you know the victim."

Mr. Stanhope clasped his hands over the ledger and stared at them. "This is rather awkward."

"Why?" I asked gently.

"I suspect you know why and it's the reason you're here." His knuckles turned white. "I owe Mr. McGuire a great deal of money."

"What for?" Matt asked. "The business seems prosperous, and as partner, you will enjoy the profits as well as a good wage."

"You are correct in all things, Mr. Glass." Mr. Stanhope's shoulders rounded and he rubbed his forehead. "The loan was for personal reasons. Reasons I'd rather no one know about."

"If you don't tell us, Detective Inspector Brockwell will come instead, and his methods of extracting information are not as gentlemanly as mine," Matt said.

I eyed him sideways and hoped Brockwell never heard himself described that way. On the other hand, he might be flattered or amused.

"Very well, but…it's rather humiliating."

"Would you like me to leave the room?" I asked.

"No, no, that's not necessary." He flattened his tie. "I like horse racing a little too much. The money I borrowed from Mr. McGuire was to repay a gambling debt. There. Now you know my secret."

"Thank you for telling us."

"What I don't understand is, why am I a suspect in the murder? The debt is still outstanding, but instead of owing Mr. McGuire, I now owe his heirs. His death doesn't dissolve my debt, merely transplants it, so to speak."

"You didn't sign a clause stating otherwise?" Matt asked.

"No, and I can prove it." He unlocked the bottom drawer of his desk and rifled through papers before handing one to Matt. "The law requires all debts be repaid to the lender's estate upon his death."

Matt scanned the document then handed it to me. It was a contract for a loan between Mr. McGuire and Mr. Stanhope. There were no special clauses to the effect the debt would be dissolved under any circumstances, let alone McGuire's death.

"Do you know why Mr. McGuire would put an asterisk beside your name in his ledger?" Matt asked.

Mr. Stanhope frowned. "No."

"Do you know Mr. Fabian Charbonneau?" I asked.

"Who?"

"A Frenchman."

"I've never heard of him."

"We just have one more question, Mr. Stanhope," Matt said. "Where were you on the night Mr. McGuire died?"

"I left here at about nine and went straight home like I always do. I was there all night. My wife will tell you."

"Nine seems rather late to be leaving the office."

"I have a lot of work to do." He indicated the ledger. "Ask Ernest."

"Ernest?"

"Ernest Ingles," Mr. Stanhope said, as if we should know. "My business partner and manager of the company. You'll probably find him in the brew house at this time of day, but he comes in here to discuss the company's financials in the early evenings."

Mr. Stanhope walked us out, escorting us to the front door. Matt asked him questions about making vinegar and associated products, and by the time we reached the exit, I knew how to brew vinegar, wine and cordial, and that Ingles was thinking of expanding into producing gas.

"It sounds complex," Matt said jovially.

"Only at first," Mr. Stanhope said. "The process hasn't changed for centuries, only the equipment has become more sophisticated."

"Does the process of making vinegar involve a particular skill?"

Mr. Stanhope gave him a blank look. "We employ chemists, of course, and engineers to oversee the engines and specialized equipment, but otherwise our staff mostly consist of unskilled labor."

"Does your equipment ever break down?"

"Of course, but fortunately not too often. If it did, we'd have to invest in new equipment, and as the company accountant, it's my job to keep such costs down." He smiled. "You seem uncommonly interested in the business, Mr. Glass. You don't work for a rival company, I hope."

"I can assure you, I don't." Matt shook his hand. "Thank you for your honesty, Mr. Stanhope."

We exited the building but instead of returning to the carriage, we followed a cart along the lane to the courtyard. The smell of vinegar became stronger and irritated my nose and eyes. Matt handed me his handkerchief.

Two workers loading barrels onto a cart directed us to the building where thick smoke billowed from large chimney stacks. The sounds of machinery grew louder the closer we got, and the odor became more intense.

"Do you want to wait outside?" Matt asked.

I shook my head and handed back his handkerchief. "I'm growing used to it."

Inside, the heat enveloped me, and the pungent smell had me reaching for Matt's handkerchief again. I blinked watery eyes and searched for someone who looked like he owned the factory. There weren't as many workers as I expected to see, but that could have been because the area was filled with several enormous vats. There was nothing for workers to do except wait for the process to complete. Each vat was connected to copper pipes that disappeared into the ceiling. The whirring, thumping and grinding sounds of machinery came from up there.

Matt asked a workman to direct us to Mr. Ingles, but the man insisted we wait while he fetched him, and he instructed us not to touch a thing as some of the equipment was hot. I didn't dare check to see if any held magical heat. Considering the warmth of the room, I doubted I'd be able to discern the different type of heats anyway.

A few minutes later, a man dressed in a waistcoat with his shirtsleeves rolled up to the elbows trotted down the stairs. He was about the same age as Mr. Stanhope, but where Stanhope was all orderly neatness, this man looked rather wild with his unkempt hair, long stringy beard, and crooked teeth. He greeted us with a cheerful if uncertain smile.

"You were looking for me?" he asked.

"Your partner, Mr. Stanhope, said we'd find you here," Matt said, raising his voice so it could be clearly heard over the machines. "I'm Matthew Glass, and this is my wife, India. May we speak to you somewhere quieter?"

"Of course, of course. I expect Mrs. Glass would prefer to get away from the smell, too." His smile turned sympathetic, and he indicated we should walk with him outside. "You get used to it, so I'm told. I was brought up here so I've never really known fresh air. It would probably smell as putrid to me as this does to you." He laughed and directed us to the shady side of the building.

"This is your family business?" Matt asked.

"All this was started by my grandfather." Mr. Ingles stood hands on hips and surveyed the buildings, carts and activity. "It was in trouble when I inherited over thirty years ago, but we turned it around. Now look at it. We employ over a hundred staff."

"You said 'we' turned it around," Matt pointed out. "Are you referring to a brother or other family member?"

"I mean Hubert Stanhope. He's like a brother to me. We've known one another for fifty years. His father worked here before him, but without Hubert, this place would still be languishing. The man is a financial genius. I think he sleeps with his ledgers." He rocked back on his heels, chuckling into his beard.

"Is that why you made him partner?" I asked.

"Best decision I ever made, aside from marrying Mrs. Ingles. Hubert brought more than capital to the partnership, he brought his brain too. I might be the one with the chemistry know-how, but that's worthless without sound business sense. Is that enough information for your article, Glass, or do you require more nuts and bolts?"

"Article?" Matt echoed.

"Aren't you the fellow who wrote requesting an interview for your book about London's factories?"

"We're private inquiry agents assisting the police to find a killer."

Mr. Ingles' face fell. "Killer?"

"A money lender by the name of Douglas McGuire."

"I—I don't know what you're talking about. I don't know a McGuire. Why are you asking me questions when the fellow's death has nothing to do with me?"

"Mr. Stanhope knew him," Matt said.

"You think Hubert killed him?"

"We're not suggesting it."

"Then why are you here at all?"

"We're just asking questions, Mr. Ingles, nothing more. We've already spoken to Mr. Stanhope and he directed us here to you."

"Very well." He rolled down one of his sleeves. "Ask me anything. I have nothing to hide and nor does Hubert."

"Where were you Monday evening?"

"Here until a little after nine, then I went home. Hubert was with me, but I'm sure he already told you that. We often work together in the evenings, going over the financial reports he prepares. Is there anything else? I have to return to the brew house."

"Do you know how Mr. Stanhope knew Mr. McGuire?"

Mr. Ingles rolled down his other sleeve. "I've never heard of a man named McGuire, so how would I know of a connection?"

"McGuire was a money lender," Matt said. "Mr. Stanhope borrowed a large sum from him."

"That's not a crime."

"You don't look surprised to hear that your business partner borrowed a large sum from a money lender," I said.

"What Hubert does with his money in his time is not my concern. But I would like to point out that the money lender's death doesn't absolve Hubert of the debt. I know the law, and the law states that he will still have to pay it. So why are you accusing him when he has nothing to gain?"

"We're gathering a picture of Mr. McGuire's life, and that means talking to his associates. Sometimes a seemingly insignificant piece of information can turn out to be a vital clue."

"Oh. Very well." He drew in a deep breath. "Murder is a horrid business. Sometimes I feel isolated from the city, working long hours here and living just next door, but when I hear of the unpleasant goings on out there, I'm glad I rarely have to leave the premises."

"You say you're a chemist," I said. "What does a chemist do here?"

"Everything, including taste the final product." He winked and chuckled. "The brew house is the heart of the operation. It's where the chemistry takes place. I test the liquids at various stages of the process, adjust aeration and room temperature accordingly, add more mother of vinegar if necessary."

I'd never heard of chemistry magic before, but it wasn't that long ago I'd never heard of any kind of magic beyond storybooks. If Mr. Ingles were a magician, he could use spells during the process to refine the flavor or speed up the process.

"You have a lot of equipment," Matt said. "Who is your supplier?"

"Various companies," Mr. Ingles said, frowning. "The vat

manufacturers supply the vats and pipes, there's a barrel maker, of course, and crushing machines, coppers. The list goes on. Why? What does this have to do with your investigation?"

"Nothing. I just like to learn about these things." Matt smiled, and Mr. Ingles smiled too, his concern alleviated. "Are the suppliers English?"

"Most likely, although I can't say for certain. Hubert would know."

We thanked him and walked off, neither of us speaking until we reached the carriage. Matt gave our coachman instructions to drive to Scotland Yard. The traffic crossing the bridge slowed our journey but neither of us minded. It gave us time to be alone.

We should have closed the curtain, however. The carriage came to a complete stop on the bridge approach. A pedestrian passing by rapped on the window, startling us.

"You ought to be ashamed of yourselves, behaving like that in public," she scolded.

Matt pulled the window down. "Madam, the lady is my wife. If you do not approve of a husband kissing his wife, avert your gaze and walk swiftly on. All you've achieved is to call attention to us. Not that I mind. I rather like the world knowing that I adore my wife."

She huffed, hurrying off with pinched lips and flushed cheeks. We finally moved ahead too, but neither of us was in the mood to resume our kiss.

"Ingles and Stanhope are right," Matt said. "There's no reason for any of McGuire's debtors to kill him. Their debts still have to be paid back."

"That absolves Fabian of the murder too."

"Except for the matter of his handkerchief being found at the scene."

"We're back where we started, with no suspects," I said on a sigh.

"Except Mrs. McGuire."

I sighed again. "I don't want it to be her, but I agree that she is our main suspect. Not only did her husband hurt her, she's also the beneficiary unless a will states otherwise. Now all McGuire's debtors owe her. The sum is considerable."

"She has two motives for murder," Matt said. "She frees herself from a tyrant and sets herself up financially."

It was a sobering and disheartening thought.

CHAPTER 8

"Mrs. McGuire is a small woman," Matt said. "It's hard to think of her as physically capable of stabbing a man. He'd be able to fight her off."

"Not if he didn't realize until too late," I said. "If they were being intimate, she could have hidden the knife and stabbed him by surprise. There was only one stab wound, according to the reports."

"I'm not sure what handbook on wifely duties you read before our marriage, but intimacy between husband and wife in an alley is not common. Just in case you weren't aware."

I nudged him with my elbow and fought back a smile. "We're discussing murder."

"Right. Sorry. I'll be more dignified lest a busybody raps on the window again."

"What are your impressions of Stanhope and Ingles?" I asked.

"Ingles seemed nervous," he said.

"I thought so too. Mr. Stanhope was nice enough. I wonder if his wife would vouch for him being home at the time of the murder."

"Brockwell will ask her."

We handed over Mr. McGuire's ledger to the inspector in his office and received a genuine smile from him as thanks.

"You did it," he said. "Well done, Mrs. Glass, I knew it was the right thing to do to come to you for assistance with Mrs. McGuire. You are an excellent private inquiry agent."

"Thank you, Inspector." I felt like a traitor for taking all the praise when it was Matt who'd retrieved the ledger, but I couldn't tell him how we'd really gained entry into her house. His policeman's ethics wouldn't approve.

"How did you get Mrs. McGuire to trust you?"

"Being a woman helped."

"No doubt." He opened the ledger and skimmed down the first pages, skipped to the last entries, then returned to the list at the front, just as we had done. He tapped his finger on Mr. Stanhope's entry. "This one has an asterisk."

"We took the liberty of calling on Hubert Stanhope at his place of business," Matt said. "We hope you don't mind."

Brockwell slammed the ledger closed. "Don't mind! Glass, you had no authority to interview my suspect."

"He's not really a suspect," Matt said. "His debt isn't dissolved."

"Nor is Fabian's," I cut in. "Mr. McGuire's beneficiary inherits them. Is that his wife?"

Brockwell nodded. "I still object very strongly to your interference. I asked Mrs. Glass to retrieve this from Mrs. McGuire, nothing more."

"We wanted to find a connection between the killer and Charbonneau," Matt said. "Considering the people who know about him in London also know he's a magician, it seemed logical that the killer is also a magician. Mr. Stanhope is a partner in a successful vinegar manufacturing business, so it's possible magic is involved in the process. Alternatively, it could be the equipment which contains metal magic. If we could prove the equipment came from Charbonneau Industries in France, we would have our link."

"And did you prove anything of the sort?" Brockwell asked, clipping off each consonant.

"No."

"We had to try," I said in an attempt to remove the scowl from his brow. "Fabian is our friend."

"You should not have spoken to anyone without talking to me first," Brockwell said. "Is that understood?"

"Come now, Inspector," Matt said smoothly. "Not only have we worked together with great success in the past, you're a very special person to my cousin. Can we not help one another?"

Brockwell's cheeks pinked. "Leave Miss Johnson out of this."

Matt put up his hands in surrender.

Brockwell opened the ledger again and read a few pages. "We've been trying to pin down McGuire's movements on the night of his death. Without Mrs. McGuire's assistance, we have not had much success. A neighbor saw the victim entering his own home at about six and we know he was drinking at the local pub from nine until midnight."

"He could have been accosted by a ne'er do well on his way home," I said. "It could have been an entirely random attack."

"That is certainly a possibility, but McGuire wasn't on his way home from the pub. The alley where the murder took place is in the opposite direction from his house."

"He was meeting someone," Matt said, nodding slowly. "Was anything found on his person to indicate he had an appointment?"

"No, but if he kept that sort of thing at home, we don't have access to it until Mrs. McGuire lets us in."

"I'll visit her again," I said, being very careful not to look at Matt. I didn't want him sneaking into her house a second time. The disguise of sanitary inspector might not work again.

"Thank you, Mrs. Glass. Tell me, in your professional opinion as a magician, do you think the Ingles Vinegar Company uses magical equipment from France?"

"It's impossible to say, Inspector. Perhaps you can check Mr. Stanhope's books to see if they use a French manufacturer."

"An excellent idea. Thank you for the suggestion." He came around the desk and put out his hand to assist me to my feet. "As always, you've been very helpful. I'm glad I came to you."

The moment we were in the carriage and the door closed, Matt turned to face me. He looked a little bemused. "Have you noticed how he still flirts with you but he gives me short shrift?"

"Don't be ridiculous," I said. "He's simply being polite."

"Polite to you and the opposite to me."

I snuggled into his side. "Are you still jealous, even now? Matt, that is sweet."

He grunted. "I'd be more worried about Willie's jealousy, if I were you."

* * *

DUKE WAS asleep when we arrived home, having undertaken the night shift at Chronos's house. Cyclops was watching it now, and we found Willie keeping Aunt Letitia company in the library. Aunt Letitia sat with a large atlas open before her, while Willie studied it over her shoulder.

"See!" Willie cried, stabbing her finger on the page. "Tombstone. I told you it was real."

Aunt Letitia made a miffed sound through her nose and slammed the book closed. "Ridiculous name." She beckoned me to take her hand and assist her to stand. "Shall we go through preparations for tonight's dinner, India?"

"We already have," I said. "Mrs. Potter has it all in hand."

"Forget the food. That's not as important as the setting."

"There'll be roses as centerpieces and the wedding china will be used. Mr. and Mrs. Bristow will have the dining room looking elegant and refined."

"Yes, yes, that's all well and good, but are you certain Hope will be placed beside Lord Coyle? It's imperative she's given the best opportunity to shine."

Willie snorted. "Ain't no problem with her shining, but scratch the pretty surface and you see the ugly base metal underneath."

"We don't have to worry about her base metal showing tonight. Hope will do her duty and charm him. The sooner we secure Coyle, the better."

"Before the gold rubs off," Willie agreed.

"Very astute. I'll have to think of some conversation openings just in case the evening stalls."

"I'll help you," Willie said. "There's paper in the sitting room."

They headed off together, leaving Matt and I staring after them. "Sometimes those two astound me with their similarities," Matt said.

"Sometimes those similarities worry me," I added. "They're rather diabolical together. I almost feel sorry for Lord Coyle."

Matt grunted. "Save your sympathies for the both of us. We have to sit through this dinner."

Bristow entered with Oscar Barratt. The last time we'd seen the ink magician and reporter for *The Weekly Gazette*, he'd been angry that the printer he'd secured to print his upcoming book on magic had canceled the contract. Oscar blamed Matt at first, accusing him of threatening to expose the printer to his guild, thereby putting his printing license in jeopardy. We'd assured him it wasn't Matt, but someone had certainly threatened him. We suspected Lord Coyle. His lordship didn't want magic exposed in such a public way for fear it would diminish the value of his collection.

"You look happy," I said as we settled into the armchairs.

"I have news," he announced. "I wanted you to find out through me, India, before you hear it from someone else. The book will go ahead after all. I've found a new printer."

I wasn't sure what to think or feel. On the one hand, I was hopeful that a book about magic would be the beginning of the end of persecution from the guilds. It would show the world that magicians were not to be feared.

But I suspected it would have the opposite effect and lead to public clashes between magicians and artless guild members. Former friends would become enemies, livelihoods would be affected, and neither magicians nor the artless would be completely happy with the outcome.

"I'm...pleased for you," I said carefully. "But my concerns haven't changed. I don't think it's a good idea yet. England isn't ready for magicians."

He waved away my concerns, and that was the end of that.

Except Matt wasn't prepared to let the matter end. "Are you using the same printer?"

Oscar hesitated before shaking his head. "This is another fellow. We had to offer him more money, but we felt it was worth it."

"'We?'" I asked. "Do you mean Professor Nash?" The professor of history had a keen interest in magic and was writing a chapter in the book about its origins and history. I'd met him through Lord Coyle and his collectors' club friends, but he wasn't a member, merely an occasional lecturer. Unlike Coyle and his ilk, Nash wanted magic to be exposed to the wider public for the same reasons as Oscar.

"Not Nash." A smile played at Oscar's lips, not quite forming but not disappearing altogether either. "My benefactress is Lady Louisa Hollingbroke. I believe you two are friends, India."

"Louisa!" I blinked hard. "When did you meet her?"

"She came to the *Gazette* only yesterday. She said she'd read my articles and enjoyed them, and she wanted to help me get the word out about magic. I explained to her the lack of support from my editor, and all the editors in the city, then told her about my book. She offered me some money then and there. This morning we went to her bank to retrieve the funds then on to a printer I know and gave him a substantial advance payment. He agreed to print the book when it's ready. It all happened very quickly."

"That's Louisa," I said weakly. "She operates swiftly and without mercy."

"Is that all she offered?" Matt asked.

Oscar frowned. "What do you mean?"

"Is that the only reason you're so happy?" I asked. "Because you've secured a new printer?"

"Yes." His frown deepened. "Should I have another reason?"

I wasn't quite sure how much to tell him, but I did feel I needed to warn him as we'd warned Gabe. "Be careful with her. She'll do anything to get what she wants."

"As long as our interests align, as they do with the book, then it doesn't matter if she's as ruthless as Attila the Hun."

Matt huffed a laugh. "You have a way with words that must make the ladies swoon, Barratt."

"From what I know of Lady Louisa, she would appreciate being compared to one of history's great rulers." He rose and buttoned up his jacket. "Please keep this news to yourselves. Not only do I not want the guilds to find out about the printer, but Lady Louisa also doesn't want her friends learning of her involvement with me. For some reason they don't like me. Don't know why. I'm charming." He winked.

I couldn't help my laugh. Oscar and I didn't always agree, but when he was happy, he was good company. His moods depended on the success of his work, however, and whether he was able to spread knowledge of magic through articles and, now, his book.

"We have no interest in telling anyone," I assured him.

"Speaking of Louisa, she told me she's a friend to Fabian Charbonneau. She said he was sent to Newgate for not repaying a debt but escaped and is now a suspect in the murder of the money lender he borrowed from. What a story."

"What else did she tell you about him?" Matt asked as we walked Oscar to the front door.

"Just that he came to London to work with you, India, and no one can find him now. She hoped he would go to her but he hasn't. Do you know where he is?"

"No," Matt growled before I could answer. "And we don't appreciate you coming here fishing for information about his whereabouts."

I was about to protest that he was being unfair, and that Oscar wasn't doing anything of the sort, but realized he was probably right. Oscar had no need to visit to tell me about the book.

"Just being friendly," Oscar said lightly. "If you need help hiding him, let me know. I have discreet friends."

"Mr. Barratt is leaving," Matt said to Bristow. "Please see that he does." He put out his hand to me and we didn't linger to see Oscar go.

"He doesn't get better on longer acquaintance," Matt muttered as we headed up the stairs. "I wish Louisa had proposed to him. They deserve one another."

"She could be waiting to get to know him," I said. "Or she could be waiting to see if she advances with Gabe first."

"Perhaps Oscar's magic isn't strong enough, like Fabian's, or rare enough, like Gabe's. Oscar can't do much with his ink magic unless he wants to drown someone in it."

I circled his arm in mine, hugging it. "I have the afternoon free before our guests arrive. I think I'll pay Louisa a visit. Perhaps she'll divulge her marital plans to me."

"And I think I'll spend a more enjoyable afternoon listening to Willie and Aunt Letitia plotting every minute of the evening."

* * *

LOUISA WAS AT HOME, but I had to wait for her caller to leave before I could speak to her privately. She introduced me to her guest as the future Lady Rycroft, which I didn't think was necessary. It did generate an instant change in the way the lady regarded me, however. As plain Mrs. Glass, I barely even rated a glance and a slight upturn of the top lip, but as the wife of the heir to the Rycroft title, I was smiled at and included in the conversation.

Louisa looked pleased with herself. "Thank goodness you showed up when you did," she said after the visitor departed. "You saved me from London's most notorious matchmaker."

"Is she trying to find you a husband?"

"She already has one in mind, and he just happens to be her nephew who came of age over the summer. She wanted to know if I'll be staying in London this autumn and winter and if not, would I like to visit her at her country estate." She pulled a face. "No doubt the nephew will just happen to arrive while I'm there."

"Is that so awful?"

"It is when I have no intention of marrying him."

"Why not? He might be charming and handsome. Perhaps you should meet him."

"He'll be just like all the others," she said.

"Do you have many suitors to choose from?"

"Dozens. That's the benefit of having a fortune, you see. I can take my pick of eligible young bucks from the best families. The problem is, none of them interest me."

"Because they're not magicians."

She smiled into her teacup. "You do know me well, India."

It was too late to back away from the topic now. I was in it up to my neck. "You proposed to Fabian and have intentions of doing the same to Gabriel Seaford."

"Fabian turned me down, and Dr. Seaford is making all sorts of excuses to avoid seeing me again." Her tone was bland, almost unemotional, but her eyes flashed. "You wrote to him, warning him not to become friends with me. Didn't you?"

I swallowed.

"Don't look so worried, India. I'm not going to throw you out, or throw anything at you. Indeed, I suspected he would ask your opinion of me. I had hoped you would give me a favorable report, but it would seem we're not such good friends, after all."

I gulped down the rest of my tea and gathered my jangling nerves. I'd come to confront her and this frosty reception wasn't unexpected, yet I felt worse than I imagined. "I didn't like you using my name to gain his friendship. It's clear that you want to marry him simply because he's a magician. He didn't need my warning to know that. It was quite obvious to him that something was...amiss in your approach."

She laughed softly. "I'm not terribly put out by Dr. Seaford's lack of communication anyway. He wasn't quite right for me. He didn't want to talk about his magic, and I strongly suspect he'll refuse to use it again. A pity, since his magic is so rare, but not unexpected considering the implications. I want someone who is not only willing to talk to me about their magic but to learn together, similar to what you and Fabian are doing."

I set down my teacup and regarded her. "Are you jealous of my relationship with Fabian?"

She set down her teacup too and regarded me with a

strained smile. "I suppose I am. You don't know how lucky you are, India." She looked away and huffed out a humorless laugh. "The funny thing is, we both have our pick of men, but in different ways. My wealth makes me attractive to bachelors, while your magic makes you attractive to magicians. Bachelors want to marry me, and magicians want you to extend the life of their magic."

"Not all magicians."

"No. Not Dr. Seaford. He is a unique man." She gave me a sly look. "Anyway, I do hope you'll forgive me for using your name, as I have forgiven you."

I was about to ask her what she meant but closed my mouth again. She was referring to the letter opener. I was wondering when I'd have the opportunity to return it, or, in fact, if I should return it at all. It would mean admitting I stole it.

I removed the letter opener from the large reticule I'd brought and handed it to her. "Did your butler notice it missing?"

She laid it flat on her palm, balancing it. "He said a parcel arrived in the mail before you called and was missing after you left. I told him not to fret but he dislikes having the wool pulled over his eyes."

"I'll apologize to him on my way out," I said.

She turned the opener over and studied the inscription then turned it over again to inspect the numbers. "Why was it important?" she asked.

"The numbers contain magical heat."

She sat back heavily and blinked wide eyes at me.

"Just the numbers," I clarified. "Claridges engraved one side to mark their property, and Fabian used a spell to manipulate the metal on the other to reveal his room number."

She closed her fingers around the handle. "I'm afraid you've got it all wrong. This isn't from Fabian. It's from his brother."

I gasped. "His brother? How do you know?"

"Because I sent him a telegraph the instant I learned Fabian went missing. He sent one back to say he would leave immediately and that he'd let me know when he arrived."

"Why wouldn't he just call on you here? Why send that and not a note?"

She shrugged. "To avoid the notice of the police, I suspect. He can't very well look for his brother if the police are watching him to see if he makes contact."

"I see," I said. "He would squirrel Fabian out of the country if he found him, not caring that it would mean he might never clear his brother's name."

"The Charbonneaus are a proud family," she said. "They would be appalled by the scandal and ashamed if word of it reached France. Maxime would be desperate to find Fabian as quickly as possible and leave, without attracting the attention of your detective inspector. And now I have no way of finding him and helping him. I assume he's no longer at Claridge's?"

"Does it matter?" I shot back. "You can't help him find Fabian since you don't know where he is. Do you?"

She pivoted the point of the letter opener on her fingertip as she studied the numbers again.

"Do you?" I pressed.

"Why would Fabian come to me now?" she asked without removing her gaze from the letter opener. "He rejected my proposal of marriage."

"But not your friendship."

She said nothing as she set the letter opener down again, and she thrust out her chin in defiance. Yet her swimming eyes spoke a different story. Perhaps she cared for him more than she liked to admit. Perhaps she'd asked him to marry her because she loved him, not because of his magic. They might not have met before he arrived in London, but they had communicated by mail, and their fathers had been friends.

That connection meant something to her, and his rejection might have wounded her deeply.

Wounded her enough to get revenge on him by making it look like he murdered McGuire?

The more I thought about it, the more the pieces clicked together. Louisa had been there in Fabian's cell when we visited. She'd heard him say he would not be staying in prison long. Where we had thought he meant he'd get out by paying his debts, she might have realized he was talking about using his magic to fashion a key and escape. If she had suspected, then it was only a matter of setting up a meeting with McGuire, stealing Fabian's handkerchief, and planting it on McGuire's body after stabbing him.

It seemed like a complicated and dangerous way to get revenge. So many things could go wrong, and there would be easier ways to punish Fabian for his rejection.

Perhaps revenge wasn't the motive, then. Perhaps she murdered McGuire and planted the handkerchief to implicate Fabian so that she could then help him leave the country. All she had to do was find him before the police, before us or his brother, and take the glory for his rescue herself. And his gratitude. A gratitude that might have him changing his mind about marrying her.

It was the same theory Matt and I had discussed and discarded, but this time the motive was love. It could make people do mad, desperate things they wouldn't normally do and made more sense to me than simply wanting an object infused with Fabian's magic.

I gathered up my reticule and hastily made my excuses to leave. "I have a dinner party to organize," I said, backing toward the door.

She stood, the letter opener in hand. She gripped it so hard her knuckles were white. "Of course. But India..." She rushed toward me, the knife pointed outward, not down for safety.

I backed away quickly, stumbling over the edge of the carpet, straight into the arms of the butler. He lost his balance and we would have fallen if not for the solid chair stopping us.

"Sorry," I muttered, pulling myself upright.

Louisa grabbed my arm, pinning me. Her huge eyes stared into mine, unblinking. For a woman who always looked so composed and sure of herself, this wildness was new.

I jerked free and hurried down the stairs to the front door.

"India!" she called out. "India, wait!

"I—I have to go. So much to do."

I reached the door and wrenched it open. She caught up to me, just as I was about to cross the threshold, and grabbed my arm again. Her chest rose and fell with her heavy breathing and her face was flushed. Her eyes no longer looked quite so wild, but that sharp edge to them was back, the spark of fierce intelligence and confidence that was no less intimidating.

"Tell me if you receive a message from Fabian," she demanded. "Is that understood?"

"Let me go," I snapped, pulling away.

She blinked and took a step back. "Sorry. I'm sorry, India, I'm just so worried about him. Please, just let me know if you find him. I want to help."

I hurried off to my waiting carriage, and I didn't look out the window to see if she watched me drive away.

CHAPTER 9

Polly Picket arranged my hair and assisted me to dress for dinner. Aunt Letitia's ladies' maid had taken on the role of my maid too when I moved in, although I rarely required her services. I could manage most outfits on my own, but Aunt Letitia insisted I use Polly for special occasions. Tonight's square cut bodice fastened up the back, but it was otherwise rather simple with no overlaying sections that required separate fastenings.

"You look beautiful," Matt said once Polly left. He kissed my throat above the pearl necklace and rested his hands on my hips. "I can't wait to thoroughly inspect this gown later. Very, very thoroughly."

"You have an interest in ladies' fashion?" I teased.

"Only yours."

A few minutes later, I convinced him we needed to talk about something—anything—or risk undoing Polly's work. I hadn't seen Matt privately after my visit to Louisa's, so I told him how the afternoon had transpired. He sat on the bed against the pillows, legs outstretched and ankles crossed. I did my best to remember the afternoon's conversation, but it wasn't easy. The combination of formal eveningwear and casual pose was distracting. I found my gaze wandering his length without me realizing it.

He noticed too, the devil, and teasingly prompted me to stay focused and continue. When I finally finished the narration, he said, "Love and revenge, two of the most popular motives for murder, and Louisa has reason for both."

"You think her capable of stabbing someone in an alley?" I asked, perching on the edge of the bed.

"I think her capable of many things, but it's possible she paid someone."

"She's quite a unique woman. Tell me honestly, Matt, is she attractive?"

"She's reasonably pretty."

"I mean is her confidence attractive. Does she have an allure that goes beyond her physical attributes?"

"Not to me."

I tilted my head to the side and regarded him. "It's all right if you think she does. I want an honest answer."

"I am being honest. I don't find her alluring."

"Why not? Is her self-confidence too much?"

"I like confident women." He took my hand and started plucking off the glove. "You're a confident woman, and I love that about you."

"Is she *too* confident? Arrogant, perhaps?"

"Probably." He sounded distracted as he slipped the glove off.

"Matt, are you listening?"

He drew my hand to his lips. "Mmmm."

I plucked my hand away. "I don't think you are. Concentrate."

He sighed. "How can I when all I'm thinking about is that gown and how wonderful it will look tossed on the floor?"

I laughed. "I think we should go downstairs before either of us gets too disheveled."

* * *

DUKE AND CYCLOPS found excuses not to attend the dinner, but Willie declared she wasn't going to miss it. She greeted Lord and Lady Rycroft with enthusiasm, seeming to relish in their disgust of her. She had refused to dress like a woman, much to Aunt Letitia's horror, but she had no men's eveningwear either, so she wore the same clothes she wore to the wedding—a fitted jacket that was the height of fashion for equestriennes, and a pair of trousers. The outfit was actually rather fetching on her, but not really suited to a formal dinner—for a lady or a gentleman.

Lady Rycroft gave Willie a cursory glance before turning her back on her, while Lord Rycroft appraised her openly. His lips lifted in what could only be described as a vicious smile.

"I see they let one of the monkeys out for the night," I overheard him mutter to his wife.

Thankfully Willie didn't hear or the night would have been over before it began.

Lord Coyle arrived last, pausing in the doorway to the drawing room as Bristow announced him. He took in the family of Rycrofts and looked like he'd turn around and march out again. He stayed, however, and settled for throwing sharp glares Matt's way. Matt looked smug.

"We hope you don't mind the extra guests," I said quietly to Lord Coyle.

He leaned heavily on his walking stick. "I don't mind, although I do wonder why."

"Can you not guess?"

His thick features settled into ponderous pouches as he inspected Matt's aunt, uncle and cousins in turn. "They're a social climbing pack," he said, matter-of-factly. "I see I am to be the ladder."

"Only if you wish it."

He grunted. "Why would I wish it? To win your favor?"

He turned to me, his eyes gleaming beneath the fatty lids. "I am already owed a favor by you, Mrs. Glass."

My chest felt heavy. "I've fulfilled my obligation to them by inviting you. What happens next is your choice."

I walked off, passing Lady Rycroft, her gaze locked on Lord Coyle. Lord Rycroft came from the other direction so that they converged on Coyle at the same time, trapping him between them. I smiled at Willie. She winked back.

We had far too many ladies for a well-balanced table, but we made do. Hope sat next to Lord Coyle, but I was surprised when Lady Rycroft insisted Charity swap with her and sit on Coyle's other side. I suspected she wanted a spare, in case Coyle wasn't taken in by Hope's charm.

Charity wasn't required. To my utter surprise, Lord Coyle didn't need any prompting to engage in conversation with Hope. They conversed almost the entire evening, sometimes alone and in low voices. Lady Rycroft looked like she'd burst with pleasure at the sight of them getting along, and Charity looked relieved. She spent the evening drinking and eating as much as she could.

The meal finally ended, and I announced that it was time for the ladies to move into the drawing room and the men to retreat to the smoking room. They rose and waited for us to leave. Willie didn't look as though she would join us, but Aunt Letitia grabbed her by the elbow and marched her out of the dining room.

"That went well," Lady Rycroft declared as she sat on the sofa. She flattened her velvet skirt around her and smiled at her youngest daughter.

Hope lowered herself onto the sofa with effortless grace. "It did," she said.

"What did Coyle say? Did he invite you to call on him? Did you arrange to meet for a walk or ride? Tell me everything, Hope. I *must* know."

"Yes, Hope," Charity said as she flopped onto a chair. "Did he ask for your hand yet?"

"Do stop talking, child," Lady Rycroft said without looking at her middle daughter. "Well, Hope?"

"We talked about scientific advancements," Hope began. "Specifically in the medical field. We talked about America and what it must be like there, and that led to a conversation about his travels to France and Italy some years ago. We discussed the history and art of those countries, and we touched on politics."

Lady Rycroft's smile froze. "Is that all?"

"You don't think that enough?"

"It's a start, but what of more personal matters? Did he tell you why he's never married?"

"No and I didn't ask."

"I specifically told you to find out! How do you propose to get him to marry you if you don't know why he has avoided the institution all these years?"

Hope sighed. "Mother, I think I should make something clear. Lord Coyle isn't interested in me as a wife."

Lady Rycroft scoffed. "He spoke to you all night. Of course he's interested."

"He told me at the beginning of the evening that he knows why he's here. I confirmed his suspicions."

Lady Rycroft's head tilted forward, as if her turban had suddenly become too heavy. She looked up at her daughter through her lashes, her eyes dark, forbidding. "You *silly* girl. You told him our plans and now we're on the back foot."

"This isn't a battle, Mama, and he isn't the enemy."

Charity snorted then hiccupped.

"Could you not feign ignorance?" Lady Rycroft whined.

"No," Hope said. "He would have realized anyway."

"It's true," I chimed in. "He would have."

Aunt Letitia shook her head at me ever so slightly, warning me to stay out of it.

Hope cast a glance toward the door, as if expecting to see the men walk in. Or perhaps she only wished they would. "We conspired to pass the time in conversation and make it look as though we were interested in one another's company," she said.

"Why?" Lady Rycroft asked.

"To appease you and Father. Otherwise you would have tried to control the evening and force conversation. This way we talked about the things that interested us."

Charity gasped. "You *like* him!" She showed us what she thought of that notion by screwing up her face.

"Don't be ridiculous. I liked talking to him, but I don't want to marry him. You warned me he was old, Mama, but you didn't mention he was fat and ugly. I've seen mangy dogs with more appeal than him."

"But you said you'd consider him," her mother protested.

"I have, and I've come to the conclusion that I don't wish to marry him."

"But…but it's too soon! And you promised, Hope."

"I promised to *consider* the match."

"*Carefully*. One evening is not enough time to come to a conclusion."

"I assure you, it is," Hope said, looking away, dismissing her mother.

"Look at me!" her mother all but shouted. Hope turned to her, her face composed but her body rigid. "You will give this due consideration. You will look beyond his physical attributes."

"Or lack of," Charity muttered.

"You will consider *all* the benefits of marriage to an earl, with his vast wealth. Is that understood?"

Hope paused then nodded. "I'll do as you ask."

Lady Rycroft looked relieved. "Good girl."

"Don't sabotage it," Charity said slyly. "Perhaps you

should chaperone them, Mama, to make sure she doesn't do or say anything to put him off."

"An excellent notion. Of course, when the time comes, I'll discreetly leave the two of you alone."

Hope's lips pinched.

"Where are they?" Lady Rycroft said, glancing toward the door. "Letitia, send the butler to the smoking room."

"The butler isn't mine to command," Aunt Letitia said. "Not when India is here."

"The gentlemen will come when they're ready," I said.

Conversation stalled until Willie suggested a game of cards. Hope, Aunt Letitia and I joined her at the card table, but Lady Rycroft remained on the sofa, while Charity slouched in the chair, looking bored. They both cast frequent glances toward the door.

"Do you know Texas rules?" Willie asked Hope.

Hope blinked at her. "Rules for what?"

Willie shuffled the deck, her fingers deft and quick as the cards passed between her hands like a small accordion. "Poker."

"We're not playing poker," I scolded. "Choose something more appropriate."

"Poker is appropriate for ladies," Willie muttered.

"I'd like to learn poker," Hope said. "Will you teach me?"

Willie smirked. I resigned myself to her gloating.

It wasn't long before Lord Coyle arrived, alone. "Rycroft wanted a word with Glass," he said as he lumbered toward us, stamping the end of his walking stick into the floor with a thud.

"Do you play cards, my lord?" Lady Rycroft asked.

"I prefer to keep my money, not gamble it."

"How about a little game just for fun?" Lady Rycroft maneuvered the spare fifth chair next to her daughter. I had to shift my chair over to make space. "There you are," she all but cooed. "Now, what game are you playing?"

"Poker," Willie said. "Five stud."

Lady Rycroft pulled a face. "What about a more refined game, like whist or loo?"

"I prefer poker," Hope piped up. "It appears to be a game of chance."

"On the contrary," Lord Coyle said. "It's a game of judgment, of your own hand and that of your opponent. Being able to read your fellow player is an advantage."

Willie nodded along as she dealt. "Being a good liar helps."

"You cheat?" Lady Rycroft cried.

"Lie," Aunt Letitia cut in. "Not cheating. Beatrice, come away and let's leave the young—" She glanced at Lord Coyle. "Leave them alone."

Coyle's chuckle shook the fatty folds of his neck. Hope turned away from him, but I saw the hint of disgust on her face.

Charity sidled over as we inspected our cards. "Move aside, Sis," she said, wedging herself between Hope and Willie. "Go on, shift your chair towards Lord Coyle." She crowded against Hope, forcing her to lean away or be smothered. "Don't peek, my lord. You can't see what she has until you've laid out your money."

"We're not playing for money," Lord Coyle said without looking up from his cards. "As well you know. Kindly step away. I don't think your sister wants you looking over her shoulder."

Charity smiled down at Hope. "Isn't he the dashing gentleman, coming to your rescue?"

"Charity," her mother snapped. "Come and sit with me."

Lord Coyle glanced at Hope at the same moment she looked at him. She gave him a small smile. "I believe you're starting, Miss Glass," he said.

"Thank you," Hope said, discarding two of her original hand. "Two cards, please."

Matt and Lord Rycroft entered, their faces flushed, their mouths set. Matt came to stand by my chair and rested a hand on my shoulder. His thumb skimmed the bare skin above the back of my bodice.

Lord Rycroft stood by the fireplace and focused his attention on the floor. The only activity in the room was the game. Willie won most hands, but since we played for nothing, it was impossible to tell who came second. I saw a side to Lord Coyle I'd never seen before. He was gracious in defeat and charming, particularly toward Hope. His gaze never once dropped below her chin, even though her bodice was cut a little too low, and he engaged her in conversation as we played. She responded in kind, smiling at the appropriate moments and giving her opinion when he asked for it, which he did often.

It almost looked as though she enjoyed his company and he hers. If I hadn't heard her speak with disgust about him earlier, I wouldn't have believed it. Either she was very good at playing the part required of her, or she had changed her mind already. I suspected the former. She was one of the most devious people I'd ever met, capable of lying quite convincingly.

At a faint sound coming from the depths of the house, Charity suddenly straightened. She'd been leaning against the doorframe for some time, yawning frequently. Now she was alert, her attention focused outside the drawing room.

"Excuse me while I get some fresh air," she said as she pushed off from the doorframe.

Like a hawk swooping on its prey, Lady Rycroft dashed across the room and grabbed her daughter's arm. "There is a window over there where you can get all the fresh air you need."

Charity tried to wrench free, but Lady Rycroft didn't let go and Charity gave up with a *humph*. She settled for staring daggers at her mother instead.

Lord Coyle used his walking stick to push up from the chair. "I must go. It's been a thoroughly pleasant evening. Thank you for inviting me, Mrs. Glass."

He kissed my hand then took Hope's. He lingered a little longer than he had over mine, but not for an inappropriate amount of time.

Matt tugged the bell pull by the fireplace to summon Bristow before giving Lord Coyle a curt nod. Coyle nodded back, and that was the end of their exchange. Instead of moving off, he caught sight of the clock on the mantel. He removed his watch from his waistcoat pocket, checked the time and adjusted it before returning it to his pocket.

"It was a little slow," was all he said.

Lord and Lady Rycroft and their daughters left too, thankfully. Once they were out of sight, it felt like a weight lifted from my shoulders. I hadn't realized how anxious the evening had made me until then.

"I think it went very well," Aunt Letitia said. "You were an excellent hostess, India. No one would have known you were new to the role."

"They did know," Willie told her. "Her past ain't a secret to any of them."

Aunt Letitia rose. "I'm going to bed. Tomorrow we'll discuss how next to proceed, India."

"Proceed?" I echoed.

"In the matter of Coyle and Hope."

"I will not be involved any further. I've done my duty and that is where I bow out. If you wish to see them thrown together again, then you and Lady Rycroft must orchestrate it without me."

"I'll help," Willie piped up. "Them two belong together."

"Those two," Aunt Letitia corrected her. "*Those* two belong together." She walked out, parting Cyclops and Duke who'd been about to enter.

"Dinner went well then?" Duke asked.

"Seems so," Willie said, beckoning them to the card table. "I reckon he's half in love with her already."

"I'm not so sure," I said. "Not on her part."

"She looked amenable," Matt said.

"It was all for show. She told us in no uncertain terms when you were in the smoking room. He's fat and ugly, according to her."

"And *she's* ugly on the inside," Willie said as she shuffled the cards. "So they're a good match."

Duke chuckled and took a seat at the card table. "You playing, Cyclops?"

Cyclops sat too. "Did he look at Charity, or just Hope?"

"He showed no interest in Charity," I said. "Nor she in him."

"Pity."

Matt clapped Cyclops's shoulder and eyed me over his head. I nodded and together we said our goodnights and left.

"Is everything all right?" I asked as he helped me undress. Polly Picket was assisting his aunt to prepare for bed, but I didn't want to wait for her. It felt odd having a maid undress me while my husband watched on or waited in another room. I'd rather have Matt help me instead.

"My uncle wanted to know if I've thrown Cyclops out of the house," he said.

I gasped. "The nerve of him!"

"I told him I didn't believe Cyclops had done anything to harm Charity's virtue, and that he was more in danger from her than she was from him."

"I'm sure he didn't like that."

"Not in the least." He placed my necklace on the dressing table and proceeded to unfasten my dress. "The problem is, I can no longer use the leverage I had. Coyle and Hope have met, the dinner is over."

"I see your point." I leaned back into him and reached up

to cup the side of his face. "Let's worry about it tomorrow. I recall you wished to toss my dress on the floor."

He offered me his first smile of the evening, and it was devilish.

* * *

WITH NOTHING TO do in the investigation, we decided to take stock of what we knew in the library after breakfast. Recapping facts and discussing theories had often worked in the past to shake loose fresh approaches, but I wasn't so sure it would work this time. We had so little to go on.

Cyclops, Duke and Willie had been reasonably sure that Chronos wasn't hiding Fabian, although they couldn't be positive. They agreed to resume shifts watching his house. I told them what I'd learned from Louisa and my suspicions about her involvement, but also my doubts.

"The fact remains, the killer wanted to set up Fabian for the murder," Matt said.

"So it must be someone who hates him," I pointed out.

"What about the brother?" Cyclops asked. "Lady Louisa says the brother sent her the letter opener, so we know he's here in London. Could the brothers hate each other so much that one wants to see the other hang for murder?"

"Fabian always spoke fondly of his family," I said.

"And the timing is wrong," Matt added. "Louisa informed the family *after* Charbonnenau's escape and the murder."

"What about the jilted girl in America?" Willie said. "If I were his fiancée, I'd want to rip out his guts and serve them to the pigs."

"Aye, but you're mad," Duke said.

She kicked him under the table.

"I can't see anyone killing a stranger just so he can blame someone else," I said. "Mad men and women aside."

"You ain't met an angry jilted American," Willie said. "You

won't remember our cousin Mary Ella, Matt. She left town before you arrived. Her fiancé never showed up to the church and she got so mad, she broke every window in his house then set fire to it. She watched it burn with a smile on her face."

"My God," I said. "That's vindictive."

"Her fiancé didn't get to appreciate how vindictive on account of him already being dead. That's why he never showed up. Turned out another man who was in love with Mary Ella accused him of stealing then challenged him to a shootout. The fiancé lost. It all turned out fine in the end, though. The second man took the fiancé's place and after a quick courtship, they married and moved away."

"Love," Duke muttered with a shake of his head. "It ain't worth the trouble."

"Amen," Cyclops said.

"You don't believe that, Cyclops," Willie scolded him. "You neither, Duke. So both of you quit your moping and do something about the lack of lovin' in your lives."

They both looked at her like they were trying to think of ways to make her stop talking.

"Like I did," she added with a grin.

"Speaking of Brockwell," I said, before she told us more than we wanted to hear, "perhaps we should speak to him again, Matt. He might require our services."

"I doubt it," Matt said. "He only came to us because the widow didn't trust him. We delivered McGuire's ledger, as asked."

"But Mrs. McGuire could give him more information. Why don't I talk to her again?"

It was agreed that I should try.

I called on her later that morning. She took one look at me and refused to let me in.

"Go away," she said. "I don't want to say anything."

It was a curious choice of words—she didn't *want* to say

anything, not that she had nothing to say. Last time, she'd told me she didn't *want* to betray her husband. This woman was frightened, even though Mr. McGuire was dead. Frightened of the police because she murdered her husband? Or because he'd treated her so badly that she could no longer trust anyone?

"Go away," she said again, and went to close the door.

"It's not a betrayal of his memory to speak to someone who knows what he did to you," I said quickly.

She paused, leaving the door open a crack. She peered back at me through the gap, her eyes narrowed.

"It's not a betrayal of his memory to be glad he's dead, or to help the police," I added.

"He hated the constabulary," she said defensively. "He won't want me talking to them, even if it's to help catch his killer."

"But he's not here, Mrs. McGuire, and he can't hurt you from the grave."

She swallowed and I thought she'd open the door, but instead she shook her head. "He wouldn't like me talking to you," she said again.

"I know how you feel."

"You don't." She pushed on the door to close it.

"My situation was similar to yours," I said on a rush of breath. When she hesitated, I continued. She was listening, and that was a start. "I don't pretend to completely understand what you're going through, but I do know how it feels to be betrayed by someone you trusted, someone you gave your heart to. My former fiancé stole my shop and my livelihood then broke off our engagement, all after the death of my father. I needed him, trusted him, and he hurt me deeply."

Unlike Mrs. McGuire, I had never been afraid of Eddie Hardacre. I'd confronted him and been satisfied when he was forced to give back what was mine by the court. She hadn't reached that point yet. If the abuse had gone on for years, then it was understandable it would take time for her fear to diminish, to undo the damage he'd caused to her sense of self-worth.

"*He* betrayed *you*, Mrs. McGuire. He did not fulfill his side of the marriage bargain when he hurt you. You owe him nothing, least of all your loyalty."

Mrs. McGuire's eyes pooled with tears. She hugged the door, blinking furiously, then stepped back. She opened the door wider.

She led me through to the parlor and asked the housekeeper to make tea. We passed a few minutes in idle chatter. I told her a little more of my past with Eddie and how that had led me to meeting Matt.

"Wonderful things have happened to you," she said as the tea arrived.

"Yes," I said. "Matt and his friends restored my faith in the world, and men in particular."

"Like your friend who's being blamed for murdering my husband?"

I nodded. "Fabian didn't do it."

"I believe he escaped from prison."

"And I'm sure he wishes he was still there now, as it would give him an alibi. He wouldn't hurt anyone, Mrs. McGuire. I hope you can help me prove it."

She sipped her tea.

"Will you help me prove his innocence?" I prompted.

"I'm not sure how I can. I don't know anything. I'm useless."

"Not at all. You're in possession of important information, you just don't know it yet."

"I don't see how I can be. My husband didn't share anything about his business affairs with me." She stared into the teacup, cradled in both hands. "He said I wouldn't understand. It was too complicated for me."

"Then let's discuss what you do know. What time did he leave the house on the night of his murder?"

"Around six," she said to her teacup.

"Did he eat dinner before he left?"

She shook her head. "He didn't like what I cooked."

I suspected there was more to the story but it was hard to gauge when she wouldn't look at me.

"Do you know where he went?" I asked.

"No."

"How did he seem? Was he angry?"

"No."

"Are you sure? Was he angry with you for cooking something he didn't like?"

Another shake of her heard. "Usually he would be. Sometimes he would throw the plate across the room, or shout at me for being a hopeless wife, but that night...he just pushed it away, got up and left."

"And what did you do?"

"Tidied up. My housekeeper is only here during the day. Then I went to bed. I took a sleeping draught and slept until the morning. I noticed he hadn't come home when I woke up, but it's happened before and I wasn't worried. Then the police came..." The teacup rattled in the saucer from her trembling hands.

"It must have been a shock."

She nodded. "I know I should have let them in, but it didn't feel right. He wouldn't have liked it. He doesn't like people touching his things."

"Have you looked through his things?" I asked.

"Lord, no."

"He can't hurt you now, Mrs. McGuire."

"I know." She stared down at the cup. "Can we do it together?"

My heart lifted. "Yes."

She fetched a key from the escritoire by the window and

led the way down the corridor. "The police found this key on him and returned it to me. I knew it was for his office. He kept it locked at all times and cleaned it himself."

Matt must have picked the lock when he and Duke entered to steal the ledger, then relocked it.

Mrs. McGuire hesitated then inserted the key into the lock and opened the door. She sucked in a deep breath and took a giant step across the threshold.

"Where shall we start?" I asked.

"The desk."

McGuire's office was much smaller than Matt's. Where Matt had some business periodicals and books on the shelves, McGuire's office had no shelves at all. Aside from the desk and one chair, there was a large filing cabinet, the drawers of which were locked. I wondered if Matt had picked the locks and searched through them.

"Do you know what your husband's business entailed?" I asked as I inspected the papers on the desk.

"Lending money to those in need." She rifled through the top drawer of the desk. "People like your friend."

"My friend is a good man who found himself in a difficult financial situation through no fault of his own, but I suspect your husband loaned money to others who were not so honorable. I suspect many were probably gamblers who'd lost more than they won."

"Do the police think one of them killed him?"

"I don't know what they think," I said. "I do know the debts are not dissolved by your husband's death."

She looked up. "I don't understand."

"You inherit them, Mrs. McGuire."

"Then…that makes me a suspect." She blinked down at the cards in her hand.

I took them from her, but they were merely calling cards of bankers, lawyers, and various gentlemen. One of them gave me pause, but I put it back with the others and opened the second drawer. It contained a single key.

I tried it in the top drawer of the filing cabinet and was thrilled to see that it fitted. Until I realized Matt would have done the same and already looked through the documents.

"They appear to be contracts filed in alphabetical order by surname," I said, closing the top drawer and inspecting the contents of the second and third.

I found Fabian's contract and Mr. Stanhope's. Each contract listed the amount of the principal, the interest rate, and personal details of each debtor, including reasons why McGuire assumed they should be able to pay. In Fabian's case, it was noted that his family were wealthy, and in Stanhope's case, McGuire had written that he was partner in the Ingles Vinegar Company. Again, there was an asterisk on his document, where Fabian's had none.

I pulled out a large number of other files and searched them for asterisks too. None bore any. I went to put them back and noticed a large envelope lying flat on the bottom of the drawer. The files had been slotted vertically above it, hiding it.

Charbonneau had been written on the front followed by *September tenth* and *£500,* the exact amount of Fabian's debt. Inside was a large sum of money, probably £500. Fabian had repaid his debt.

Yet he couldn't have. Not on September tenth. So the question was, who did?

CHAPTER 10

"Is this written in your husband's hand?" I asked.

Mrs. McGuire nodded then peeked inside the envelope. "Good lord," she murmured. "So much."

I tried to give her the envelope but she refused to take it.

"You'd best put it back where you found it," she said.

"It's yours now."

"I don't know…"

I returned to the desk and searched through the calling cards. "This fellow is a lawyer. He's probably your husband's lawyer and will have a copy of his will. Pay him a visit to discuss the terms of your husband's will. You are most likely the beneficiary, so all monies owing your husband are now owed to you."

She took the card. "This man called here yesterday. I didn't speak to him."

"He probably read about Mr. McGuire's death in the newspapers and wants to discuss his affairs with you. I think you should see him."

"I will. Thank you, Mrs. Glass. Thank you for everything."

* * *

I COLLECTED Matt from number sixteen Park Street and together we drove to Scotland Yard. I refused to tell him what I'd learned, on account of not wanting to repeat myself with Brockwell. He crossed his arms and spent the rest of the journey glowering.

I recounted my meeting with Mrs. McGuire to both Matt and the inspector, finishing with the details written on the envelope full of money.

"That's the day McGuire died," Matt said.

"The day before," I pointed out. "His death occurred in the small hours the following morning."

"Did Mrs. McGuire notice her husband return in the evening and go out again?" Brockwell asked.

"She took a sleeping draught at about eleven so can't be certain he didn't return. He could have come home, deposited the envelope in the filing cabinet, and gone out again. The important point is, Fabian's debt was repaid *before* McGuire's death. I suspect McGuire was going to update his ledger later, but his death prevented him from doing so, and so the ledger in your possession, Inspector, still lists the debt as outstanding."

"The timing is interesting," Matt said, thoughtfully. "We know McGuire was at home for an early dinner, so he either brought the envelope home with him then went out again, or he went out after dinner, met with someone who repaid him, then returned after his wife went to bed before going out a second time to the pub. Either way, India's right. Fabian couldn't have repaid it. The date on the envelope was the tenth, and Fabian was in prison on the tenth, at least until late in the evening."

Brockwell flipped open his notebook and ran a finger down the page. "Last inspection by the guards was at ten o'clock. A witness said McGuire was at the pub from nine until midnight, and he didn't meet anyone there."

"So who paid off Fabian's debt?" I asked.

"Does it matter?" Brockwell said. "Whoever paid it isn't the killer because McGuire was alive when he brought the money back to the house."

"It doesn't matter regarding the murder, but it matters to us, Inspector. Fabian will now owe someone a favor for paying off his debt, and I'd like to know who."

"Find him and ask him."

"Yes, thank you, Inspector," I said wryly.

Matt hadn't been paying attention during our exchange, but now he piped up. "How did Mrs. McGuire seem? Was she upset?"

"A little," I hedged, not wanting to make her sound heartless. "I think she was still in disbelief, and somewhat under her husband's spell, even now. She couldn't meet my gaze when she spoke ill of him."

"Or couldn't she meet it because she was lying?"

"And *she* murdered him?" Brockwell finished. "Thank you for your insight, Mrs. Glass."

"I don't think she did it," I told them.

He tapped his forehead. "I have taken a note in here of your opinion."

I scowled at him, not sure if he was simply indulging me. "One more thing," I said. "Mrs. McGuire thought her husband was distracted at dinner. It might be nothing, or it might be that he was distracted because of his upcoming meeting that night with the killer."

"Thank you again, Mrs. Glass. Your insights and investigative skills are a marvel."

"You're welcome, Inspector. Oh and I almost forgot. I found Mr. Delancey's card in McGuire's desk drawer."

"Who?" Brockwell asked.

"He's with Rotherby's Bank, and sometimes loans money to magicians in a private capacity. It could be nothing, but I would like to ask him some questions about his connection to McGuire."

"I'll speak to him this afternoon."

"Actually, I'd like to visit him, just Matt and me. If his connection to McGuire has anything to do with magic, he might talk to me but I doubt he will to you."

Brockwell fingered his sideburns. "I don't like it. It's against procedure."

"Very sensitive questions must be asked about magic. He won't talk to you, Inspector, but he trusts me. Think of him as another Mrs. McGuire. You asked me to speak to her."

"Very well. I will allow it. Glass, be careful. Don't let anything happen to your wife."

"I'll do my best." Matt's tone dripped with sarcasm that seemed to slip past Brockwell altogether.

* * *

Mr. Delancey wasn't at his Rotherby Bank office. Being lunchtime, we found him at home, sharing his midday repast with his wife.

"Do join us for coffee and dessert," Mrs. Delancey said, inviting us into the dining room. "What a lovely surprise this is, India. And Mr. Glass too, of course."

"To what do we owe the pleasure?" Mr. Delancey asked as he sat at the head of the table.

His wife resumed her seat at the opposite end of the polished table while Matt and I found a place in the middle. The footmen set the table for two more and served desserts of lemon jelly, apple tart, a pudding, and late season strawberries with cream.

"I do apologize for the simplicity of the offerings," Mrs. Delancey said. "When it's just the two of us for luncheon, we prefer to eat light."

If this dessert course was considered light, the servants must eat well off the leftovers. It was too much for four, let alone two.

"You were naughty last time you were here, India," Mrs. Delancey goaded. "You knew Mr. Charbonneau had escaped from prison yet you said nothing."

"I don't like to gossip unnecessarily."

"All gossip is necessary, my dear. Sometimes it's a more valuable commodity than money."

"Steady on," Mr. Delancey said with a good-natured chuckle. "Not even Coyle believes that."

"India and Mr. Glass are here for information, Husband, not money."

"How do you know?"

"Because they've come here to the house, not your office."

Following a conversation with the Delanceys was like watching a tennis match, my head swiveling left and right as each took turns tossing remarks down the table.

"Actually we did go to the office," Matt said. "They informed us that Mr. Delancey had returned home for luncheon."

Mr. Delancey scooped up a spoonful of jelly and raised it in salute to his wife before eating it.

"What do you want to talk to him about?" Mrs. Delancey asked. "Is it regarding Mr. Charbonneau? Have you found him yet? Is he guilty of murdering that scum as the newspapers suggest?"

"Language, my dear! There's no need for it at the table."

"I do apologize," she said to us. "But such people make me angry. They prey on the desperate and weak."

I wasn't sure how McGuire was all that different to Delancey. They were both money lenders, except one worked for a large institution while the other worked alone.

"Your business card was found with the victim's belongings," Matt told Mr. Delancey. "Why would that be? Have you met him?"

Mr. Delancey licked his lips then patted them with the napkin. "I have, as it happens."

"Why didn't you tell me?" his wife blurted out.

"I didn't think it important."

"Not even after reading his name in the newspapers in connection to Mr. Charbonneau? We read the article together," she said with a pout in her voice. "You ought to have mentioned it."

"My humblest apologies, my dear. You're right, I should have mentioned it when I eventually remembered where I'd heard the name McGuire. I didn't at the time of reading the article, but some time later it finally clicked." He snapped his fingers. "McGuire came to the bank and was referred to me, because of the large amount of money he wanted to borrow."

"Usually Mr. Delancey's underlings deal with ordinary folk, while he gives the better clients his attention," Mrs. Delancey explained.

"Did you loan him the money?" Matt asked.

"I rejected his application," Mr. Delancey said. "He didn't have any means to repay such a large sum, so naturally I couldn't approve the loan. It wasn't until he died that I read about his own money lending scheme. He didn't mention it to me in our meeting."

"I wonder why," his wife said.

"Because he'd have to declare the names of his debtors," Mr. Delancey told her. "I'd wager many of them do not want it known they owe money to a ragtag lender."

She gasped. "Do you mean they're criminals?"

"Some might be, certainly."

"Not Mr. Charbonneau."

"Why not Charbonneau?"

"Because...because... India said he's a good fellow." She picked up her wine glass. "And I trust her opinion."

"Fabian is a good man," I said. "He borrowed money from McGuire for the same reason others do. He couldn't go to a bank as he had nothing to show he could repay. He was probably hoping his family would reinstate his allowance, but am I right in thinking the bank wouldn't have accepted that?"

Mr. Delancey gave a nod. "Very astute, Mrs. Glass."

"You didn't think to report your meeting with McGuire to the police?" Matt asked.

"I didn't see the relevancy to the murder."

"It shows that he owed money to someone. Most likely his creditor was asking for it to be repaid."

That was why he'd demanded Fabian repay him—the banks wouldn't lend him anything so he'd called in his own debts. Perhaps he'd asked his other debtors to repay too.

"Did he say why he needed the money?" I asked.

"To take advantage of a business opportunity that had come his way. I didn't really believe it, though. He refused to give me details of the venture and seemed rather nervous throughout the meeting. I think he needed the money to repay a debt, just as you say, Glass."

"Can you tell us anything else about your meeting?" Matt asked. "Anything at all?"

Mr. Delancey shook his head and tucked into his jelly.

"Will the information help Mr. Charbonneau?" Mrs. Delancey asked.

"If we can find who killed Mr. McGuire then Fabian can come out of hiding," I said.

"Then we *must* help." She appealed to her husband. "Ferdinand, are you sure there's not more you can tell us?"

Mr. Delancey had his mouth full but shook his head.

"You know several of London's leading businessmen?" Matt asked him.

Mr. Delancey swallowed and scooped up another spoonful. "Certainly. Why?"

"If I tell you the names of the men who owed McGuire, can you tell me your opinion of them?"

Mr. Delancey waved his spoon back and forth. "I'm afraid not. Professional confidence and all that."

"I understand," Matt said with barely disguised patience, "but this could help find his killer and prove Charbonneau's innocence."

"The answer's no, Glass. I am sorry."

"Do reconsider," Mrs. Delancey said to her husband. "For Mr. Charbonneau's sake. If he's not proven innocent, he'll hang for murder, and the world can ill afford to lose a magician of his caliber."

"My dear, you ask too much of me. My integrity is very important to the bank. Besides, I'm sure Mr. and Mrs. Glass will find the murderer without my help. They're an excellent sleuthing team."

She sighed. "Please try to convince him, India."

I wasn't sure how, until the clock on the mantel chimed one. "Mr. Charbonneau will donate a piece of magical iron to your collection. If your help leads to his freedom, it'll be the least he can do."

"Oh yes!" Mrs. Delancey clapped her hands. "Do accept, Ferdinand."

Mr. Delancey set down his spoon and wiped his mouth with his napkin. "A metal item of my choice?"

"I'm sure he'll agree, as long as it's not a bridge," I said.

He chuckled. "Very well. But it must be understood that any information I give you is not to be traced back to me. If you inform the police, keep my name out of it."

"Agreed," Matt said.

"Tell me a name then. Who was McGuire's largest debtor?"

"Mr. Stanhope, business partner of Mr. Ingles of the Ingles Vinegar Company."

"I know of the company, but I've never met either fellow. They don't bank with us." He looked away and studied his wine glass.

"What do you know about the company?" Matt prompted.

"They make vinegar and wine, I believe."

"You agreed," Matt warned him.

"Ferdinand," Mrs. Delancey barked. "Answer him."

Mr. Delancey drained his wine glass then set it down very deliberately. "I know I agreed to give an opinion, but what I know about the business came from others. I don't want to get my colleagues into trouble. We're not supposed to share information, you see."

"Who are the 'we' you're referring to?" I asked.

"Bankers, Mrs. Glass. Bankers from various banks talk to one another, at gentlemen's clubs and the like." Mr. Delancey put up his hands. "Before you tell me it's unethical, I just want to point out that it's natural for people to gossip. The information isn't used in a professional capacity."

I didn't believe that, but we couldn't judge him harshly when we were asking him to share the information. "If you want the magical ironwork, you have to tell us. We'll keep the information to ourselves, I promise."

He sighed. "The Ingles Vinegar Company is going through a difficult patch. They defaulted on repayments on a large loan taken out some years ago with another bank."

Matt sat forward. "That's not the impression we got on our visit to the factory. It seemed to be thriving. Mr. Ingles in particular was happy with the company's performance."

"They don't have the cash flow right now. I've never met the man and I don't know the structure of the company, but perhaps he isn't aware of all that goes on there. That's often the case. Sometimes when a company grows large, a manager is appointed and given too much authority. He might not inform the owners when the business is facing difficulty, particularly if its failure is his own fault. He might have taken out a larger loan, or tried to expand too quickly, perhaps spent too much on new equipment without doing a thorough analysis first. There are many reasons he might wish to keep the business's failure to himself, but I can assure you, it all comes down to him wanting to protect himself. Find out who controls the purse strings at Ingles and you will find the source of their financial woes."

Stanhope.

We thanked the Delanceys and made to leave, only to have Mrs. Delancey protest that it was too soon. "You've hardly eaten a thing, India."

"It was delicious, but we must go," I said. "Thank you for your hospitality."

"We must invite you both to dinner, mustn't we, Mr. Delancey?"

Her husband agreed with enthusiasm. "We'll invite all our friends, and your Mr. Charbonneau too when this is all over. Everyone wants to meet him."

"He can bring our magical iron piece. What shall we ask for?"

"A sculpture would fill the bare corner in the drawing room where the vase used to be before the maid broke it," he said.

Mrs. Delancey clapped her hands in delight. "Does he work in bronze?" she asked me.

"Iron and bronze are two different metals," her husband said with a shake of his head. "Do you know of a bronze magician, Mrs. Glass?"

"No," I said.

"Pity," Mrs. Delancey muttered. She tugged the bell pull to summon the butler. "I'll send out invitations when this is all over. Do tell Mr. Charbonneau when you find him that he should come to us in future if he requires money. We'll be more than happy to help."

"With the promise of more magical objects?" I asked.

She patted the lace collar at her throat. "We wouldn't be so vulgar, Mrs. Glass. It would be out of the goodness of our hearts."

Matt and I stopped for a casual lunch at a chop house, although I wasn't all that hungry having already eaten dessert. Over the meal, we discussed our approach and decided to speak to Mr. Ingles first, even though we thought Mr. Stanhope was responsible for any financial difficulties the company might be facing. We wanted to know how much Mr. Ingles knew.

We went straight to the brew house when we arrived at the South Lambeth factory. Thanks to the noise of the machinery, no one heard us and we were able to sneak past the workmen when their backs were turned. We found Mr. Ingles upstairs, inspecting a clear cup containing a liquid substance by holding it up to the light streaming through one of the large arched windows. The whir and thump of machinery came from the enormous metal vats and coppers.

There was more activity here than on the level below, and we were quickly spotted. Mr. Ingles didn't immediately greet us when his worker alerted him to our presence. He continued to study the contents of the cup, swirling the dark golden liquid around the sides then smelling it.

Matt and I approached him. "May we speak with you alone?" Matt said over the sounds of the machines.

Mr. Ingles dismissed his staff and poured the liquid into the vat through a funnel protruding from the side. The vat vibrated from the machine inside which must be either stirring or squashing the contents. "I've told you everything. What more do you want from me?"

"We have some more questions," Matt said.

"About Hubert's movements? I told you, he was here with me until about nine. He's not involved in the murder of that man, Mr. Glass. He's an upstanding fellow. I can vouch for his character."

"These are merely routine questions," Matt assured him. "There's nothing to be alarmed about. If anything, they'll prove Mr. Stanhope's innocence, since you're sure he *is* innocent."

"He is."

"Then you have nothing to worry about," I said, matching Matt's gentle, reassuring tone.

Mr. Ingles used the cloth hanging over his shoulder to wipe out the cup, which I realized was actually a beaker used in science laboratories. "Very well. How can I help you now?"

"You told us that Mr. Stanhope is the company accountant," Matt said. "He controls all the financials, approves purchases, and applies to banks for loans, doesn't he?"

"He can't take out a loan without my approval, but he does manage the company accounts. He has staff to assist him, but all major financial transactions go through him. Why? What is this about?"

"Are you aware the company has defaulted on a substantial loan recently?"

"Wh—what?" he spluttered. "No, no, that's not true. I know the loan you speak of. It was taken out years ago when we expanded. We've never struggled to meet our regular repayments. Never. Who is spreading these rumors?"

"It's true, Mr. Ingles," I said. "We regret to inform you, but if Mr. Stanhope is solely responsible for the company's finances, then he hasn't told you about the financial difficulties Ingles is facing."

"That can't be. Business is booming. We've got more orders than ever, thanks to our cordials. We're set to become the third biggest producer of vinegar and related products in the country. What you're suggesting is just not possible."

Mr. Ingles scrubbed a stained hand down his face. When it came away, he looked like a tired old man. He stared at the vats, shaking his head over and over.

"This has come as a shock," I said, touching his arm.

He shook me off. "I'll talk to him and get to the bottom of this. There's obviously been a mistake."

He went to march off but Matt caught him by the elbow. "I can't let you do that. By authority of Scotland Yard, we have to speak to Stanhope first."

Matt wouldn't meet my gaze. It was probably just as well or I might have made it too obvious to Mr. Ingles that no such authority existed.

"You told us you were with Mr. Stanhope until nine on the evening of the murder," Matt said. "In light of what you now know about your partner's cheating, do you still stand by that?"

Mr. Ingles blinked. "If your accusation of financial mismanagement is true, what does it have to do with the murder?"

"It explains why he went to Mr. McGuire for a loan."

"But it doesn't explain why Hubert would murder him as he still owes the man's heirs the money. Besides, I reread the newspaper article about the murder after your last visit, and the man died in the early hours of the morning. Whether I lied to you about him being with me until nine or not is irrelevant."

"So you did lie?" I pressed.

"Yes, I lied." He wiped his hands on the towel, once again looking like the strong and sprightly man in his sixties rather than someone who ought to take to his bed. "Hubert asked me to. He said the police would question him over the murder because he owed the fellow money. I was more than happy to give him an alibi, as you investigators call it, because I knew he was innocent. He's a decent man. But I didn't give him an alibi anyway, as the murder occurred much later. Hubert must have thought it happened earlier."

He marched off, striding toward the stairs. He no longer looked vulnerable, but furious. I wasn't sure if he was angry with us for our questions, or with Mr. Stanhope for cheating the business out of money to pay his personal debts.

Matt took my arm and lowered his head to mine. "It fits," was all he said.

He didn't need to say more. We'd discussed beforehand the question of timing. Mr. McGuire had left the house around six o'clock. Most likely he'd met with the person who paid back Fabian's debt, and perhaps others on his list of debtors. One of those could have been Mr. Stanhope, but not if he was still there, as Mr. Ingles originally suggested. It was Matt's theory that Ingles had lied for his friend. He'd been nervous the day we questioned him about it, and he had seemed uncomfortable. If Mr. Stanhope had indeed left the factory much earlier, he could have met with McGuire, who then ordered Stanhope to pay back the money. Panicking, Stanhope met with him again later and killed him to avoid repaying him.

There were two problems with our theory, however. One, why would he set up Fabian? Indeed, how could he set up Fabian when he didn't even know Fabian had escaped? And two, he claimed to be home with his wife in bed at the time of the murder. We were yet to speak to her and determine if she would lie for her husband as Ingles had done.

We followed Mr. Ingles as he marched across the courtyard. He didn't acknowledge any of the workers who greeted him, leaving them with bemused frowns as they stared after him. This man who I'd only thought of as an amiable and unassuming gentleman had turned into a lion, fiercely protecting his territory. His territory being the company.

He pushed open Mr. Stanhope's office door without knocking. "What have you done, Hubert?"

Mr. Stanhope looked up from his paperwork, sporting a similar expression as the other staff. "Ernest? What's going on? And what are *they* doing here?"

"Informing me of your embezzlement," Mr. Ingles said through gritted teeth.

Mr. Stanhope half rose then fell back onto his chair. He made a small sound of protest in the back of his throat. "Whatever you've heard, it's wrong. I don't know what—"

"Don't lie to me!" Mr. Ingles thumped his fist on the desk. A pen resting in an ink stand fell out and rolled away.

Mr. Stanhope swallowed as he picked it up. "There must be a mistake. Tell me what the matter is and we'll discuss it calmly. But those two must go."

"They have to stay," Ingles bit off. "Police orders."

Thankfully Mr. Stanhope bought our lie. "Whatever they've told you isn't true. Come now, Ernest. I'm not a liar or cheat, you know that. I would never risk the company by embezzling profits."

Mr. Ingles crossed his arms, some of the wind taken out of his sails. "The company is in excellent health. Why couldn't we repay the bank loan? Where did the profits go, if not into your pocket?"

Mr. Stanhope tugged on his cuffs. "It's complicated. Losses are carried over from one year to the next, and then there are suppliers who are paid on differing schedules, and our own customers don't always pay on time. What appears as a profit on paper is not always so in reality."

It seemed to appease Mr. Ingles somewhat, but not Matt. "Hand over your ledgers, and I'll check them. If what you say is true, I'll know in a matter of hours."

"It's far too complicated for someone without solid company accounting expertise to understand."

"I have my own international business interests. The police don't pay enough for us to live in Mayfair."

Mr. Stanhope paled.

"We have it on good authority that you defaulted on the company's loan repayments," Matt went on.

"Who told you that?"

"An informant at the bank."

"Bollocks! The bank would never give up that sort of information to you two."

"We have evidence."

I cleared my throat. "It would be best if you just admit it, Mr. Stanhope." I nodded at Mr. Ingles. "Better in the long run."

Mr. Stanhope stroked his moustache and beard, his gaze shifting between us. But it wasn't until Mr. Ingles thumped the desk with his fist again that Mr. Stanhope admitted it.

"I borrowed some money from the business, but I've paid it back. It was just a temporary loan, but it impacted our bank repayment. It's all in order now and won't happen again. I'm sorry, Ernest."

Mr. Ingles swept his arm over the desk, pushing off the papers, pens, and ink, and sending the lot onto the floor with a clatter. "This is still my company! *I* am the largest shareholder. *I* put hours and hours into the business, out there in the brew house. How dare you cheat me!"

"I—I didn't cheat you." Mr. Stanhope rose and pressed his hand to his heart. "I paid back the company money. It's all there and our repayments are up to date. Check with the bank."

"How did you pay it back?" Matt asked. "By borrowing from Mr. McGuire?"

"Yes."

"So you owed him instead, exchanging one debt for another."

Mr. Stanhope pressed his lips his together.

"Say something!" Mr. Ingles shouted.

"How did you expect to pay McGuire back?" Matt asked.

"Through hard work," Mr. Stanhope said, his gaze flicking to Ingles. "Slowly, over time, out of my own wages. I would never use company money again. Never."

"But he asked you for the money back sooner than expected," I said, choosing a more soothing tone than the men. "You panicked and killed him, not realizing the debt wouldn't be dissolved, or perhaps hoping McGuire's heir will return to a more regular, slower repayment schedule."

"I didn't kill him! I'm not a murderer, you have to believe that."

"Then why ask Mr. Ingles to lie for you and say you were here until nine?"

"I knew the police would come asking questions. I knew I'd be a suspect, that's why I asked Ernest to vouch for me."

"When did you leave the office?"

"About six-thirty."

"Did you go straight home?"

"I went for a walk. I doubt anyone saw me. That's why I asked Ernest to say I was here. Anyway, wasn't the murder later? I would have been home then, with my wife. The police have already asked her and she told them I was there, asleep alongside her all night. I assure you, I didn't kill anyone." Mr. Stanhope's eyes filled with tears. "You have to believe me."

We turned to leave but Matt paused in the doorway. "The company should have been able to pay the bank loan if you hadn't embezzled the funds. Why did you need money? What was it for?"

"Gambling," he said on a groan. "Horses. Ernest, I'm sorry. I'm so sorry."

Mr. Ingles stood very still, his fists closed at his sides, the knuckles white. His eyes blazed with fury. "Take your things and go."

"Go? I can't go." Mr. Stanhope gave a strangled laugh. "We're partners."

"I don't want a cheat as a partner. I'll be speaking to my lawyer this afternoon about dissolving the partnership on the grounds of embezzlement."

"Ernest—"

"Don't talk to me. I never want to hear your voice again." He jerked the door open and strode off.

"But Ernest, you can't do this to me! Please. I'm begging you. This company is my life. It's everything to me."

Mr. Ingles spun around, teeth bared in a snarl. "It's everything to *me*," he spat. "It's *my* family business. *My* name is on the front of this building. Get out before I call the constables and have you arrested for trespassing." He stormed off, watched by open-mouthed employees.

Mr. Stanhope sat heavily on his chair and buried his face in his hands. "What am I to do? Where will I go? My reputation will be ruined." His shoulders shook and he sounded like he was crying. "I can't believe this is happening. I simply can't believe it."

I wasn't sure if we should go, but Matt thought it best.

"See that he's all right," he said to a staff member we passed in the corridor. "Someone should take him home."

I felt a little raw as we made our way to the carriage. Had we just destroyed Mr. Stanhope's life? It was impossible not to feel as though we were to blame for Mr. Ingles wanting to dissolve the business partnership.

Matt instructed the coachman to drive us to Scotland Yard. Inside the cabin, he took my hand and rubbed his thumb along mine. "The encounter upset you," he said.

"I feel awful. Poor Mr. Stanhope."

"We're not to blame for what he did. He made his own bed."

"But he paid the company funds back. Mr. Ingles might never have found out if not for us."

"Until the next time Stanhope embezzled funds. Mr. Ingles had a right to know. If I were in his position, I'd want to know. Perhaps I'd feel like you do if I thought Stanhope innocent of murder."

I gasped and rounded on him. "You think he did it? He doesn't seem like the type to me."

"Hendry didn't seem like the type either."

He had a point, but I wasn't convinced. "Owing money doesn't seem like a compelling enough reason to murder someone. And what of the connection to Fabian? Why set it up so it looks like he did it? There's nothing linking them."

Matt remained silent. I settled into his side. Being close to him and feeling the thrum of his pulse made me feel a little better.

Brockwell wasn't in, so we left a message for him to call on us urgently. When we arrived home, we learned that Willie was watching Chronos's house and Cyclops had gone for a walk to Hyde Park with Aunt Letitia. Matt took the correspondence Bristow handed to him into the library and I followed. I tinkered with the black marble clock from the shop, trying yet again to see what could be causing it to lose time.

Duke joined us a few minutes later and closed the door. If that wasn't a sign that something was amiss, then the worried look on his face certainly was.

"Can we talk?" he asked.

Matt lowered the letter he'd been reading. "What's wrong?"

"It's Cyclops. He won't want me telling you this."

I set down my beat setting tool and gave Duke my full attention. "We won't tell him."

He glanced at the closed door. "Rycroft visited him today and threatened him."

CHAPTER 11

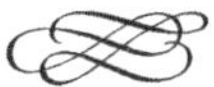

"You'd better start at the beginning," Matt said.

Duke glanced at the door again. "Cyclops was in the stables this morning when Rycroft showed up."

"You mean Rycroft's man," I clarified.

"No, his lordship himself. He must have found out that Cyclops was there. He ordered the stable hands to leave but had his own two men with him. I wasn't there and didn't see them, but I'm guessing they weren't the fancy fellows that serve inside the house."

I pressed a hand to my heart, not liking where this was going.

Matt went still. "Did they rough up Cyclops?"

"Threatened him," Duke said.

I let out a pent-up breath. "What did Lord Rycroft say?"

"He offered Cyclops money to leave London. Cyclops told Rycroft he'd done nothing to Charity and wouldn't take the money. That's when Rycroft threatened to speak to his friend, the Home Secretary."

"The Home Secretary!" I cried. "Do you think he really knows him?"

"They probably go to the same club," Matt said dryly.

"What do you reckon he wants the Home Secretary to do?" Duke asked.

"The Home Office is in charge of the police force," I said. "He might want the police to investigate."

"And risk the public finding out?" Matt shook his head. "I doubt it. He won't want Charity's reputation ruined. My guess is he wants Cyclops deported."

Duke swore. "Can the Home Secretary do that if Cyclops has done nothing wrong?"

We all knew the answer to that. The Home Secretary wouldn't care if Cyclops were innocent. If he wanted to appease a friend and deport someone who wasn't a citizen, he could. He wouldn't need proof that a crime had been committed. He could make up a minor violation.

But he wouldn't expect Cyclops to have a powerful friend to challenge the deportation order.

Duke and I both looked to Matt.

He rose. "I'll write to the Home Secretary immediately and pay him a visit tomorrow. You did the right thing in coming to me, Duke."

* * *

THE NEWS of Rycroft's threat hung over me like a dark cloud. I found it difficult to pretend to Cyclops that I didn't know, and I threw myself into trying to fix the black marble clock. My mood oscillated between worry and anger, until finally my work began to soothe me.

That's when the ideas formed. I wasn't sure of the law, but perhaps Cyclops couldn't be deported if he became an English citizen. How long did that process take? Would marrying an English girl speed it up? I even imagined an entire discussion with Catherine in which I asked her to propose to him. She'd do it too, if it meant saving him. The problem was getting Cyclops to agree. He was too honorable for his own good.

Distraction arrived in the form of Louisa and the man she brought with her. I knew instantly that he must be Fabian's brother. They were of a similar height and build with the same dark shade of hair, but his jawline was softer and he wasn't quite as handsome.

"I must apologize," Maxime Charbonneau said as we settled in the drawing room. "I should not have pushed you at the hotel, Mrs. Glass. I feel terrible for my actions."

"It's quite all right," I said.

"Why did you push her?" Matt asked, his voice edged with steel. Clearly he wasn't going to forgive as quickly as me.

"I panicked," Mr. Charbonneau said. "I did not want anyone to know I was in London."

"Anyone except me, that is," Louisa added. She sat erect and regal on the sofa beside me in an elegant sea green dress with lace panels, hem and cuffs. The matching hat sat forward so that her elaborate hairstyle could be appreciated from the back. I admired her confidence, elegance, and forthright attitude, and yet those very characteristics made me feel uncomfortable too. Perhaps it was because I'd never met a woman like her before. She was very different to anyone I knew, even Catherine.

"I was afraid the police would find Fabian through me," Mr. Charbonneau went on. "At that time, I did not know that Louisa was not hiding him. I thought he was with her and that if the police saw me go to her, they would find him."

"It's perfectly understandable," I said. "I know now that it was you who sent the letter opener to Louisa."

"She tells me you assumed it was from my brother," Mr. Charbonneau said.

"I felt the magic warmth in the inscription. It didn't occur to me that you could have sent it. I'm sorry I took it."

"Why did you, if you thought it was from Fabian?" Louisa asked, her voice light and breezy yet her gaze sharp. "Why keep news of him from me?"

"I simply wanted to speak to him first."

"But I am his friend. I could help him just as well as you could, India." I didn't like the sweetness in her tone, the smile on her lips. "Or do you not trust me?"

"Trust you?" I echoed. Perhaps if I stalled, something would come to me. Something that would get me out of the hole I seemed to be digging myself into.

"We don't trust you," Matt said.

I almost choked on my gasp. I couldn't quite believe what I was hearing. Yet I shouldn't have been surprised. Matt was not in the habit of being manipulated.

"And why is that?" Louisa asked, the airiness in her voice gone.

"In light of your failed offer of marriage to Fabian, there is now doubt that you would help him out of the goodness of your heart."

Her nostrils flared. "What has that got to do with anything?"

"You might save him then demand he marry you as thanks."

The fingers on her lap twisted together but her smile remained. "That's absurd."

"You asked him to marry you?" Mr. Charbonneau asked. "Why did you not say, Louisa?"

She laughed, a tinkling, musical sound as elegant as I expected from such a woman. "It was on a whim. It's not important now."

Mr. Charbonneau's frown deepened. "I am sorry to inform you, but he is going to marry another."

She waved a hand. "No matter. My feelings are a little bruised, but I shall recover."

"You already have recovered," I pointed out. "You introduced yourself to Dr. Seaford with a view to proposing to him, too. He's a friend of ours," I told a stunned Mr. Charbonneau. "A magician friend. He saw through her and has now distanced himself."

She narrowed her gaze. "Are you quite finished disparaging my character?"

"So you are not in love with Fabian?" Mr. Charbonneau asked.

Louisa squared her shoulders. "I think I might be. I don't know. What I do know is, I made a mistake regarding Dr. Seaford. I was upset over Fabian's rejection and hoped another man would make me feel less wretched."

I rolled my eyes. I didn't believe her for a moment.

"How is any of this relevant to Fabian's disappearance?" she pressed. "Are you any closer to finding him?"

"Fabian will only come out of hiding once he feels safe," I said.

Mr. Charbonneau nodded. "We cannot search every house in London."

"The only way to make him feel safe is to catch the real murderer."

"And pay back his debt," Mr. Charbonneau added.

"It has been paid," Matt said. Both Louisa and Mr. Charbonneau looked surprised.

"By you?" Mr. Charbonneau asked.

"No. We assumed it was one of you."

They looked at each other and both shook their heads.

That left only one likely benefactor. Coyle.

"If my brother does contact you first," Mr. Charbonneau said, "please tell him I wish to speak to him."

"Be sure to add that Maxime wants him to go home and

forget about creating new spells," Louisa added with a bitter twist of her mouth.

Mr. Charbonneau bristled. "The family have indulged him long enough. What do you call them? Whims? It is time to settle down, marry a good woman and have children."

"He isn't interested in the family business," Louisa said hotly. "He wants to explore the world of magic, to invent new spells, not make more money for people who are already wealthy."

Mr. Charbonneau stroked his jaw and pressed his lips together, as if he were holding in words that wanted to burst out. It seemed like they'd already had this discussion and that he'd said all he wanted to say to her on the matter.

"Forgive us, Mrs. Glass," he said to me. "As you can see, Louisa and I do not agree on the best future for my brother."

"He's talented, inquisitive, and has already conducted years of research," Louisa said. "It would be a crime for all of that to go to waste."

"Perhaps Fabian should decide for himself," I said.

They both looked at me as though I were mad.

I was relieved when they left. While they had arrived together, Mr. Charbonneau told Louisa he'd rather walk back to the hotel, and Louisa departed in her carriage, alone. She didn't say goodbye and he didn't even give her a passing nod.

Later, when we were telling Willie and Cyclops about the meeting, Willie said, "If I were Fabian, I'd move to New Zealand. Those two will pull him apart between them."

"He made a stance against his family when he came to London," Matt said. "And he made his position clear to Louisa when she asked him to marry her. I think he'll be fine, even if he doesn't move to the other side of the world."

"I hear New Zealand's a mighty pretty place," Cyclops said without lifting his gaze from the fireplace.

"You ain't moving to New Zealand," Willie told him. "You're staying right here, with me."

"That a proposal of marriage, Willie?"

"No, it's a threat."

He chuckled, but quickly sobered and turned back to the fireplace. "Wish I could stay in London forever."

Matt and I exchanged glances. I wanted to reassure Cyclops, but it was too soon. If he knew Matt was interfering on his behalf, his pride might have him leave London anyway.

"Because Catherine's here?" Willie asked slyly.

"No, because you and Duke are here." Cyclops winked at her. "You know you're my favorite girl."

She hooted a laugh. "Liar."

He chuckled but again, it didn't last, and he resumed staring into the fireplace.

Willie frowned. She suspected something else was wrong, but thankfully she didn't have the opportunity to ask. Bristow entered the library and announced the inspector.

Willie sat up a little straighter and touched the hair at the nape of her neck. Her tugging and teasing only made the loose arrangement messier. "You got to tell me when you're coming, Jasper. A woman's got to look her best for her man."

"I—er—right." Brockwell's face flushed. "Next time, I'll send a message ahead."

"It was a joke," she said, grinning. "I know you're here to see Matt and India about the investigation."

"I am."

She got up and stood in front of him, feet slightly apart and hands on hips. She looked as though she was about to challenge him to a duel. "Don't mean I can't have some fun with you after."

"I—uh, I..."

"Come on, Jasper, out with it. Or do you just want to kiss me? That's fine if you do. I ain't a prude. You can kiss me right here."

"Spare us," Cyclops muttered.

Brockwell cleared his throat. His face had gone so red, it was surprising steam didn't rise from his nose and ears. "I'd rather wait until we're alone, if that's all right with you, Miss Johnson."

"Miss Johnson!" Willie echoed. "Ain't no need to be so formal, Jasper. You and me know each other about as well as two people can. Come and sit down and say what you got to say."

"After you, Miss Johnson."

She rolled her eyes. "You English and your manners. If there was only room for one more on a life raft, you'd still say 'after you.'"

She turned to sit down again. Brockwell's gaze lowered, admiring her rear in trousers. If Willie knew men looked at her in that way, would she wear dresses?

"You received our message," Matt said.

"I did, and I know what you're going to tell me," Brockwell said. "I paid the Ingles Vinegar Company another visit not long after you, as it happens. Mr. Stanhope had just left after being thrown out by Mr. Ingles, and Mr. Ingles was in a fearsome mood about Stanhope's embezzlement. I had a devil of a time trying to get him to calm down and tell me what happened. It seems you two kicked over a beehive."

"Only to reveal the rotten foundations," Matt said. "It was necessary."

"Why?"

"To expose Stanhope and rattle his cage."

"My husband thinks Mr. Stanhope is guilty of the murder," I said.

"And you, Mrs. Glass?"

"I'm not sure. There are too many questions without answers for me to make a firm decision yet."

"My wife prefers solid evidence before making decisions," Matt said.

Brockwell gave me a nod. "She is a woman of similar sensibilities to myself."

Matt scowled. Fortunately, Willie appeared to think nothing of Brockwell's comment. Her gaze was too busy roaming over his face, down his length and back up again.

"I visited Mr. Stanhope at home after I left the factory," Brockwell went on. "He was in a state, let me tell you. I could hardly get a sensible word out of him, and his wife is worried."

My guilt resurfaced. We should have been more circumspect, and not told Mr. Ingles about the embezzlement. We'd ruined Mr. Stanhope's life, and I wasn't sure he deserved that. "Do you think he'll do something terrible?"

"Hard to say. Mrs. Stanhope seems like a good woman. She'll do her best to see that he recovers from this blow."

It was a relief to hear, but I didn't envy her the task.

"Did you ask Mrs. Stanhope about her husband's alibi for the time of the murder?" Matt asked.

"She says she was asleep with her husband beside her. She's quite sure she would have woken if he got up."

"That's good enough for me," I said.

"Wives have been known to lie for their husbands, Mrs. Glass. I expect even you would lie to me if I accused Mr. Glass of murder."

He had a point.

"It seems you and I are on the same page, Inspector," Matt said. "Although I do sympathize with Stanhope, in a way. If he does prove to be innocent of the murder, I'll personally do everything in my power to convince Ingles to invite him back to the factory."

I smiled at him and mouthed, "Thank you."

"Any news of Charbonneau?" Brockwell asked.

"Not yet," Matt said.

Brockwell waited for more, but Matt gave nothing away.

"Where have you looked?" the inspector prompted.

"We've checked the main hotels in the city. My friends are now taking it in turns to watch a house of interest."

"May I know which house?"

"It's under control."

"Which house, Glass?"

Matt refused to answer, and I hoped Brockwell didn't pressure me instead. I wasn't as strong as Matt, but I didn't want the police knocking on Chronos's door. If he were guilty of hiding a fugitive, he would be in enormous trouble.

"It seems to me you don't want me to find him," the inspector said.

"If we see him, we'll come and tell you," Willie piped up. "Trust us, Jasper."

Brockwell hesitated then nodded. "Thank you, Miss Johnson. That's all you had to say, Glass."

Willie gave Matt a smug smile.

Despite what he said, I doubted Brockwell would have accepted Matt's assurance as easily as he'd accepted Willie's.

The inspector made his excuses to leave, and Willie offered to walk him to the front door. "That's very kind of you, Miss Johnson. I accept."

"You don't need to keep calling me that here," she scolded. "They know what we're doing."

Brockwell cleared his throat. "I am here in a professional capacity."

She hooked his arm with her own and marched him toward the door. "That part of the visit is over now. Kiss me, Jasper."

He glanced over his shoulder at us. "That would not be appropriate."

"Prude."

"Professional," I heard him say before they were out the door.

Cyclops chuckled. "I hope he knows what he's in for with her."

"I think they're very good together," I said. "They balance out each other's extremes. He tempers her excesses and she adds fire to his otherwise cautious nature."

"Fires can get out of control."

Matt smirked. "And some explode."

"Only when added to gunpowder," I shot back. "Nobody could accuse the detective inspector of being an explosion waiting to happen."

A sound from the entrance hall caught my attention, and I peered through the doorway. Luckily I covered my mouth before my gasp alerted Brockwell and Willie that I could see them kissing. It wasn't just an ordinary goodbye kiss. It was the sort of kiss where the parties seem to want to devour the other altogether, not only with their mouths but their hands too. Hers were in his hair, over his face, then grasping his shoulders, while his were clamped on the area of her body he was admiring earlier.

"I think Brockwell has been hiding his gunpowder all this time," Matt muttered from behind me.

* * *

WHILE MATT VISITED the Home Secretary the following morning, to counter any damage Lord Rycroft might have done, I had to contend with other members of his family. Hope and Charity asked to see me, not Matt or Aunt Letitia, and I told Bristow to show them through to the drawing room.

"This will be about Lord Coyle," Aunt Letitia said as she settled herself onto a chair to receive them. The girls hadn't asked to see me alone, so I saw no reason for her to leave.

I did, however, inform Bristow to pass on a message to Cyclops to stay well clear if he happened to return from his shift watching Chronos's house. "And Willie too," I added as an afterthought. There was no guarantee she'd behave if she was in the same room as Charity.

It was quite obvious from the moment she entered that Charity had simply come along hoping to catch a glimpse of Cyclops. She couldn't stop glancing toward the door.

"He's not here," I told her.

She blinked innocently at me. "Who?"

"Don't play games. You won't be near him again so you can stop looking for him. He's wise to your tricks. We all are."

She pouted. "You're very cruel. I only told my father because I hoped he would force Cyclops into doing the honorable thing."

"You don't care for him," Aunt Letitia blurted out before I could recover from my shock. "You are a nasty little wasp, my girl. But you have been caught and your sting will be rendered useless. If you go near Cyclops again or continue with the lie, I will rip out that sting myself."

I stared at her, open-mouthed.

Charity sniffed. "Mad old bat."

"Be quiet," Hope snapped. "Honestly, Charity, you make everything worse by your mere presence. Stop it. Just stop it, do you hear me?" She closed her eyes and squeezed the bridge of her nose. After a deep breath, she opened her eyes again and seemed a little more composed. "I am sorry for my sister's actions. I truly am. She's an embarrassment to the family and I, for one, will be glad to leave her behind just as soon as I make a good match."

Charity snorted from where she stood at the window, her arms crossed.

"Has Lord Coyle made an offer?" Aunt Letitia asked.

Hope bit her lip and gave a small nod.

"So soon," I said. "Congratulations."

"You misunderstand. He has made his intentions clear to me before he asked my father for my hand, but I rejected him. I cannot marry him."

"But your pretty speech just now," Aunt Letitia said.

"I spoke of making a *good* match."

"Not to a fat, old pig," Charity piped up. She gave her sister a flat smile.

Hope sighed but didn't disagree with her.

"I don't know why my sister objects to him," Charity went on. "They are quite similar. Both are fiercely independent, enjoy telling others what to do, and like getting their own way. It might make for a fiery marriage, but I think Hope rather likes dramatic spectacles, as much as she pretends to be a biddable daughter."

"Do be quiet," Hope snapped.

"See? Aunt Letitia, you knew she was like this all along. You always saw through her act. Mama and Father never did."

Hope slumped, the fight leaving her. It wasn't a side I expected to ever see in the youngest, most vibrant of the Glass sisters.

"Why are you both here?" Aunt Letitia asked. I couldn't be sure if she didn't believe Hope's woeful turn or simply didn't care.

"Lord Coyle says he'll give me time to come to my senses, as he put it," Hope said. "But I want India to use her influence with him and ask him to look elsewhere for a wife."

"Me?" I said numbly. "I have no influence over him."

She suddenly leaned forward. "Can you not try? Please, I'm begging you. I don't want to marry him, but I don't think either he or my parents care what I want."

Why would Lord Coyle go from lifelong bachelor to wanting to marry a girl young enough to be his granddaughter? With his wealth and influence, many women must have tried to end his bachelor days over the years, so why choose to end them with Hope now? Had he truly fallen in love with her so quickly? They had certainly seemed comfortable in one another's company, and conversation had flowed freely. Many married couples didn't even share that.

"The extra time will benefit both of you," I said, rather stupidly.

"India won't help you," Aunt Letitia said with finality. "You've made your bed and now you must lie in it."

"What bed?" Hope asked.

"You flirted with him at dinner."

"That's what I told her!" Charity cried.

Hope glared at her sister. "I was merely doing what all ladies of good breeding do when seated beside a gentleman. Well, most ladies of good breeding. At least I don't flirt with the staff."

Charity merely gave her that flat smile again and turned back to the window.

"Insisting on calling Cyclops staff does you no credit," Aunt Letitia bit back. "India won't help someone who disparages her friend in such a manner."

Wisely, Hope remained silent.

"Aunt Letitia is right," I said. "You speak of Cyclops as though he's nothing. You tried to sabotage my relationship with Matt, and you've tried to stop your own sister from being happy with Lord Cox. Why should I help you?"

Hope pressed a hand to her stomach as if I'd landed a sickening blow. "I—I'm sorry, India. Truly I am. I had my reasons for doing all of that, even with regards to Cyclops. If he really is a friend then the situation for him is worse than if he is staff. As a coachman, my father would consider him beneath Charity and would do anything to keep them apart. But if Matt treats him as an equal, then my father might think him a good enough match for his strange and difficult daughter. Believe me, there are few gentlemen who would look favorably at her, and those who do are quite mad themselves. My parents want her married. At this point, they don't particularly care who to."

Charity clapped her hands. "Well done, Sister. What a performance. You should be on the stage."

Hope's throat moved with her swallow, but she was otherwise quite still.

"India may believe that my brother might try to force a union between Cyclops and Charity," Aunt Letitia said, "but I don't. I've known my brother longer than you, Hope, and I am absolutely certain he wouldn't countenance it. He'd rather send Charity to an asylum."

Charity sat bolt upright. "Asylum?"

Hope's lips curved ever so slightly. "If we decide to do nothing, we shall find out which one of us is right, won't we?"

Charity folded her arms again, but this time it was more of a hug than a show of defiance. She turned back to the window.

"We won't find out," I said to them all. "Because Lord Rycroft will leave Cyclops alone."

"I don't understand," Aunt Letitia said. "Is that where Matthew went this morning? To confront Richard and demand he end this nonsense?"

We hadn't told her or Willie that Matt was going to see the Home Secretary today, and we certainly hadn't informed Cyclops. Cyclops would feel as though Duke had betrayed his trust, and Willie and Aunt Letitia could inadvertently add fuel to the fire if they knew Lord Rycroft was demanding Cyclops be deported. It would seem Hope and Charity were also in the dark.

It was time that those in the room were made aware.

Once I finished telling them, I had to grasp Aunt Letitia's hand and stop her from marching out of the drawing room to her brother's house.

"There's another way to fix this," I told her quietly. "Please, sit down, or you might suffer one of your turns."

"I will not," she snapped. "My mind is very clear today. Very clear indeed." She sat anyway, thankfully.

"I'll talk to Lord Coyle on your behalf," I told Hope. "I'll tell him what a terrible match it will be, and I will do my best to be as convincing as possible."

She released a breath. "Thank you, India. Thank you."

"In return, Charity will tell your parents that she accosted Cyclops in the stables, not the other way around."

A bubble of laughter escaped Charity's lips. "Why would I do that?"

"That's not my concern." I turned to Hope. "It's yours."

"Me!" Hope cried. "How can I convince her? She doesn't care two straws for me."

"True," Charity said, shrugging a shoulder.

"You'll think of something," I said to Hope. "If you want me to intercede on your behalf with Lord Coyle, that is. If you fail, I might find myself telling him that you didn't want to appear too eager to accept his proposal and that he shouldn't give up easily."

Hope gasped. "You wouldn't."

"Wouldn't I? I care more for Cyclops than I do for you." I smiled serenely. "Enjoy the rest of your day. If you don't mind, Aunt Letitia and I are very busy."

Charity swanned past us, not looking quite as victorious as I expected her to. Perhaps she was worried about how her sister would convince Lord Rycroft to leave Cyclops alone. I suspected Hope had many tricks up her sleeve, some of which would involve divulging long-held sisterly secrets. Nothing was sacred for Hope, particularly when she was backed into a corner.

She and Lord Coyle had more in common than either realized.

"Well done, India," Aunt Letitia said after they'd gone. "That was masterful. I wish Matthew had been here to see it."

"Don't congratulate me yet. It won't be easy for Hope to convince Charity to own up to her deception and then to convince her father to stop persecuting Cyclops."

"Would you really tell Lord Coyle that she wants to marry him if she fails?"

I sighed. "I wish I had the fortitude to follow through on my threat, but I suspect I would crumble. As much as I dislike Hope, condemning her to a marriage with a man like Coyle would be an awful thing to do. I will try to help her get out of it."

"I suppose. But there's no need to rush, is there? No need at all."

CHAPTER 12

Matt failed to even see the Home Secretary let alone convince him that Cyclops should not be deported. "He was too busy," he bit off. "I think my uncle told him to avoid me."

"That wouldn't surprise me," I said as I loaded a plate with sandwiches for him.

"Don't be too worried," Aunt Letitia said as she poured him a cup of tea. "India has set her own plan to save Cyclops in motion, and I think it will work. It's quite clever."

We told him about our meeting with the sisters, Hope's request that I get her out of the marriage to Coyle, and the condition I placed on my assistance. Matt was smiling by the end.

"My clever little bride. I shall have to watch myself with you."

"Nonsense," I said, handing him the plate.

"You'd never employ such blackmail on me?"

"No, I mean I'm not little." I let go of the plate, smiling.

We decided to visit Lord Coyle after luncheon, but not to speak to him about Hope. Her name was the first on *his* lips, however.

"Your cousin is a delight, Glass," he said as he led us through to the small library. It was the room he received visitors in, and was the one with the hidden door that led through to his magical collection. Unlike the Delanceys, he kept his magical objects a secret, only allowing a select few to see them. As far as I knew, only other members of the collectors club had viewed them, aside from Matt and me.

"Hope is a unique young woman," Matt said.

"Unique indeed. I've never met another lady like her, not in all my years. She's clever and witty, beautiful and well bred. She matched me on any subject, and we have discussed many, many things in our brief acquaintance. I feel as though I know her very well already."

"I'd caution you to act slowly, my lord," I said. "There are many sides to her, and I'd wager you haven't seen them all yet." I wasn't sure if I was warning him for his benefit or hers.

"If I do not act, someone else will snatch her up. I'm not a fool, Mrs. Glass, nor am I blind. I know why you're warning me; I'm too old for her. But I don't care."

Matt tensed. "Does *she* care?"

Lord Coyle's moustache lifted with the stretch of his lips. "Whatever reservations she has now will pass in time. We are a good match. She knows it already, I can tell, and she will see that I can give her everything she wants."

A small shiver slithered down my spine.

"We're not here to talk about my cousin," Matt said as he refused the chair Coyle offered. "We want to know if you paid back Fabian Charbonneau's debt."

"The one that landed him in prison?" Lord Coyle lowered himself into one of the armchairs with a groan. "Now why would I do that?"

"So that Fabian will owe you a favor," I said. "You like to collect them, particularly from magicians."

"Please do sit down, Mrs. Glass. You're upsetting my gentlemanly code of honor by remaining standing. If you do not sit, I will have to stand, and my knees will protest most vehemently."

"This won't take long. Please, do not get up on my account. I insist."

He pointed the end of his walking stick at a chair opposite. "Come now, let's be friends. Sit."

Matt snatched the stick off him. "She doesn't want to sit," he growled. "Answer us honestly. Did you or did you not pay off Charbonneau's debt?"

Coyle settled into the chair, filling it. "I did."

"How did you know who he borrowed from?"

"I asked him."

"You visited him in prison?"

"It was shortly after you two were there, I believe."

"Not according to the police investigation," I said. "He had no visitors after us and Louisa."

Coyle's smile was slippery. "You'll find wardens are not paid well, Mrs. Glass. They'll say anything if you slip them a few bob."

"Why hasn't Charbonneau come out of hiding and told the police that the debt is repaid and he has no reason to commit murder?" Matt asked.

"Because he didn't know I was going to repay the money lender. I didn't tell Mr. Charbonneau my plan. That would have been presumptuous."

"Nonsense," I spat. "You kept the information back from him deliberately. Why?"

Coyle heaved his shoulders in a shrug.

"Because he either knew or suspected that Charbonneau would use his magic to fashion a key and escape," Matt said. "Perhaps Charbonneau hinted that he wouldn't be in prison much longer, and you guessed why. Now you're simply biding your time, waiting for him to be cleared of the murder and come out of hiding. At that point you'll tell him you repaid his debt and that he owes you. Are you hoping he'll give you the key in return? Or will you ask for something more from him?"

"Like a favor that you can call in at a later date," I added tartly.

Lord Coyle's smile grated my nerves. "I don't owe you an explanation."

"The police should have been told," Matt said.

"Why? It's irrelevant. It doesn't clear his name because he didn't know I'd paid his debt."

"Where and when did you meet McGuire?" I asked.

"Six forty-five in the evening in an alleyway. Not the same alley in which he later died."

"You went into an alley to meet a money lender?" I scoffed. "You're not that foolish."

"I waited in the carriage while my man fetched him. McGuire then came to me. I believe alleys were his favorite meeting place for conducting business. That's where Charbonneau first met him. Highly unprofessional, if you ask me, but if one likes to keep one's affairs a secret then I suppose they suffice."

"How did he seem?" Matt asked. "Anxious?"

"He was surprised I was there to pay off the debt. He didn't realize I knew Charbonneau."

Matt raised a brow. "That implies you and McGuire already knew one another before that evening."

Lord Coyle's fingers flexed around the silver head of his walking stick.

"How did you know him?" Matt asked.

"I didn't say that I did. You said it."

"We have reason to believe McGuire owed someone money, and that person wanted to be urgently repaid. That's why he suddenly called in his debts. He didn't ask you about Charbonneau, out of the blue, did he?"

"I wonder if that's why he was anxious," Lord Coyle mused. "Perhaps he was worried about his creditor. Some of the money lenders in this city are dangerous, Glass. You'd best stay well away from them. They shouldn't be crossed."

"Was it you, Coyle?" Matt pressed. "Did he owe you money?"

His lordship leveled his gaze with Matt's, neither looking away. The air in the small room thickened with tension, shredding my already frayed nerves.

"I'd never met McGuire before that evening," Coyle finally said. He leaned forward on his walking stick. "There is something that might interest you about that night. He tried to hurry along our meeting. When I asked him why, he informed me he had another meeting to go to where he expected another debtor to repay his debt. He seemed relieved about it."

"Why do you suppose that is?" Matt asked.

"Perhaps it would help repay this debt you seem so sure he had. As I said, some money lenders are dangerous. If McGuire owed one of them a substantial amount, he had every right to be frightened if he couldn't repay."

"Do you know of any capable of murder?" I asked.

"Murdering the fellow who owes you money isn't good for business, Mrs. Glass. If I were one of those money lenders, I would threaten McGuire in another way, such as to hurt his family or ruin his business or reputation. Perhaps if I knew something about him, something illegal or immoral that he'd done, I would threaten to expose that. But not commit murder."

The shiver ran down my spine again. This man knew how to make threats and use information to get what he wanted. I had no doubt *he'd* made such threats before.

"India," Matt said, holding out his hand to me. "If you have no more questions for Coyle, we should go."

I took his hand and thanked Coyle. Matt didn't say a word until we were inside our carriage and on our way to Scotland Yard. He could hardly contain his excitement.

"You look like a boy who has won a prize at the fair," I said. "What is it?"

"Coyle gave me an idea for the motive."

"You think *he* killed McGuire?"

"No, but I do know why one of McGuire's debtors would. That's where we've been failing. We haven't pinned down a motive for the murder. Not for Charbonneau, Stanhope or any of McGuire's debtors. After all, their debts are not dissolved upon his death."

"Is it because they couldn't repay it quickly and they hoped his heirs would return to the usual repayment plan, something that allows them more time?"

"That's a possibility, but now I have another theory, thanks to Coyle. Perhaps McGuire was killed because of the information he threatened to reveal about one of his debtors if the debt wasn't repaid."

"You think he made such a threat and his killer murdered him to ensure the secret never got out?" It was a good theory, and I warmed to it with every passing moment. "What if McGuire met his killer after he met Lord Coyle in the alley? If the killer told McGuire at that meeting that he couldn't repay, McGuire might have threatened to reveal his secret then."

"And who do we know with a big secret that could ruin his life if it became public?"

"Stanhope," I said on a breath.

It made sense. He knew his business partner very well, and knew that if his embezzlement came to light, Mr. Ingles would not only hate him but take action to remove him from the company. For a man such as Mr. Stanhope, who loved his work, it was a dire consequence. He would do anything to keep the embezzlement a secret.

Perhaps even commit murder.

Part of me felt sorry for him. He'd been backed into a corner; he was desperate. He didn't seem like a bad man, just someone who couldn't control his gambling, and that had led to his financial difficulties.

"We still don't know why he set up Fabian," I said, "or how he was able to slip away from his wife in the night."

"She could have lied for him."

"She'd have to be a good actress for Brockwell to fall for it. He's no fool."

"Some women beguile the inspector," Matt said. "Both you and Willie have him wrapped around your finger, so why not Mrs. Stanhope too?"

I had to meet her to know for certain. Brockwell might not be as immune as Matt to the charms of manipulative women, but he hadn't become detective inspector by having the wool pulled over his eyes by a woman with a pretty face.

"What do you think about Coyle?" Matt asked. "Do you think he's lying when he said he never met McGuire before that night, and that he wasn't the one who loaned him money only to call it in?"

I sighed. "I don't know. It wouldn't surprise me if he lied to our faces. Nor would it surprise me if he has a finger in the money lending pie in this city."

"It makes sense that a small lender like McGuire would be in debt to a wealthy man like Coyle. McGuire would need cash flow and Coyle could give it to him."

"For a price."

"Indeed."

We met Brockwell in his office, surrounded by photographs of the murder scene, spread on his desk. He quickly gathered them up and tucked them away beneath other papers.

"My apologies, Mrs. Glass," he said. "You shouldn't have seen that."

I dismissed his concerns and got straight to the point. "We know why Stanhope killed McGuire."

He listened to our entire explanation, only to shake his

head at the end. "I like it as a motive, Glass. I do. But it's a motive that could apply to most of McGuire's debtors. I'm sure Stanhope wasn't the only one with a secret. And there is also the matter of his alibi and his connection to Charbonneau. We've so far failed to find one. Anyway, it's possible McGuire threatened Charbonneau with something too."

"Such as?" I prompted.

Brockwell shrugged. "Something magical? To inform his guild that he is a magician?"

"I don't know if that's a threat for the Charbonneaus."

"Their business is so successful, they don't need the guild's approval," Matt added. "They could go directly to their government for a license. I believe the family are good friends with important people; people much higher than the guild leader."

"Something else, then. Something that could ruin Charbonneau."

Or destroy something he wanted, I might have said but did not. All Fabian cared about was his magic research and making new spells. What if McGuire threatened to take that away?

No, it wouldn't matter. Fabian wouldn't murder anyone. Not even for that. I was sure of it. "Fabian is no murderer," I said. "I give you my word, Inspector."

Matt tapped his finger on his thigh, his brow furrowed. "It *is* Stanhope. I'm certain of it. I couldn't work out why he asked Ingles to lie for him and say that he was at the factory until nine. The murder happened well after nine. The approximate time of death was in all the papers the following day, and Stanhope admitted to reading them. So why did he ask Ingles to lie? It didn't make sense then, but it does now. Coyle gave us the clue."

"Stanhope's meeting with McGuire," I said, realizing his point.

Brockwell wagged a finger at Matt. "Stanhope met

McGuire earlier in the evening. It was probably at that meeting that he told McGuire he couldn't pay, and McGuire informed him that he would tell Ingles about the embezzlement. Stanhope formed his murderous plan then and there, but he didn't want us to know he even met McGuire."

"Hence getting Ingles to lie about the time he left work," I added. "Do you think Stanhope was the man McGuire met immediately after Coyle in the alley?"

"It's likely," Matt said.

Matt and I exchanged nods of agreement, but Brockwell shook his head. "It is also possible that Stanhope asked Ingles to lie about the time he left the factory simply because he was afraid we'd jump to this very conclusion. That if we learned he met McGuire early in the evening, we would also assume he killed him later."

"Why are you defending him?" Matt asked.

"Because I have met his wife, and I'm certain she didn't lie to me. Nor does it explain why Charbonneau's handkerchief was placed at the scene of the crime. Let us assume, for the sake of argument, that McGuire told Stanhope about a French fellow who also owed him money. Let us also assume Stanhope knew the Frenchman was in prison and found out where he lived, and even that he went there to steal the handkerchief. How did he know Charbonneau was planning to escape? Or indeed, that he had? It is a mystery, is it not?"

"Then you'd better put on your hat and solve it, Inspector." Matt stood abruptly. "India and I will continue to do what we can. I propose we call on Mrs. Stanhope."

"No!"

"We'll wait until her husband is out—"

"Absolutely not!" Brockwell slapped both hands on the desk in a most uncharacteristic display of emotion. "Mrs. Stanhope is a good woman and should not be bothered any more than she already has been."

"You're too chivalrous for this job, Brockwell."

"It is not chivalry, Glass, it's common sense. I have questioned her thoroughly and she kept to her story. I saw no cracks in it, no doubt in her mind. Unless we have new, *solid* facts, I will not question her again. Nor will either of you. Is that understood?"

I grabbed Matt's arm and dug my fingers in, hard. "It's very clear, Inspector. We'd best be on our way."

I wasn't sure who steered whom out of the building, but we were both glad to be in the carriage and driving home.

"You wanted me out of there because you plan on us speaking to Mrs. Stanhope," Matt said. "Don't you?"

"No, Matt, I do not. I agree with Brockwell. If she lied to him, she'll lie to us. Unlike you, I don't think him capable of being beguiled by a woman. If he believed her story then she was either telling the truth or she's such a good liar that we won't be able to detect her lies either. So if we're going to question her, we need proof."

"Very well. How do you propose to get it?"

That was the problem. I didn't have a clue.

* * *

I HOPED OCCUPYING my mind would allow my inner thoughts to find a solution, but it seemed working on the language of magic occupied my mind too much. After an hour, I set aside my notes and settled at my writing desk, my horology tools at hand. This type of activity would be more soothing.

I worked on my watch first, simply taking it apart and putting it back together again. Then I turned to the black marble clock. It was two minutes and twenty seconds too slow. That was unacceptable.

I used one of the spells Chronos had taught me as I returned the inner workings to their rightful place then adjusted the hands. It was the first time I'd used a spell on this clock. Indeed, it was the first time I'd used the spell at all, except in practice. All other clocks and watches I touched seemed to simply work when I finished tinkering with them. This clock had proved obstinate. Perhaps the spell would fix it. I'd know by tomorrow.

Peter arrived and informed me that Catherine was waiting in the drawing room. I packed away my tools and headed down the stairs, but I stopped just outside the drawing room door. It was open and Cyclops's resonant voice could be clearly heard.

"I don't need your help," he said.

"You don't *want* my help, Nate," Catherine said. "But you do need it. There's a difference."

He grunted. "I won't let you get tangled up in this mess. Lord Rycroft is dangerous."

I peeked around the corner and saw them standing very close together near the fireplace. Closer than mere friends.

Catherine frowned up at him, chewing on her bottom lip. "Surely there's something I can do. Speak to Charity, perhaps?"

"She won't listen to reason," he said. "India and Miss Glass have already tried."

"But I must do something!"

Cyclops took hold of Catherine's hand and she immediately closed her other hand over the top. "Listen to me." Cyclops's voice was all warm honey. I'd seen him use the same tone to soothe frightened horses and it seemed to work on Catherine too. "My greatest fear was that you wouldn't believe I was innocent. Knowing that you do is all I need from you. It's all I want."

Catherine's lip wobbled. "Of course I believe you. There was never any doubt."

He kissed her forehead and removed his hand.

But Catherine wasn't ready to release him altogether yet. She blocked his exit as he tried to leave. Her moment of weakness had vanished, and the fire I knew she possessed in every bone had returned. "Why?" she asked.

"Don't," he growled back.

"Why do you say such wonderfully sweet things then push me away?"

"You know why." He strode past her toward the door, spotting me. It was too late for me to pretend I hadn't heard them.

She turned to us, hands fisted at her sides. "You're a coward, Nate."

"India," he said in greeting as he passed me. He didn't stop or look back.

Catherine threw her hands in the air. "How can he say such things then pretend he feels nothing for me?"

"At least his words give you hope," I said, joining her. "It shows he cares."

"He's infuriating."

"Give him time."

"I have given him time, India." She released a ragged breath and allowed me to pull her down to the sofa to sit beside me. "I've given him time and space in the hope he will come to his senses and admit there's something between us, something worth exploring, but he's too stubborn. What more can I do?"

"Understand why he's keeping you at arm's length."

"I do understand. I just don't agree with his reasoning or like it."

"He's doing it for you, Catherine. He's worried that being with him will cut you off from your family, from society. That's not the life he wants for you or your children. If that's not a sign of love then I don't know what is."

My words did nothing to ease the tension in her fine features. "Ronnie wouldn't abandon me and nor would you or Matt, Duke or Willie. Even Miss Glass would support us. We have more friends than most. As to any future children, they will have two parents who love them and a wider family in all of you, too. That's far more than many poor children have in this city."

I sighed. It was impossible to argue with her when she was right.

Catherine didn't stay for long. Although she said she'd come to see me for a friendly conversation, I suspected she'd really come to see Cyclops. Having accomplished that, she returned to the shop and the home she kept above it with her brother.

Another visitor replaced her, however. This one wasn't as welcome, particularly since he didn't greet me before shouting at me.

CHAPTER 13

"Tell your husband to call off his dogs, India," Chronos snapped before he'd even set a foot inside. "Do it now. I'm tired of being watched. I feel like a criminal."

Bristow stepped between Chronos and me, blocking my line of sight. "Perhaps Mr. Steele would prefer to wait outside until Mr. Glass arrives. Fossett," he said to the hovering Peter, "fetch Mr. Glass from his study. Tell him Mr. Steele would like a word."

"This is my granddaughter's house!" Chronos cried. "Let me in!"

"Not until you calm down, sir."

"India!"

"It's all right, Bristow," I said. "Chronos will cause more trouble outside than in. Our neighbors get quite enough excitement from us already."

Bristow stepped aside and Chronos moved past him into the entrance hall. He slapped his hat into the butler's chest. "Hang that up then run along and fetch me a drink. Something strong from Glass's liquor cabinet. Make it the good stuff. I deserve it after the last few days."

"Chronos!" I cried. "Don't be childish. Bristow, set another place for dinner. It's too early for liquor."

Chronos grunted as he watched the butler leave with his hat.

"So you've spotted Duke," I said, knowing he was the one watching the house.

"Not just him," Chronos said as he followed me to the drawing room. "All three of them. It's been going on for days. Tell your husband Charbonneau isn't with me and to call off the watch."

"It's not Matt's fault. It was a joint decision between all of us."

"Don't take the blame for him."

"Nothing I say will change your mind, so if you won't be quiet, you may leave."

"Before dinner?" He grunted again. "Think I'll stay."

Matt entered, followed by Duke.

Chronos jutted his jaw in Duke's direction. "So your spy followed me here. I should have known."

Duke rolled his eyes. "I didn't follow you. Willie took over."

"We're not interested in your movements, Chronos," Matt said with a calmness I envied. "We're interested in those of the person hiding in your house."

"No one is in my house except me!"

Matt hitched up his trouser legs and sat. He held out his hand to me with a smile and I sat beside him. His relaxed demeanor only seemed to rankle Chronos. He huffed and clicked his tongue and shook his head, refusing to sit down.

It was Duke who finally spoke up. "Someone else is in there. I saw the curtains flutter when you weren't home this morning."

Chronos finally chose a chair and lowered himself into it. "A draft."

"It moved too much for a draft."

"My housekeeper, then. She sometimes cleans when I've gone out."

"She was out too. There was someone else in your house. Someone who knows I was watching."

"Everyone knows you're watching my house! The entire neighborhood is abuzz with it. None of you know the art of being inconspicuous. It's their American-ness," he said to me. "Cowboys in London are an oddity. Not to mention girls dressed as cowboys and giant pirates."

I bit my lip to stop my smile from spreading. Chronos had just turned the conversation from heated to ludicrous. It was a timely reminder that he was all bluster and no substance. Matt knew it all along, hence his unruffled feathers.

Chronos scowled at me. "Why are you smiling?"

"I'm not."

"This is not amusing." He sniffed. "It's an invasion of my privacy."

"An invasion of your privacy would be if we stormed inside and searched your house. If you push us, we might very well do it."

He sniffed again.

"Is Fabian staying with you?" I asked. "Answer me or you are not welcome to stay for dinner."

"You think I can be bought with food?"

"Is Fabian staying at your house?"

He got to his feet. "I don't have to listen to these accusations."

"It's not an accusation, it's a question."

He marched off, only to be met in the doorway by Bristow, carrying Chronos's bowler hat.

"Don't leave without your hat, Mr. Steele."

Chronos snatched it off Bristow. "It's damp."

"It fell into a pail of water."

"How?"

"I can't recall."

"It will keep its shape," I said to Chronos before his temper exploded. "It's well made."

"I can't wear it home now, can I? I'm not putting a damp hat on my head." With a huff, he pushed past Bristow.

"Give Charbonneau our regards," Matt called after him. "Tell him not to peer through windows again until we can clear his name."

Chronos's only reaction was to slam the front door closed.

I rubbed my forehead and sighed. "He may be an old man, but that gives him no right to be rude to the staff. Or us."

Matt rubbed my shoulder and kissed my temple. "He's under some pressure."

"You don't have to defend him," I said. "He's quite capable of doing it himself."

"I can't believe he left before dinner," Duke muttered. "If I were him, I'd have saved the denials until after dessert."

* * *

A LETTER from Mrs. McGuire arrived the following morning, asking for my help in going through the rest of her husband's business papers. She wanted someone who understood his affairs to explain the contracts to her, but she didn't want a man's help. She wanted me to go alone.

I had a devil of a time convincing Cyclops and Duke that I would be all right when I read out the note to them and Matt in the sitting room.

"She might be the murderer," Duke said.

"I don't think she is," Matt said.

Cyclops agreed with Duke. "You can't rule her out. India shouldn't go alone."

"She's frightened of men," I told them. "She might not talk to me if I arrive with one of you in tow."

"Then take Willie with you," Cyclops said.

"She's not here and didn't come home last night."

"She'll be at Brockwell's."

"I ain't so sure," Duke said. "He doesn't seem to want the distraction during a big investigation. She probably found another bed to sleep in."

"Duke!" I cried. "Willie may be a lot of things, but she wouldn't conduct a liaison with someone else while she's with the inspector."

Cyclops and Duke exchanged looks.

"I don't particularly like it," Matt said. "But I agree with you, India. You should go alone. But let it be known to Mrs. McGuire that she'll suffer my wrath if any harm should come to you."

"I'll be sure to weave those words into the conversation."

I smiled at him but he scowled back. "This is serious," he muttered.

I kissed the top of his head. "I'll see you all later."

* * *

Mrs. McGuire looked different, but I couldn't place the reason. She wore the same black crepe mourning dress that I'd seen her in twice, with a long black veil attached to a bonnet and cascading down her back.

It wasn't until she began to speak that I realized what had changed. She fixed her gaze *on* me rather than lowering it, and she spoke with a steady, strong voice, not a tremulous one. Mrs. McGuire's confidence had returned, or it had at least begun to. Her brute of a husband hadn't destroyed it altogether.

We went straight to her husband's office where tea and biscuits had been set out for us on the desk. There was no sign of the housekeeper, but I heard the thud of a door closing somewhere in the house.

"I hoped you would come," Mrs. McGuire said, pouring

the tea. "I know it's presumptuous of me, but I made the tea and set it all out in the hope you would."

"Didn't your housekeeper make the tea?" I asked.

If she thought it an odd question, she didn't let on. "I gave her the day off so we wouldn't be disturbed. She left some time ago."

I accepted the cup and saucer only to put them down again. I didn't want her to notice my shaking hands. "Are we alone here?"

She blinked at me. "Yes. Why?"

"I heard a door closing just a few moments ago."

"Oh. I didn't hear anything." She smiled. "Perhaps Mrs. Roston left just now. It would be like her to wait for your arrival. She worries about me being alone since Mr. McGuire's death."

"She didn't worry about you before his death?"

She leveled her gaze with mine over her teacup. "She didn't have the courage to worry. Not with my husband the way he was."

"Yes. Of course."

We both sipped.

"Shall we get started?" I said, setting down the cup. "My husband doesn't want me gone for long. He'll send out a search party if I don't show up in a reasonable time." I laughed but she looked horrified.

"What is a reasonable time?" she asked.

I waved off her question. "It changes with the wind."

"Then we must hurry. I wouldn't want your husband to… worry." She put down her cup too and picked up the top document from a pile on the desk. "I removed these from my husband's filing cabinets. They appear to be contracts for his clients. I hoped you could explain some of the terms to me. It's all so complicated."

"I'll try," I said, accepting the document.

She sat alongside me, and I told her what some of the

phrases meant. It wasn't too complicated. The terms were clear and not bogged down by heavy legal jargon. Mrs. McGuire should have been able to work out most of it herself.

"I know you think I'm stupid," she said when I explained a particular clause for the second time.

"Not at all," I said.

She lifted a hand and I reeled back, but she only touched her forehead before lowering it to her lap again. Thankfully she hadn't noticed my reaction.

"I wasn't educated," she told me. "I could read only a little when I married, just enough to run a household with the help of a housekeeper. Mr. McGuire didn't tell me anything about his business affairs. He said I wouldn't understand." She lifted her hand again, this time passing it across her jaw, as if touching the ghost of a bruise.

I offered her a comforting smile. "A lack of education doesn't mean you're stupid. You simply weren't given the opportunity to expand your knowledge, and I'm sure your husband didn't encourage you to learn."

Her eyes swam with tears. "He said I didn't need to know anything except how to be a good wife. But I failed in that too, in his eyes. We never had children," she added.

I thought it just as well that a cruel man like McGuire never fathered children, but it would be unkind to say so to his childless widow, so I changed the subject.

"Did you visit the lawyer whose name was on that card we found?"

She nodded. "He was my husband's lawyer. He says I am the beneficiary of my husband's will. Everything comes to me now. This house, his belongings, and all the money people owe him."

"As well as any debts he owes to others."

"The lawyer mentioned as much, but he didn't know of a debt. I was hoping to find details of it amongst all this paperwork, if a debt exists at all."

"Our inquiries would suggest there is one, and it was called in suddenly."

She surveyed the papers. "Then we'd better find out if it was paid or not."

I forgot my reservations about Mrs. McGuire by the time we'd finished with the documents from the filing cabinet. She seemed genuinely in need of my help to explain the terms of the contracts and to understand her new financial position. If the housekeeper had still been in the house when I arrived, I was quite sure she left when I heard the door close. Mrs. McGuire had most likely been telling the truth when she said the housekeeper had stayed until she knew her employer was safe with me. Considering what the widow had been through, it was understandable.

"That's it," I said, placing the last contract on the pile. "Are you sure there are no more documents in the filing cabinet?"

"Quite sure, but you may check for yourself."

I rifled through each drawer while Mrs. McGuire watched on from the study doorway. There were no more documents. I then opened each of the desk drawers, but found nothing. I sat back on my haunches on the floor, and looked around the room.

"If I wanted to keep something secret, I would hide it," I said. "Your husband was in a dangerous business, Mrs. McGuire. It's possible that the man he owed was ruthless, and some of the men who owed him money were also undesirable characters."

"Gamblers," she said with a nod at the pile.

"He must have a hiding place either here or elsewhere. Was there another room in the house where he went and did not want anyone to follow him?"

She shook her head. "This was his sanctuary. He was in here all the time when he was home, except when he ate and slept."

"What about outside the home? A deposit box at a bank, for example."

"I suppose one might have existed but we've found no paperwork or a key, and the lawyer didn't mention one."

The information had to be in this room. I crawled under the desk and checked the underside. Nothing had been nailed to it and I couldn't see any extra partitions. I crawled out again.

"Help me up, please, Mrs. McGuire. We're going to tear this place apart."

She assisted me to my feet then glanced around the room. "Where do we start?"

"Tap the walls. If a section sounds hollow then there might be a storage cavity behind it."

We tapped the walls, checked under the chairs, inside the desk and filing cabinet drawers for false bottoms. We rolled up the rug and stamped our feet over every exposed inch of the floor. The only section we couldn't check easily was under the filing cabinet. It was heavy and we couldn't lift it between us.

"I never heard furniture scraping on the floor," she said.

"He might have waited until you were out." I eyed the filing cabinet, hands on hips. "It *must* be under there."

It crossed my mind to fetch Matt, Duke or Cyclops, but that would only take time. Besides, I wanted to conquer the filing cabinet without their help.

I placed my shoulder against its side and pushed as hard as I could. The cabinet lifted a little only to fall back again. I grinned. "I don't think he moved it. He *tipped* it. Help me move the desk over to the other side to stop the cabinet putting a hole in your floor when it falls."

We maneuvered the desk into position then put our shoulders to the cabinet. On the count of three, we gave an almighty shove, raising the side of the cabinet closest to us. It crashed down on the desk, splintering the wood.

Neither of us cared. On the floor was a square shaped panel with a ring set into the wood. A trapdoor.

Mrs. McGuire pulled on the ring and the panel lifted, revealing a small cavity under the floor. Inside were two documents. We unfolded one and poured over it together.

"It's a contract for a financial arrangement," I said. "It says that your husband owed the lender five thousand pounds."

Mrs. McGuire gasped. "How will I ever repay such an amount?"

"It doesn't matter." I pointed to a clause at the bottom. "The debt is null and void if he dies without paying it."

"That is a relief. Do you think that's odd?"

"I don't know. The world of money lending is new to me." I searched the document for a name, but there was none. Whoever loaned McGuire the money didn't want to be identified. Perhaps that was why the amount was never to be repaid after McGuire's death.

"What about this one?" Mrs. McGuire said, unfolding the second document. "It's different. It's not a contract."

It was a single paragraph of text with a signature at the bottom.

Mr. Hubert Stanhope.

Mrs. McGuire read out the paragraph. "'I hereby acknowledge that I embezzled funds from my place of business, The Ingles Vinegar Company of South Lambert, to the amount of one thousand pounds.' That's all it says." She handed the document to me and I reread it. "What does it mean?"

"It means your husband could produce this signed note if Mr. Stanhope didn't repay his debt. Most likely he would show it to Mr. Stanhope's business partner, Mr. Ingles." It meant Matt was right, and Stanhope had a very good reason to murder McGuire. McGuire must have told him at their early evening meeting that he would show the signed confession to Ingles if he didn't repay the debt in its entirety. Stanhope had met him again later, probably telling McGuire he had the money, but had instead killed him to prevent his business partner from learning his shameful secret.

It must have been a double blow for Stanhope the day we told Mr. Ingles. Not only did Stanhope lose his position at the company, but he realized he'd committed murder for nothing.

"Perhaps that's why Stanhope had an asterisk on his contract," Mrs. McGuire said. "It was referring to this, a sort of reminder for my husband."

I nodded but my mind was elsewhere. I was more convinced than ever that Stanhope had murdered McGuire. But the unanswered questions bothered me too much. I couldn't go to Brockwell with this. Not yet. Not until I knew I wasn't condemning an innocent man.

We still needed evidence linking Stanhope to Fabian, and there was also the matter of his alibi.

It was time to talk to Mrs. Stanhope. Matt might be right about that too, and Brockwell couldn't detect her lie.

I asked Mrs. McGuire to deliver an urgent message to him to meet me at the Stanhopes' address in Hammersmith then proceeded there myself in the carriage. I instructed Woodall, the coachman, to wait a little up the street but within sight of the townhouse's front door.

I knocked on the basement service door and told the young maid who answered that I needed to know how many staff worked in the house. "The information will be used as part of a statistical analysis on the employment of domestic servants in London conducted by the Foundation for Retired Domestic Workers."

She wrinkled her nose "I've never heard of it."

"We're a newly formed charitable institute that raises funds to support live-in domestic workers after their years of servitude come to an end. There's a great need in this city to care for those who've cared for others over many years and who find themselves without a home when they are no longer of use to their employers."

"Well it's about bloody time someone did something for us. Come in and meet everyone for yourself."

"I only require numbers, at this point."

"Come in and have a cup of tea anyway. It's the least we can do for someone on our side. Come on, Mrs....?"

"Glass," I said without thinking.

"Come in, Mrs. Glass, and we'll tell you everything you need to know about the servants on this entire street."

I glanced over my shoulder and nodded at Woodall. There was no sign of Matt, but I had no plans to speak to Mrs. Stanhope without him. Staying in the service rooms would be a good way to learn if Mr. Stanhope was at home, however, while remaining out of his sight.

"We're a small group," the maid, Martha, said as she led the way down the dark corridor. "I'm the only live-in staff. Mr. and Mrs. Crupper used to live in but when they married last year, they found their own accommodations and commute every day. He's the butler and she's the cook. I do the cleaning and help out Mrs. Crupper in the kitchen." We reached the kitchen where a woman sat at the table with a man dressed in outdoor clothes. "This is Mrs. Crupper and Reggie, the stable hand, coachman, maintenance man. You name it, Reggie does it. He lives above the stables."

I gave them my spiel again about the foundation. Mrs. Crupper was as enthusiastic as Martha had been, but Reggie merely hunkered down over his bowl of soup, tucking it close to his chest as if he were afraid someone would take it from him. He didn't seem to be listening at all. When he finished, he placed his bowl into the washing tub then left without a word.

Mrs. Crupper tapped her forehead. "He's not all there," she said as she poured my tea. "Poor fellow. He's a good man, though, and a hard worker. He'll benefit from your foundation's funds, that's for sure. Long time away, of course, him being only in his thirties, but some day."

"Are your employers kind?" I asked.

"Kind enough," Mrs. Crupper said, taking her seat again. "We don't see much of Mr. Stanhope during the day, on account of his work."

"Where does he work?"

"A vinegar factory. He's a real important man in the company. Isn't that right, Martha?"

"It is," Martha said, dipping a biscuit in her tea. "Mrs. Stanhope's very proud of him. She likes to tell all her friends how important too, which is probably why few friends come round nowadays."

"Martha!" Mrs. Crupper clicked her tongue at the maid. "That's not why they don't come." To me, she said, "Mrs. Stanhope is ill. She doesn't leave the house much on account of the pain in her legs. The poor thing, they give her so much trouble these days."

"She's still in good spirits," Martha said. "Always cheerful, that's Mrs. Stanhope."

"You like them both?"

"She's kind."

"And Mr. Stanhope?"

Martha shrugged. "I don't have much to do with him."

"He's all right, as masters go," Mrs. Crupper said. "He's never hurt any of us, never treated us unfairly, and he's good to Reggie. I've never seen him shout at Reggie, and poor Reggie sometimes needs to be shouted at or he doesn't know what's what."

It wasn't glowing praise, but I'd heard some horrific stories of the way maids had been treated by their employers, so it was no wonder they thought Mr. Stanhope a good man simply because he left them alone. They'd be shocked to learn he was a murderer.

Footsteps sounded on the flagstone corridor and a man dressed in black coat and tie with white gloves appeared. "Where's Reggie?" he asked. "He needs to bring the carriage around. Mr. Stanhope is returning to the factory now." This must be Mr. Crupper, the butler.

"In the stables," Martha told him.

"Who're you?" Mr. Crupper asked me.

"This is Mrs. Glass," Mrs. Crupper said. "She's with a charitable foundation that helps retired servants. She's just sharing a cup of tea with us before she goes on her way."

"I hope you're not gossiping."

"We'd never," Mrs. Crupper said with a secretive smile.

Her husband gave her a good natured grunt. He turned to go, only to stop again and stand to attention as more footsteps sounded along the corridor. "Sir, I was just about to go in search of Reggie and give him instructions to bring the conveyance around."

Mr. Stanhope appeared in the doorway.

I froze. I had nowhere to go. Facing the door meant I couldn't even present him with my back. I could only sit there and hope he didn't bother to look further than the butler.

"There's been a change of plans," Mr. Stanhope said. "I won't be returning to the factory this afternoon. I have other business in the city to attend to."

"I'll inform Reggie, sir."

Mr. Stanhope turned to go and in so doing, his gaze swept around the kitchen. It flicked over me then snapped back.

I swallowed and tried to look calm.

His face paled and the slack skin beneath his jaw shook. I waited for him to order me out, but he didn't. He simply stood there, staring, his breaths coming hard and fast. He didn't know what to do, I realized. If he acknowledged me he'd have to explain how he knew me, and it was clear that he hadn't told the staff he no longer worked at the factory. Perhaps he hadn't even informed his wife.

"This is Mrs. Glass," Mrs. Crupper said quickly with an anxious glance at her husband. "She works for a charitable institute—"

"This space is for staff use only," Mr. Stanhope said through a clenched jaw. "Not for idle chit chat with friends."

Martha made a sound of protest. "But she's not—"

"Martha!" Mrs. Crupper hissed. Martha pressed her lips together.

I smiled at her. "Thank you for the tea," I said rising. "It was a pleasure to meet you all." I pushed past Mr. Stanhope, half expecting him to grab my arm and haul me to a stop.

But he let me go without a word.

Outside, I gave Woodall a signal to indicate that he was to continue to wait, then I took up a position between two neighboring houses opposite and a little up the street from the Stanhopes' house. Shielded by a set of front steps, I could safely watch their house. With Mr. Stanhope about to leave, it was the perfect opportunity to speak to his wife.

Matt ought to arrive at any moment too. Together, we could ask her questions about the night of the murder. But everything hinged on Mr. Stanhope leaving. Now that he'd seen me, there was a very good chance he'd decide to stay.

The front door opened, but instead of Mr. Stanhope emerging, the butler appeared. He glanced along the street toward a lane, perhaps waiting for Reggie to bring around the carriage. Good. Mr. Stanhope still planned on leaving.

Mr. Crupper scanned the street, his gaze halting when it got to me. I'd thought myself well hidden behind the steps but it would seem not. Damnation.

I should have left then, perhaps even tossed him a wave. But I did not, and I paid for my hesitation.

My only warning came in the form of a sudden and inexplicable chime from my watch in my reticule. Finally it worked as my old one had. No, not quite. It chimed but did not save me from the attack.

Just as I registered the significance of the chime, pain ripped through my skull. My vision blurred and I slumped forward against the steps.

CHAPTER 14

Through the fiery ache in my head and the ringing in my ears, I could make out a man's voice, shouting, and running footsteps. A figure blocked out the light and something lightly slapped my cheek.

"Mrs. Glass?" came Woodall's panicked voice. "Mrs. Glass, wake up! Blimey, if you're dead, Mr. Glass'll kill me."

"I'm not dead," I managed to say.

He helped me to sit up. The poor man looked terribly worried, and I smiled to reassure him, even though my head felt as though it had split open. I touched the back of my skull. No blood, thankfully, although a lump had begun to form.

"India?" Matt jumped out of a still-moving hansom and raced toward me. "My god, are you hurt?" He cupped my face and searched my eyes. His own were filled with worry.

"I was hit on the head from behind," I said. "I didn't see his face. Or hers."

"It was a man," Woodall said. "But I was too far away to see who. He ran off in that direction." He pointed down the street. "He's long gone. I came to Mrs. Glass as soon as I saw her fall."

"Thank you, Woodall," Matt said. "Your attention to my wife is appreciated."

"I best get back to the coach, sir."

Matt checked me over again, inspecting the wound. "Do you feel ill?" he asked.

"No."

"Dizzy?"

"Not anymore."

"Can you see properly?"

"Yes."

He gently drew me into a hug, as if he expected me to shatter. He expelled a deep breath, ruffling my hair.

"I know what you're going to say," I said.

"And what is that?" he asked, voice rolling through me like thunder.

"That I should have waited for you before going inside."

He drew away and frowned at me. "You went inside?"

It was too late to take it back and pretend otherwise. "Just to the service area."

"Christ, India, why couldn't you wait?"

"I thought it wouldn't matter if I spoke to the servants without you. They might have some information, and there was little chance of coming across Mr. Stanhope down there."

"So what went wrong?"

"The odds didn't work in my favor. Mr. Stanhope came downstairs and recognized me."

"You think *he* hit you?"

"It's too much of a coincidence for it not to be him."

He scrubbed a hand over his face. When he drew it away, the worry in his eyes had been replaced by simmering anger.

"On the bright side," I said, opening my reticule, "my watch chimed just before I was hit. It warned me, Matt. Isn't that wonderful. My magic worked."

He grunted. "It didn't save you."

"The reticule was closed."

He rubbed his face again. "I'm going to have a word with Stanhope."

"I think he's already gone. Help me up, Matt. We'll speak to his widow as we intended."

"You should rest here a moment then Woodall can take you home."

I cocked my head to the side, bringing on a fresh wave of aches that I hid behind a glare. "I'm going to speak to her with you. In the mood you're in, you might not follow the script."

"Don't treat this lightly, India."

"I'm not. I want to catch a killer and that means completing what we set out to do—determine if Mrs. Stanhope is a liar. Now, help me up."

"You're stubborn." He settled his hands on my waist and lifted me to my feet. Either by accident or by design, I ended up standing very close to him. "But I am very glad to have my stubborn wife with me at all."

I was about to make a quip about him being overly dramatic but one look at his hard features, his dark swirling eyes, and I decided it was best not to. I kissed him lightly instead then took his hand.

We crossed the road as Mr. Crupper emerged from the Stanhope house. He looked worried as he trotted down the stairs to meet us.

"Are you all right, Mrs. Glass?" he asked. "My mistress says she saw you'd fallen."

"She didn't fall," Matt growled. "She was hit on the head by an assailant. Did you see him?"

Mr. Crupper took a step back beneath the force of Matt's ire. "I—I didn't, sir. I saw someone approaching Mrs. Glass but thought it was an acquaintance of hers, so I returned inside. My employer, Mrs. Stanhope, told me just now that she saw Mrs. Glass on the ground."

"This is Mr. Crupper, the butler," I told Matt. "Mr. Crupper, meet my husband, Matthew Glass. May we speak to Mrs. Stanhope?"

"She is not receiving callers."

"She'll see us," Matt snapped.

Mr. Crupper pulled himself up to his full height, which was far less than Matt's. "I don't think so. Mrs. Glass may go to the basement entrance and receive a cup of tea from the staff."

Matt's gaze turned icy. "Step aside."

"I'm not from a charitable foundation," I quickly said to Mr. Crupper. "We are assistants to Detective Inspector Brockwell of Scotland Yard. We have his authority to question Mrs. Stanhope over the murder of Mr. McGuire."

Mr. Crupper's eyes grew wider with every word, his jaw slacker. "But the inspector has already been here and asked his questions. What can he possibly need to know now?"

"That is not your affair," Matt said.

Mr. Crupper swallowed. "Follow me."

We headed up the stairs and inside to a sitting room. A woman with gray streaks through her hair and deathly pale skin welcomed us. She reclined on a chaise by the window, a blanket covering her from the waist down.

"Please excuse me for not getting up," she said. "My legs, you see."

"Mr. and Mrs. Glass to see you, madam," the butler said. "They're with Scotland Yard."

Mrs. Stanhope's brows arched. "The police again? Whatever for this time?"

Mr. Crupper backed out of the room, leaving the door open.

"I don't understand," Mrs. Stanhope said as she indicated we should sit. "Crupper thinks you work for a charity, I saw you crumpled on the footpath, you've been watching the house, and now you're here claiming to work for the police. What is going on?"

"Did you see who hit my wife?" Matt asked.

"No. I was reading." She picked up the book on the table beside her. "I looked up for a moment and saw a woman on the ground, a man running towards her. Your coachman?"

I nodded. "You saw no one running off?"

"I'm afraid not. Somebody hit you, you say? That's shocking. You poor thing. Are you all right?"

"I feel fine now, thank you."

"I'll have Crupper bring in tea." She reached for a little bell beside the book.

"It's not necessary," I said before she rang it. "I don't want tea. Mrs. Stanhope, we're here to ask you questions. I admit to lying to your staff to gather information on behalf of the police."

Her lips pinched. "So I gathered."

"I'm sorry, but it was necessary to learn more about the household."

She rubbed her forehead and sighed. "My husband didn't murder that man, Mrs. Glass. I've been through this with the detective inspector. Hubert was at home, in bed. He sleeps beside me. I would have noticed him get up, and I assure you, he did not."

"Forgive us for not believing you," Matt said flatly. "But my wife has just been attacked outside your house after meeting your husband downstairs. That's not a coincidence."

"Why would my husband attack her? It doesn't make sense if she is here to ask a few questions. He'd be mad to hurt anyone in broad daylight. What if he was seen?"

She had a point. Even if he realized I suspected he was guilty of murder, he wouldn't risk assaulting me. He gained nothing from it.

"Those are the facts, Mrs. Stanhope," Matt said. "And I don't like coincidences."

She blinked rapidly and rubbed one of her legs through the blanket. "Yes, of course. This is an awful business. Truly awful. The murder, the suspicion surrounding my husband, and now the attack on Mrs. Glass. I don't understand it. I truly don't."

If she was acting, she was incredibly good at it. My heart softened, and even Matt's dark mood seemed to evaporate. He shifted in the chair and looked away.

"I don't think you know everything there is to know about your husband," I ventured.

She bristled then gave a small wince of pain. "I'd know if he were a murderer or not."

"Did you know he no longer worked at Ingles?"

She stilled. "Pardon?"

"He was ordered to leave by Mr. Ingles after your husband's embezzlement came to light."

"Embezzlement!" She scoffed. "That's ridiculous. You can't say such things about my husband. They're simply not true!"

"Speak to Mr. Ingles, if you like," Matt said. "You wanted facts, madam, and we're presenting them to you."

"But he went to work this morning and came home for luncheon as he sometimes does." She rubbed her leg again. "He's gone back there now."

"No, he hasn't. I don't know where he is going instead, but it's not to the factory. He and Ingles had a falling out over the embezzlement. Ingles is going to dissolve the partnership."

Mrs. Stanhope choked on a sob. Matt handed her his handkerchief and she pressed it to her quivering lips. The veins on her cheeks stood out, deep blue against stark white, and her eyes reddened with her tears.

"Poor Hubert. This will hurt him deeply. The company is everything to him. It's his life." She dabbed the handkerchief to her eyes. "Why didn't he tell me?"

"He's probably ashamed," Matt said.

"This is awful. Simply awful. When news gets out, how will he ever show his face again?"

Matt and I exchanged glances. I nodded at him but he

gave a slight shake of his head. He wanted me to ask the questions now.

I crouched next to Mrs. Stanhope and took her hand. "What has your husband's mood been like these last few days since the inspector questioned him?"

She lifted a shoulder. "As you would expect. He's been on edge, worrying that the police will find so-called evidence against him."

"So-called?" I echoed.

"They need to blame someone, so why not him? And now this embezzlement... It'll look like he had a reason to kill that man, won't it?"

I squeezed her hand.

"Now I know why he was acting oddly before the police arrived," she went on.

"He was?"

"Yes. Anxious, harried. He jumped at the slightest sound. He must have been worried Mr. Ingles would find out about the embezzlement." She dabbed her eyes again. "Why did he do it? We have enough money. I've never gone wanting."

"Gambling," Matt said.

She looked as if she was about to protest but thought better of it. I suspected Mrs. Stanhope knew her husband liked to gamble, but didn't know his gambling had become a problem.

"He owed a lot of money to someone," Matt went on. "So he took it from the company."

"With the intention of paying it back," she assured us.

"Of course. But he got caught out at the bank when the company couldn't make a regular loan repayment. He knew if he was going to keep the embezzlement a secret, he had to pay back the company. So he borrowed from Mr. McGuire, but McGuire called in the debt too soon, and your husband found he had no way to fund that repayment."

She rubbed her leg through the blanket again. "So you

think he killed the money lender?" She shook her head. "No, Mr. Glass, he couldn't have. I would have noticed him get out of bed. I know you think I'm simply saying that to help him, but I assure you I'm not lying. Ask Martha. She helps me into bed and then out of it again in the morning. I would have told her I'd had a terrible sleep because Mr. Stanhope woke me. But I didn't. I haven't had an interrupted sleep in a long time." She picked up the bell and rang it.

Mr. Crupper entered immediately.

"Fetch Martha," Mrs. Stanhope said, once again rubbing her leg.

"Doesn't the pain keep you awake at night?" I asked.

"I sleep through it, thank God."

I glanced at Matt as I headed back to my chair. He didn't look at me, however. He stared at Mrs. Stanhope, his forehead deeply furrowed.

It was still furrowed when Martha entered. She dipped a curtsy to her mistress, glanced at Matt, and completely ignored me. It was understandable considering the trick I'd played on her and the other staff.

"Martha, tell Mr. and Mrs. Glass about our morning routine," Mrs. Stanhope said.

Martha looked taken aback. "There's not much to tell. After Mr. Stanhope goes to work, I bring your breakfast on a tray. I come back again when you're finished and assist you out of bed, getting dressed, that sort of thing."

"How does Mrs. Stanhope seem in the mornings?" I asked. "Refreshed? Tired?"

"She looks like she had a sound sleep," she said, her gaze dead ahead.

"Has that been the case all week?"

"Yes. And for weeks before this one. Mrs. Stanhope never complains of a poor night's sleep."

I couldn't think of any other questions, and Matt didn't look as though he wanted to add anything. His troubled gaze settled on Mrs. Stanhope and remained. It would have unnerved me, but either she didn't notice or she was pretending not to. She simply slowly rubbed her thigh through the blanket.

"How long have your legs given you pain?" I asked.

"Some months now," she said. "The doctor said there's no cure."

"I am sorry."

"Thank you, Mrs. Glass. Sometimes the pain is...trying."

"Can the doctor give you something to ease it?"

"He prescribed a tonic but I stopped taking it. It affected my mind and I'd rather have my wits about me than be oblivious."

What a difficult choice to make, yet I admired her for it. Indeed, my admiration for Mrs. Stanhope had grown with each answer she gave, and with the way she interacted with the staff. It was clear why they liked working for her.

"It's fortunate your legs don't trouble you during the night," I said.

Her brow creased but she nodded.

Martha shifted her weight from one foot to the other.

"You may go," Mrs. Stanhope said to her.

"Just one moment, Martha." Matt had finally found his voice again, although that troubled look remained in his eyes. "Please stay while I ask Mrs. Stanhope another question."

Mrs. Stanhope nodded at Martha and the maid resumed her position, only this time the hands clasped in front of her knotted together.

"Can you describe to us your evening routine, please, Mrs. Stanhope," Matt said.

She blinked. "Of course, but I don't see the relevance. I dine with Mr. Stanhope unless he is working late at the factory. Then I read alone or we play cards until I retire at ten. Martha assists me into bed and I read for thirty minutes or so which is when Mr. Stanhope comes to bed too."

"Do you take a sleeping draught?"

"No," she said. "As I've already told you, I don't have trouble sleeping."

Martha's knuckles went white, her eyes huge.

"Do you consume anything in that half hour of reading?" Matt asked.

"A cup of tea. It's Mrs. Crupper's own recipe which she leaves in the kitchen for Martha to make up for me before bed."

"Martha?" Matt prompted. "You have something to add to the conversation?"

Martha chewed on her lower lip.

"Martha?" Mrs. Stanhope asked. "What is it?"

"The tea." Her eyes swam and her face twisted as she tried to hold back her tears. "Mrs. Crupper told me there's something in it to make you sleep better."

Mrs. Stanhope's lips parted with her sharp intake of breath. "You've been medicating me without my knowledge?"

"Mr. Stanhope said it was a good idea when Mrs. Crupper told him about it."

"My husband *knew*?" Mrs. Stanhope pressed a hand to her stomach. "Martha, why didn't you tell me?"

"We thought you might refuse it." Tears dripped down Martha's cheeks. "We all remember how you were before you drank the tea. You were in so much pain you couldn't sleep and that made the days worse. You were going to fade away from exhaustion. Please, madam, don't blame us for wanting what's best for you." She took a step toward her mistress, but Mrs. Stanhope dismissed her with a lift of her finger.

"I'll speak to you later. Go. I wish to speak to Mr. and Mrs. Glass alone. Close the door."

Martha obeyed, silently crying as she backed out of the drawing room.

Mrs. Stanhope sank into the chaise, her shoulders

slumped, her body so thin it seemed to become part of the upholstery. "I don't know what to say," she whispered.

"You don't have to say anything," Matt said gently. "We're deeply sorry it has come to this."

"Thank you, Mr. Glass."

"Forgive me," he said, "but I now have more questions."

She nodded.

"Do you still believe your husband wouldn't harm my wife just now?"

Of all the questions I expected him to ask, that wasn't one of them. I'd expected something that would resolve our final piece of the puzzle—the connection between Stanhope and Fabian.

"He wouldn't," she said. "But I'm afraid I wasn't entirely forthcoming before. Although I doubt my husband could physically harm anyone, Reggie is another matter."

"The servant?" I asked.

"He is my husband's man to his very bones. Mr. Stanhope has always treated him well, kinder than anyone has ever been to poor Reggie. People can be cruel to simpletons, and Reggie suffered more than his share of torment before he came to work for us as a boy."

"He's been with you a long time," I said.

"Twenty years."

I touched the back of my head where the lump had taken on the proportions of a swallow's egg. It throbbed like the devil.

"He used to get into scrapes when he was younger. I saw for myself how good he was at defending himself when he felt threatened. If it weren't for my husband taking him off the streets, he would have ended up in prison."

"Why him?" Matt asked. "There are hundreds of youths in need of a home, so why did your husband employ him twenty years ago?"

"It was a favor for our previous coachman and odd-job

man. Reggie is his brother-in-law. He and his wife, Reggie's sister, used to despair of Reggie and worry about his future. Their parents had long since passed, and she was Reggie's only family. When he left our service to work as a guard, he asked Mr. Stanhope to take on his wife's brother. Reggie has been a loyal and valued member of the staff ever since. He dotes on my husband."

Matt sat forward. "Your previous man became a guard?"

She touched her forehead and closed her eyes, as if she too had an aching head. "The wages are quite good, so he told us at the time."

My pulse quickened as I followed the path Matt was taking. "Where does he work now?" I asked.

She lowered her hand and frowned, clearly puzzled by the line of questioning. "Newgate, I believe. Why?"

Matt and I both rose at the same time. "Thank you," he said. "Your candor is appreciated."

"Goodbye, Mrs. Stanhope," I said. "We wish you well." It sounded empty, but I couldn't have been more convincing. Her life was about to be shattered.

She knew it too. "What happens now?"

"The detective inspector will want to speak to Mr. Stanhope when he returns," Matt said.

She pressed the handkerchief to her lips then, remembering it belonged to Matt, held it out to him.

"Keep it," he said.

The butler saw us out, his dislike of us clear in his stony silence and the slamming of the door behind us. I didn't blame him in the least.

"That was awful," I said, taking Matt's elbow.

"Stanhope did it," he said, scanning the street. "Where's Woodall?"

We looked in both directions, but our carriage was nowhere to be seen. It was unlike Woodall not to follow instructions.

"I have a bad feeling about this." Even as I said it, a carriage rumbled toward us at full speed.

The hooves of the four horses kicked up mud and muck and the wheels spun dangerously close to the pavement. The coachman, dressed all in black with a black hood, applied the whip with cruel regularity.

Matt pulled me back out of the way, almost tossing me aside as the coach ground to a halt in front of us. He hardly had a moment to settle into a fighting stance when two men jumped out.

Mr. Stanhope and Reggie.

Reggie set upon Matt, but Matt easily deflected the blow and landed a punch to Reggie's gut. He reeled back but didn't fall, and he came at Matt again. Matt ducked out of the way of Reggie's punch and deflected a swing of his left fist, only to be hit by the right.

"Stop!" I cried.

Matt bared his teeth and landed a blow on his assailant's jaw. Reggie stumbled into the carriage behind him, sending the cabin rocking. He shook his head, dazed.

"It's over, Stanhope!" Matt said without taking his gaze off Reggie.

Stanhope turned flat, dead eyes onto me. "Yes. It is." He pulled out a pistol from his inside jacket pocket and pointed it at Matt.

"No!" I screamed. "Don't!"

"Get in the carriage, Mrs. Glass, or I'll shoot him."

"Don't move, India," Matt said.

Mr. Stanhope cocked the pistol. "I will shoot unless you do as I say."

Oh God, oh God. "This is madness." I hated the tremble in my voice. I wanted to be strong for Matt, I wanted to be defiant in the face of this monster, but every fear I'd ever had during Matt's ill health came flooding back. All I felt was sick to my core.

The door behind me opened. "Get back inside, Crupper," Mr. Stanhope snapped. The door shut again. "Get in the carriage, Mrs. Glass. I won't ask again."

"No, India, don't." Matt's voice was commanding yet I heard the panic edging it. "If you go with him, I can't follow you."

"If you don't go with me, I kill your husband here."

"Matt," I managed to say through the tears clogging my throat. "I have to."

"Don't do it," he ground out through gritted teeth. "I'll be all right. You know I will." He was talking about his watch saving him. But that had only worked in the past because he hadn't died instantly, and I had been able to place the magic watch in his hand. If the bullet pierced his heart, he would be dead. If I couldn't get to his watch in time, he would be dead, and I suspected Mr. Stanhope wouldn't let me get close enough to try without using the gun on me.

"I have nothing to lose, Mrs. Glass," he said. "Nothing at all. You have pushed me beyond the point of return."

He was right. There was no reasoning with him now. I stepped forward.

"No, India." Matt's voice shook, shattering my nerves altogether.

I couldn't look at him as I climbed into the carriage. Reggie shoved me and I fell onto the seat. Mr. Stanhope climbed in behind me, his back to me, the gun still pointed at Matt.

"Don't hurt her," Matt growled. "I'll do whatever you want, say whatever you want. Just don't hurt her."

Mr. Stanhope shut the door and spoke to Matt through the open window, his pistol still aimed at Matt's head. "Get the police to look elsewhere for their killer. Fail and your wife won't live."

He was a fool if he thought the police would look elsewhere now. The neighbors would have seen this; the staff certainly had, and Mrs. Stanhope too. She stared at us through the window, her eyes full of unshed tears, the blanket pulled up to cover her mouth.

Mr. Stanhope thumped on the ceiling and the carriage rolled away.

I spun around and watched Matt's bleak figure through the rear window. He stood there, face bloodied, fists closed at his sides, looking utterly lost.

CHAPTER 15

The Royal Victoria Dock workers had finished for the day and the warehouse precinct that spread from the jetties into the surrounding streets and lanes was eerily quiet. Birds squawked overhead, searching for scraps, and somewhere in the distance a train whistle blew. The lamps had not yet been lit, but daylight had already fled from the narrow lane down which I was forced. The brick warehouses looming on both sides of it weren't the giant buildings used to store wool and grain. Those were on the concourse, easily accessible by cranes and carts. These buildings were divided into smaller warehouses, their doors numbered in white paint. It was into one of these that Reggie shoved me.

"Careful. She's a lady," the coachman said.

"Thank you," I muttered. "May I see the face of the man showing me kindness?"

His only response was to pull the brim of his hat lower. I suspected he was the brother-in-law jailor, going by the way he ordered Reggie about.

"Stop talking," Mr. Stanhope said. "Someone might hear us."

His gaze darted back and forth before he followed me

inside. He had pocketed the pistol in the carriage, no longer seeing the need to brandish it. He knew I couldn't escape three men.

The warehouse smelled like vinegar. The bitter stench seemed to come from the walls themselves but more likely it was from the barrels stacked up at the far end.

"Get some light," Mr. Stanhope told Reggie. "Then shut the door."

Reggie lumbered around the warehouse, igniting the lanterns. He was bigger than I first thought, his hunched shoulders and lowered head deceiving me. He'd shown no qualms in hitting Matt and had not said a word the entire time, not even to acknowledge Mr. Stanhope's bidding. He simply did as ordered.

My hope lay with the coachman. He stood by, watching his brother-in-law from beneath his hat brim. Still he didn't remove his hat, despite being indoors.

"Please, don't do this, sir," I begged him. "Mr. Stanhope is a murderer."

The coachman said nothing.

"My husband will be frantic." Tears pricked the backs of my eyes at the thought of Matt going mad with worry. "Please, sir. Don't participate in this madness."

"It's too late," the coachman said heavily. "I made my mistake some time ago. Now I have to continue or go to prison. Believe me, Lady, they don't treat men like me well in jail."

As a former prison guard, the other prisoners would be brutal. But I made no comment, not wanting him to know I knew who he was and why he was involved. If he thought he could walk away, there was a good chance he would be sympathetic and fetch Matt.

"You will release her, won't you?" the coachman said to Mr. Stanhope.

"Once her husband convinces the police of my innocence," Mr. Stanhope said.

"What if he can't? What if they don't believe him? Not all of Scotland Yard's inspectors are fools."

Mr. Stanhope shrugged. "We'll cross that bridge when we come to it. You can go now."

"Don't leave me here with them," I pleaded. "He'll kill me, just as he killed the money lender."

The coachman hesitated then shook his head. "Not my concern."

"Keep your ears open, and come back when the police state they no longer think I did it," Mr. Stanhope said.

The coachman nodded then left. The door slammed shut behind him.

"This is madness," I said to Mr. Stanhope. "How long do you plan on keeping me here?"

"As long as necessary."

"Someone will come. Someone will want this vinegar, or make a new delivery."

"Not for another week."

"You plan to stay in here for an entire week? You are mad."

"If I am, then it's you who made me this way. You and your husband." He strode up to me, stopping a mere inch away. The light from the gas lamp behind my head illuminated his eyes and cast shadows in the hollows of his cheeks. With his bared teeth, he did indeed look like a madman, or a devil risen from Hell.

"We were only trying to help the police," I said as calmly as possible. "You cannot blame your fate on us."

"You told Ingles about the money!" He grabbed my shoulders and shook me. "You told my wife!"

My watch chimed, just a single pure note that was out of place in the dim, wretched warehouse. Mr. Stanhope released me. I clutched my reticule and slowly eased the drawstring open. If the watch had chimed then it might also save me, just as my previous watch had done. I slipped thumb and finger inside the opening and felt for it.

Mr. Stanhope ripped the reticule from my hands. "What was that infernal sound?"

"My watch," I said quickly. "It's broken and chimes at odd times."

He pulled out the watch and held it up to the light. It chimed again.

"Damned annoyance." He went to throw it.

"No!" I grabbed his wrist. "Please don't. It was a gift from my husband. I'll stop it chiming, I promise."

He jerked free and tossed the watch at me. "See that it doesn't make any more noises." He strode over to Reggie, lurking in the shadowy corner. "If the watch makes another sound, destroy it. If she talks again, make her stop. I don't care how."

I swallowed my gasp and clutched the watch to my chest as Reggie lurched toward me. The watch warmed to my touch, but it wasn't as reassuring as I'd hoped. My previous watch only saved me when I was in immediate danger and I didn't expect this one to be any different. If I threw it at my captors now, while they weren't directly harming me, it would do nothing. It may well do nothing no matter what they were doing to me. I couldn't rely on it to work at all, let alone the way my old one had.

Reggie crowded me, backing me into the barrels. I sat but he did not move away. The stink of his sweat overwhelmed me as much as his physical presence, but it was his vacant stare that chilled me. Without the capacity to think, he couldn't feel, and if he didn't feel sympathy then he would do whatever Stanhope demanded.

My watch remained silent, thank God. I clutched it so tightly that my fingers became numb, yet I still didn't relax my grip. I tried to remain as still as possible, not wanting to catch Mr. Stanhope's attention. He paced the floor, head bowed, his teeth biting his lower lip. His footsteps and Reggie's breathing were the only sounds in the warehouse.

The light filtering through the high narrow windows faded away altogether. The lanterns struggled to keep the darkness at bay, only managing to create deeper and more ominous shadows.

I wanted to check the time, but I wouldn't be able to see the watch's face. I guessed we'd been in the warehouse for forty minutes. If Matt had successfully convinced Brockwell to let Mr. Stanhope go, or pretend to, then this could be over soon. If Mr. Stanhope kept to his agreement of releasing me, that is. And if Matt could find some way to get the message to him.

Too many ifs.

A movement in a high, narrow window caught my attention but I didn't get a chance to register what it was. A gunshot rang out. Stanhope ducked. Reggie spun around and I shrank back, trying to see who'd fired and if anyone was hurt.

My heart pounded, praying Matt had arrived yet not wanting it to be him either. If he got hurt…

Another shot rang out, this time from Mr. Stanhope's pistol. The window shattered. It had been closed earlier, but now stood open. Shards of glass rained down on the floor below, shattering into thousands of pieces.

"Get her, Reggie!" Mr. Stanhope shouted as he aimed at the window again. "She's our insurance!"

Reggie grabbed my arm, pulling so hard my shoulder screamed in pain. I didn't cry out. I didn't want to worry Matt, or get him to change whatever plan he was enacting. Reggie swung me in front of him and whipped out a knife from his jacket. The blade raked the skin at my throat. I tried to steady my breaths, to sink away from the knife, but that only forced me back into Reggie's chest. The arm that snaked around my waist squeezed as if he wanted to cut me in half.

My breathing labored to draw in air, and that only made the blade press harder.

Mr. Stanhope squinted into the darkness, searching for the figure through the window. But there was no more movement there. No signs of life.

Matt!

The lock on the door suddenly clicked and the door itself crashed back on its hinges. Mr. Stanhope swung around, pistol at the ready.

"Watch out!" I screamed.

But no one entered. There was no sound from the doorway or the window.

Mr. Stanhope moved to a position where he could see through the door. That was his mistake. The person at the window fired another shot into the warehouse.

Mr. Stanhope fired back.

In the same instant, the figure at the door burst inside and ran at Stanhope, crashing into him, tackling him to the ground. I knew without seeing his face that it was Matt.

My heart kicked into a rapid rhythm as panic set in. Matt might be stronger and younger but he wasn't armed.

I needn't have worried. Matt wrestled Stanhope's hands above his head, rendering the pistol useless. He should have rendered him unconscious instead. He could still give orders.

"Reggie! Kill her!"

"No!" Matt released Stanhope.

But it was too late. The muscles in Reggie's shoulders and arms tensed, and the blade bit into my skin.

"Shoot him!" Matt shouted as he raced toward me. "Shoot Reggie NOW!"

Stanhope aimed his pistol at Matt. He'd be dead before he reached me.

I swung my watch upward. It arced behind me, out of my line of sight.

A gunshot rang out.

"Matt!" I screamed.

But it was Stanhope who crumpled to the floor. Matt was very much alive, although his ashen face worried me. But he wasn't bleeding.

Reggie suddenly released me. He dropped the knife and crashed back into the barrels. They rolled away as he too collapsed, my watch chain wrapped around his neck.

No! Please no, don't be dead because of me. Reggie was Stanhope's creature, too simple and loyal to think for himself. I didn't want to kill him.

I reached for my watch and tugged. The chain released him and he gasped in air, choking and coughing as he rolled over. I closed my eyes and blew out a shuddery breath of relief.

Matt's arms surrounded me and pulled me close. His hands stroked my hair, touched my face, and his voice filled me. "It's all right," he murmured. "You're all right, it's over."

It was soothing, his arms a comfort, yet I couldn't stop shaking. I placed my palm to his racing heart in an effort to calm it, and my own.

"Is Stanhope...?" I swallowed the rest of my sentence.

Mr. Stanhope groaned in response.

"Course he ain't dead," came Willie's voice.

I glanced up to see her leaning through the window, her gun pointed at Stanhope. She grinned at me.

"If I wanted to kill him, he'd be dead already," she went on. "But Matt said to maim him unless killing were the only option." She waggled the gun. "Matt, get his pistol so I can come down."

Matt kissed my forehead then did as she ordered. He checked the barrel for bullets then pointed it at Stanhope. "Reggie, get over here where I can see you both."

Reggie knelt by his groaning master, the red mark of my watch's chain clearly visible above his neckerchief. Stanhope groaned again and clutched his arm. Blood dampened his sleeve and smeared the floor but not enough to be worrisome.

"Get up, coward," Willie said as she entered through the door. "It's just a scratch."

I flung my arms around her and hugged her. "You saved our lives."

"I only saved Matt's," she said quietly. "I had time for just one shot and I reckoned if I saved him, he could then save you. It weren't an easy choice." She blinked watery eyes at me, every last shred of her cockiness gone.

"It was the wisest decision. You made the right choice." I hugged her again.

She squeezed me tightly then released me, almost pushing me away. "Don't go all soft on me, India. It were nothing."

"It wasn't nothing. We'd be in serious trouble if your shot had missed."

She pushed the front brim of her hat up with her finger. "I ain't missed a shot that easy since I were big enough to hold a Colt."

"Ha!" came Duke's voice from the doorway. "You boasting again, Willie?"

She grinned. "You missed all the fun."

Duke entered the warehouse with Brockwell and six constables. The inspector's eyes widened upon seeing Willie still holding the gun.

"That was just like the old days back home," she said. "Only no one died. Pity."

The inspector's gaze narrowed ever so slightly. "You just happened to have your gun on you?"

"What's the point having one if you don't take it with you?" She winked.

He scratched his sideburns. "An interesting yet dangerous philosophy."

Willie's jovial mood evaporated. "I could've killed him if I wanted, but I didn't. I was saving you from the commissioner's questions, *Inspector*." She stormed out of the warehouse, trailed by Duke.

The inspector gave orders to his men to escort Reggie outside but not Stanhope.

"You thought putting the life of Mrs. Glass in danger would stop me arresting you?" Brockwell said. "All you achieved was another charge against your name, and a very angry husband."

Matt had hardly moved since grabbing Stanhope's gun. He stood over Stanhope, his chest still rising and falling with his heavy breathing. I took his hand and rubbed my thumb along his. He finally lowered the pistol and drew me to his side. He kissed my forehead.

"Are you hurt?" he murmured.

"No. You?"

"I don't think so."

I stood on my toes to whisper in his ear. "I'll check you over later. Thoroughly."

His lips twitched into a hint of a smile.

"How did you find us?" Stanhope snapped at Matt.

"I went to Ingles and asked if he knew of a place you might go. I assumed the factory somewhere, but he claimed he hadn't seen you arrive and he'd been there all afternoon. He suggested one of the warehouses. There are two leased to Ingles," he told Brockwell. "This one and another at St. Katherine's docks. We came here first after a brief visit home to get Willie and send Duke to Scotland Yard."

His hand squeezed mine as he drew it to his lips. He pressed a deep, longing kiss to it.

"Duke told me about your visit to Mrs. Stanhope," Brockwell said.

"You should have left my wife out of this!" Stanhope growled. "She is innocent!"

"And you have just ruined her life with your actions," I told him. "How will she recover from the shame?"

His nostrils flared, and he lowered his head.

"You killed McGuire because you couldn't repay him," Brockwell said.

"And because McGuire threatened to tell Ingles about the embezzlement," Matt added. "McGuire had his own debts that needed to be repaid. He was desperate and probably afraid of his creditor."

Stanhope grunted. "He should have been afraid of *me*."

"Who was his creditor?" Matt asked.

"I told you, I don't know."

"Who?" Matt snarled.

"I don't know!"

"Why did you set up Fabian Charbonneau to take the blame?" I asked. "What has he ever done to you?"

"I've never met him. He wasn't important, just a convenience." He wiped his fingers across his sweaty forehead. "I read about him going to prison in the newspaper. The article named his creditor as McGuire, and that's when I first got the idea. One of the Newgate jailors owed me a favor."

"Reggie's brother-in-law," I said.

Stanhope gave a single nod. "Dean. I asked him about the Frenchman and he told me the man was convinced he wouldn't be there much longer. All the jailors thought he was mad, but I wondered if there was some truth in it. Even so, I forgot about him for several hours. I was not in my rightful state of mind that afternoon. It wasn't until Dean came to me and claimed the Frenchman had escaped that I hatched my plan."

"Was this before or after you met with McGuire in the alley the first time?" Matt asked.

"After but before I— Before the second time."

"Go on," Brockwell said. "What did you do once you heard of the escape?"

"It was easy enough to find out where the Frenchman was staying after the newspaper report of his incarceration. It even pinpointed the street he lived on. I broke into his house and stole the handkerchief. You can guess how the rest of my evening transpired."

"Indeed," Brockwell bit off. "You met McGuire a second time, after midnight, and killed him, leaving behind the handkerchief to incriminate Charbonneau."

"Yes," Stanhope said without a hint of remorse. He reminded me of Reggie, with his vacant stare and expressionless features. They were suffering a loss of mental capacity, yet it had come about in quite different ways. I wondered if Stanhope's would be as permanent or if he would come to his senses again.

"Did you hit my wife outside your house?" Matt snapped.

"Not me. Reggie did it. I was worried about her speaking to my wife and told him so. He took it upon himself to try and stop her, but your coachman—"

Matt punched him in the jaw.

"Glass! Desist!" Brockwell said. "Remember you are a gentleman."

"Not at this moment," Matt growled.

I took his hand again and held it tightly.

The blow triggered something in Stanhope. His eyes suddenly brightened. "Reggie is unpredictable. I can't control him. Indeed, I lied earlier when I said I killed McGuire. Reggie took it upon himself after I told him I had to repay the money and couldn't."

"Enough!" Matt shouted. "Take responsibility for your own actions."

Stanhope ducked his head, cowering. When he realized Matt wouldn't hit him again, he straightened. He ought to have remained vigilant.

I stepped up to him, lifted my skirts, and gave him a swift kick to the shin. "That's for manipulating Reggie."

Stanhope grunted and rubbed his leg.

Brockwell ordered his men to take the Stanhope and

Reggie away in the police carriage. "Arrest the Newgate jailor by the name of Dean, too."

We joined Willie and Duke outside, while Brockwell remained behind to gather evidence inside the warehouse. Willie leaned against the carriage, her arms crossed, her hat pulled low.

"She's in a foul mood," Duke muttered to us. "On account of Brockwell calling her dangerous."

"He's not entirely wrong on that score," Matt muttered back. "But on this occasion, I'm glad I didn't have to waste time waiting for her to fetch her gun. Another moment later and..." He blinked at me. "This could have turned out differently."

I stood on my toes and kissed him lightly on the lips. He smiled properly for the first time in days.

"If Willie shot Stanhope, then what happened to Reggie?" Duke asked. "How'd he end up on the floor?"

I opened my fingers to reveal the watch. I wasn't willing to put it away yet. "The chain wrapped around his throat when he attacked me."

"Good to see your magic works like it used to."

"Ha!" Willie barked, proving she was listening. "And Jasper thinks *I* carry a dangerous weapon."

Brockwell emerged from the warehouse but paused as he spotted Willie. She pulled her hat brim lower and turned her face away.

He cleared his throat. "Seems like I'll have to word my report carefully."

"You don't have to on my account," she said. "Tell your superiors I shot him. I don't care."

"I can't do that."

"Why not?"

"Because if they find out you and me are...acquainted, they'll tell me to give you up. And I'm not ready to do that."

Her mouth twisted to the side and her finger tapped a

rapid rhythm in the crook of her arm. She grunted in what I suspected was meant to be indifference. But I knew Willie well enough to know her emotions were very close to the surface. She'd been rattled by having to make a choice between Matt and me, and now she was struggling not to show it to all of us, but to Brockwell most of all.

"Are you ready to give up on us?" he prompted. "To walk away?"

"I don't know."

"Willie," I scolded.

Duke thumped her shoulder. "Give him a kiss and let's go home."

Brockwell looked horrified. "This is a crime scene. And I have to return to the Yard to process the paperwork. Thank you for your efforts in the investigation, Mrs. Glass. You too, Glass. It is appreciated, as always."

He walked off. Willie opened the carriage door and indicated I should get in ahead of her.

"Willie," I hissed at her. "Stop being petty and go after him."

"He doesn't want me to," she said, a pout in her voice.

"Of course he does," Matt told her. "Besides, he needs a ride back to Scotland Yard and it'll be awkward if you sit close together but don't speak. So either go and invite him nicely or make your own way home. It's your choice."

She stared after Brockwell, retreating along the alley. "I s'pose it's a long way to walk." She trotted after him. After a brief conversation, she took his face in her hands, pulled his head down and planted a kiss on his lips.

They returned and climbed into the carriage. She was all smiles while he baffled.

* * *

THE FIRST THING we did after depositing Brockwell at Scotland

Yard was visit Chronos. He wasn't happy to see us at first, but a quick explanation of the evening's events lifted his spirits.

"This is excellent news!" he declared. "Fabian! Fabian, you can come out now. The danger is over. The real murderer has been caught."

Fabian appeared at the top of the stairs. "India? Is this true?"

"Yes," I said. "The police are no longer blaming you for the murder. Another man has been arrested."

He came down the stairs and clasped both of my hands. He kissed them then grasped Matt and kissed his cheeks. Matt took it in his stride, no doubt used to the European custom from his youth.

"This is wonderful news." Fabian dragged his hand through his mop of hair. It had suffered from lack of care and Makassar oil. His eyes looked tired and his cheeks drawn, but his smile was big and genuine.

"Your men can stop watching my house now, Glass," Chronos said. "Tell the police to leave me alone too."

"I am still an escapee," Fabian told him.

"Your debt has been paid," I said.

He frowned. "Who paid it?"

"We suspect Lord Coyle."

He blinked. "Not my brother?"

"No."

"Be careful, Charbonneau," Matt said. "Coyle will use it against you one day. He likes people to owe him favors, particularly magicians."

"You could repay the debt with a piece of magical iron," I said hopefully.

Fabian nodded. I didn't have the heart to tell him it might not be enough to satisfy Coyle.

"How did you find the killer?" Chronos asked.

"It's a long story," Matt said. "And it involves India's bravery."

"Mine?" I said, laughing. "I was terrified."

"No one would have guessed." He kissed the top of my head.

Chronos beamed at me. "Come in, come in. India, you deserve a strong drink. I don't doubt you were brave. You might have the Glass name now, but you're a true Steele, through and through."

"Are you going to tell me I get it from you?"

"Lord no. From your grandmother. Her bravery was frightening at times. Truly frightening." As his voice faded, I thought he'd become lost in distant memories, but he shrugged it off and smiled. "Let's have that drink."

"Not tonight," I said. "I want to go home and dine with Matt. There is something I want to tell you, however. Both of you." I pulled the watch out of my reticule. "This is my new watch, the one Matt gave me after my last one broke. It not only chimed tonight, but saved my life. Just as the other did."

"I knew it." Chronos smacked his hands together. "I knew you were powerful and that it wasn't your father's or grandmother's magic in that old watch." He beamed and took both my hands in his. "My granddaughter, master magician."

"Don't say that out loud," Matt warned him.

"That is good news," Fabian said. "Good news, indeed. Soon, we shall begin our experiments. Yes?"

I smiled. "Yes."

* * *

I FELT REFRESHED the following day. It was a relief to have the murder solved and Fabian free. I spent the morning with Matt, walking through Hyde Park and boating on the Serpentine, followed by luncheon at Café Royal in Regent Street. In the afternoon, Aunt Letitia and I paid a call on a friend. While I itched to return to my spell making with Fabian, today wasn't the day to restart. He needed time to recover and look for somewhere to live, and I needed time to reflect.

Aunt Letitia and I returned home late in the afternoon to find Duke and Willie arguing with Cyclops in the entrance hall. Upon seeing us, they fell silent. Duke shuffled his feet, Willie crossed her arms, and Cyclops wouldn't meet our gazes.

Aunt Letitia didn't appear to notice their awkwardness and retreated to her room to rest.

"I'm going to my room too," Cyclops muttered.

"I'm going out," Willie said, pushing past me.

Duke shrugged and followed her.

I stood in front of the door, blocking their exit. "None of you are leaving until you tell me what's happened." I pointed at the library. "In there. Now."

Duke and Cyclops wordlessly complied but Willie grumbled all the way. "You're a shrew now you're married."

"I prefer to think of myself as more assertive. Do you know if Matt is home yet?"

"He ain't."

"Then I'll have to deal with you three on my own." I shut the library door. "So who'll start? Why are you arguing?"

CHAPTER 16

Cyclops perched on the edge of the table and folded his arms, his lips pressed together. I wouldn't get an answer from him.

"Cyclops is being pig-headed," Duke said.

"That's nothing new," I said. "Is this to do with Catherine?"

"Rycroft. He sent his men here again today."

"What happened? Are you all right, Cyclops?"

He nodded then shot a glare at Duke. "Traitor."

"He's your friend and has your best interests at heart," I said.

"Aye," Willie chimed in. "And friends help each other. You got to let us help you, Cyclops, or this could end in disaster."

"What did Rycroft want?" I asked.

"Rycroft wasn't there," Cyclops said. "Just his men. They followed me to the stables."

"Did they set upon you?"

"No."

"We stopped them," Willie said, hands on hips. "If we hadn't been there, there ain't no telling what they might have done."

It didn't bear thinking about. Cyclops was a powerful man and could defend himself, but not if he was outnumbered.

"Why didn't you want to tell us?" I asked him. "Matt and I need to know or we can't fix it."

"I don't want to come between you and Matt's family," Cyclops said. "He needs them if he's going to fit into English society. He can't make enemies of someone like Rycroft. Not on my account."

"That's absurd. Matt doesn't *need* Rycroft. Anyway, marrying me was a far worse *faux pas* to commit in their eyes than being friends with you."

"And *we're* Matt's family," Duke added. "Maybe even more of a family than them."

Willie clapped Duke on the shoulder. "They're right, Cyclops, and you know it, only you won't admit it. So, are we going to tell Matt when he gets home?"

Cyclops expelled a breath. "He's going to get mad, and then he's going to call out Rycroft. It ain't going to end well."

"He is not medieval," I said. "He won't challenge anyone to a duel. He will simply see that Rycroft leaves you alone."

They were strong words and seemed to reassure Cyclops, but they felt hollow to my ears. Matt had tried and failed to speak to the Home Secretary after Rycroft threatened to have Cyclops deported. He would try again, but there was little else he could do. We had to rely on Hope to convince Charity to tell her parents the truth. It was such an enormous task that I doubted she'd succeed.

If she failed, what could be done?

"Until this is resolved, you should remain in the house," I told Cyclops. "If you must go out, take both Willie and Duke."

"I ain't going to be a prisoner, and I ain't dragging you and Matt into this."

"You're not dragging anyone. Besides, it's Matt's uncle, so Matt is already involved. You could say *he* dragged *you* into it."

"I can't wait around here to be at Cyclops's beck and call," Willie said. "I got things to do, friends to meet, and poker games to win."

"I'm sure the three of you can all go together."

She arched a brow at me. "Jasper'll like that."

"Oh. Perhaps you can conduct those visits alone. Are you and Brockwell, er, friends again?"

"Sure are." She winked. "He can't resist my—"

"Don't tell me!" I put up my hands. "I don't wish to hear it."

"I was just going to say he can't resist my American charms."

Duke snorted and Cyclops chuckled. "Aye, *that's* what he can't resist," Cyclops said.

Willie blushed, which only made the men laugh more. She stormed off. "It ain't like that between us," she shot back over her shoulder. "We ain't giddy lovebirds like Cyclops and Catherine, or Matt and India. We're just two people who get along."

"As do Matt and I," I said.

"But we ain't getting married, and we don't want to. That's the difference between you and us."

"You say that now," Duke said. "But I reckon he'll have you walking down the aisle by this time next year."

Cyclops nudged Duke with his elbow. "More like *she'll* march *him* down the aisle. Think we should warn him before it's too late?"

"You ain't funny!" She jerked open the door and strode out of the library.

Duke and Cyclops grinned like schoolboys.

"What have I missed?" Matt asked, his gaze tracking Willie's exit. "Why does she look like she wants to shoot something?"

"Jasper Brockwell," Duke said.

Matt smiled. "Say no more." He looped his arm around my

waist and kissed me. "Did I miss an important meeting?"

Duke crossed his arms and arched his brows at Cyclops, but Cyclops merely focused on the floor. It looked like they were leaving it up to me to tell Matt.

When I finished, Matt sat on the edge of the table beside Cyclops. "I'll see that this ends," he told his friend. "And soon."

Cyclops nodded once then left, followed by Duke. I took Matt's offered hand and found myself pulled gently into his chest. He trapped me in his arms and gave me a grim smile.

"Any suggestions?" he asked.

"We wait for Hope. If she fails, we'll think of something else."

"I can't believe he wasn't going to tell me."

"You know what he's like. He wanted to spare you, protect you."

"I don't need protecting."

"That hasn't always been the case. When your watch stopped working properly, you were vulnerable. The three of them worried about you and were prepared to do anything for you."

He conceded the point with a shrug and his lips curled up at the corners with his smile. "I'm not vulnerable anymore. In fact, I feel very healthy," he murmured against my mouth. "Very healthy indeed."

* * *

IT FELT good to sit down with Fabian again and resume my lessons. He looked like his usual well-groomed self, with sleek hair swept off his forehead and neatly pressed suit. There was no sign of Newgate's misery in his cleanly shaved jaw or the brightness of his smile. He was as enthusiastic to get started as me.

However, it was not ideal to undertake our lessons

beneath Chronos's roof. My grandfather had insisted Fabian continue to live with him, and being without his family's allowance, Fabian couldn't afford to refuse. We did our best in the parlor, but Chronos's hovering and constant interjections became too much for me. I growled at him, snapped at him, and ordered him to go away, only to find that he either didn't listen or came back within minutes.

"I'm just going to sit here silently and listen," he said after I asked him to leave again. "You won't even notice me."

Fabian and I continued to discuss a point of pronunciation, attempting to say a particular word with various accents and emphases. It was almost impossible to tell if we were saying it right until we inserted the word into a known spell. If it worked, then we had the pronunciation correct, but if it didn't, we had to try a different way. The process of trial and error was incredibly slow, especially since we didn't know what the result would be.

The enormity of the task before us loomed like a mountain, one I wasn't entirely sure I could climb. I did know I wanted to try, however. Learning the language and practicing new words to make new spells fulfilled me in a way little else did. It was like tinkering on my watches. Somehow it just felt natural, right.

Chronos knew it too, and he watched me with a knowing smile. It had been he who told me I needed to be actively involved in spell casting and the world of magic or suffer the emptiness that resulted in leaving it all behind. I hadn't told him he was right, and I didn't plan to. He was smug enough.

There was a knock on the door, answered by Chronos's housekeeper. A moment later, a set of heavy footsteps clomped along the hall. The footsteps were accompanied by the thud of a walking stick.

"Good morning," Lord Coyle said. "I wasn't expecting to see you here, Mrs. Glass."

"Nor I you, my lord."

"Bring in tea," Chronos said to the housekeeper. She bobbed an awkward curtsy for Lord Coyle, but his lordship wasn't looking at her. He was looking at the papers we'd spread out on the table.

I hastily tidied them up. "Are you here to see my grandfather?" I asked.

"I want a word with Mr. Charbonneau. In private."

"You may speak in front of my friends," Fabian said, matching Coyle's regal tone. He didn't look in the least intimidated by Coyle. Perhaps that was the French way, or it was simply borne from a lifetime of wealth and privilege almost equal to Coyle's.

Lord Coyle lowered himself into a chair without being invited and indicated we should all resume our seats. Chronos frowned at him but sat wordlessly. As much as my grandfather thought of himself as superior, thanks to his magic, he was a true middleclass Englishman and somewhat in awe of the nobility.

"Are you here to tell Fabian that he owes you for paying off his debt?" I asked. "Don't deny it. We know you paid it off."

Lord Coyle's lips flattened, disappearing beneath his white moustache. "You have taken the wind out of my sails, Mrs. Glass." To Fabian, he said, "My friend told you that I will want something in return for helping you?"

"I am not your friend," I said.

"No doubt she has warned you against owing me anything."

Fabian met his gaze. "I will repay you as soon as I am able. Until then, my gratitude will have to be enough."

Lord Coyle lifted a dismissive finger off his walking stick. "Of course, of course. A small token of that gratitude is sufficient."

"What sort of token?" I hedged.

"Nothing too extraordinary. A piece of iron with your

magic in it, Mr. Charbonneau, that's all. Shall we say the key you used to escape from Newgate?"

Fabian frowned as if he couldn't quite believe it. Nor could I. Where was the demand for a favor to be called in at a later date?

"You see, Mrs. Glass?" Lord Coyle's smile sickened me. "That is all I want. Just a piece of magic iron from Mr. Charbonneau." He rocked back and forth in the chair then pushed himself to his feet. "I'll collect it another time. Enjoy your studies." He nodded at the stack of papers and books on the table. "Mrs. Glass, will you walk me out, please."

"I will," Chronos said, stepping forward.

I shook my head at him and led the way. "What do you want to say?" I asked his lordship at the front door.

He plucked his hat off the hat stand and tapped me on the shoulder with it. "Did you think I'd bother asking him for a favor?" He shook his head. "The man could be back in France soon and out of my reach. Then I'd have nothing. The key will do nicely. See that he doesn't renege on the deal."

"Only if my agreement to do so frees me from my own obligation to you."

He chuckled. "Well done for trying to negotiate, Mrs. Glass. Well done indeed. Good day."

He opened the door only to balk upon seeing the man on the other side, about to knock. It was Fabian's brother, Maxime. Lord Coyle couldn't have failed to notice the family similarity as he stepped aside to allow Maxime in.

"You must be Mr. Charbonneau," he said, putting out his hand. "Fabian Charbonneau's brother."

Maxime shook it, frowning. "And you?"

"Lord Coyle."

At the mention of a title, Maxime hesitated. His gaze flicked to me then back again. "I am pleased to meet you, my lord. Are you a friend to Fabian?"

Fabian emerged from the parlor, followed by Chronos.

The housekeeper also appeared, carrying a tray with teapot and cups, making the small entrance hall quite crowded. Chronos shooed her away and she retreated to the parlor to deposit the tea tray.

"He is not my friend," Fabian said to Maxime.

"And he was just leaving," I added, opening the door wider.

Lord Coyle grunted. "A shame we cannot be friends, Mr. Charbonneau, considering all I have done for you, and for so little in return. So very little."

Fabian straightened. "I have promised you the key. That is all you will get."

"Assistance?" Maxime asked. "Is he the reason you are free, Fabian? Did he help the police catch the killer?"

"You didn't know?" I asked.

"This is the first time I have seen my brother," Fabian told me. "He does not yet know of your great assistance and that of your husband."

"Ah, I see." Maxime took my hand and patted it. "On behalf of my family, I wish to thank you, Mrs. Glass. If there is anything I can do, anything at all, please ask."

Lord Coyle grunted a laugh.

"May I ask how you have assisted my brother, sir?" Maxime asked Coyle.

"That is not your concern," Coyle said.

Maxime bristled. "He is my brother, my family. It *is* my concern."

"If you were so worried about him, why didn't you come to his assistance?"

"I am here now."

"You're too late to do any good."

I swallowed my gasp. These two men were both powerful in their own countries. They were probably rarely challenged or doubted. Neither was going to back down from this war of wills.

"Lord Coyle is right," Fabian said to his brother. "You are too late, Maxime. You may return to France. I am out of prison, out of danger, and only wish to continue studying magic with India."

Maxime's nostrils flared then he spoke in rapid French. Fabian's response was to shake his head. "Fabian!" Maxime shouted.

"Seems these two have some family issues to resolve," Lord Coyle said. "I shall leave them to it."

Fabian and Maxime continued to speak in French, this time directing their gazes toward Lord Coyle. Coyle must have understood because he paused inside the doorway.

Chronos held his breath. "In English," he said. "So India can understand. Your parents should have taught you some of the language," he muttered to me.

"Now is not the time," I whispered back.

"My brother asked me why I owed Lord Coyle," Fabian explained. "I told him Coyle paid off my debt, so I do not have to return to prison. He then suggested he pay Coyle back."

"And I am going to refuse the repayment," Lord Coyle said cheerfully.

Maxime cocked his head to the side and gave a tight smile. "No, sir, you cannot refuse. I will have my bank—"

"I said, I refuse," Coyle bit off, all cheerfulness withered away. "This is my decision. You will accept."

"Why?" Fabian asked. "I will still give you the key in gratitude, and you will have your money too."

Lord Coyle's fingers tightened around the walking stick head.

"Because he doesn't want the key," I said. "Or the money. He lied earlier. He *is* hoping your gratitude will continue, Fabian, and that you will one day feel obliged to grant him a favor of his choosing. Isn't that so, my lord?"

Lord Coyle didn't get a chance to answer before Maxime's temper exploded.

"No! This is not how a gentleman behaves. This is not how my family does business."

"This is not business," Lord Coyle said lightly. "It is something far more substantial."

Maxime stabbed a finger at Coyle. "I will pay you back. My brother will owe you nothing, not even the key he talks of. Is that understood?"

Lord Coyle brushed Maxime's finger aside. "I refuse your offer."

"You cannot refuse!"

"Maxime," Fabian warned. "Your temper…" He spoke to his brother in calm, soothing tones in French but it had no effect on Maxime.

Maxime's chest rose and fell with his heavy breaths and he clenched his fists. Would he hit Coyle? I found myself disinclined to interfere, and I almost wished Fabian would stay out of it and see how the situation played out.

Lord Coyle looked unperturbed by the pending eruption of fury. "Now I see why you wished to escape your family," he said to Fabian. "I cannot imagine the pressure this fellow put on you to marry the woman of his choosing."

Fabian winced and glanced anxiously at his brother.

Maxime's face turned red and a vein in his throat bulged above his collar. He stepped up to Coyle, stopping within inches. Coyle didn't move, but simply continued to smile in that nasty, conceited way of his. He may not be as young as Maxime, but he was a large man brandishing a walking stick. He was also influential and could have Maxime thrown in jail in a trifle for assaulting him.

"You will accept my repayment of the debt," Maxime said through a clenched jaw. "I will not ask again."

Coyle took his walking stick in both hands and pressed it lengthways against Maxime's chest, pushing him away.

Maxime stumbled backward but quickly recovered. He uttered something in French, spitting out each word as if they were poison.

"*Non*!" Fabian shouted, glancing frantically around.

The sound of grinding metal came from outside. It grated my nerves, hurt my ears, and sent a shiver up my spine. I looked through the door toward the sound and let out a gasp. A foot-long rod of the wrought iron fence came flying toward me.

Maxime wasn't speaking French, he was casting a spell.

I ducked but it changed course before reaching me and smacked into Lord Coyle's chest with such force that he took a step back into the hat stand, sending it to the floor with a crash. He fell against the wall which thankfully held him. He stared at Maxime, his mouth ajar, his jowls wobbling either in indignation or shock, I couldn't tell which.

Fabian helped him to stand. "Please, sir, accept my apologies. My brother has a terrible temper when he does not get his own way."

I had a sudden image of the two of them fighting as boys, hurling iron implements at one another. Their poor mother.

"There is more iron out there," Maxime spat. "Do not tempt me to use it."

Lord Coyle eyed the fence and made to leave.

"*Non*," Maxime said. "Accept my money."

Coyle cleared his throat. "I accept your offer." He pulled a card out of his pocket and instructed Maxime to get in touch with his man of business. Then he left, but not before inspecting the fence.

I closed the door and leaned back against it, my heart pounding in my chest. The flying magical piece of ironwork reminded me too closely of the papers Melville Hendry had flung at me mere weeks ago. The situation could have ended up far worse, if Maxime had chosen so.

Fabian picked up the rod. "My humblest apologies, Mr.

Steele. This should not have happened in your home. Please forgive us."

"Forgive *me*," Maxime said with a bow for Chronos. "I am to blame. Please, accept my apology."

"You have quite the temper." Chronos sounded awed and not at all worried by the power he'd witnessed. "It's no wonder your company is so successful." He waggled his fingers at the iron rod. "That spell...does it only make iron fly? Or is it also used to bend iron?"

"That spell is different," Maxime said.

"You should try to incorporate some of the words into other known spells," Chronos said to Fabian. "Maxime, did you know my granddaughter can do what you just did *without* a spell?"

Maxime shook his head but seemed disinterested in my capabilities. I suspected the art and science of magical spells didn't excite him in the way it did his brother.

"Mrs. Glass, you look pale," Maxime said. "Did I frighten you?"

"I'm all right," I said. "Somewhat...surprised, but otherwise all right."

Maxime dipped his head. "I do not lose my temper often."

"Thank goodness for that."

"I do not like to be manipulated."

"Nor do I," Fabian told him darkly. "And yet that is what you have been doing to me ever since you told me I must marry the woman *you* chose."

"That is different."

"No, it is not. I will not return with you, Maxime. I want to be here in London, learning more about magic with India."

Maxime threw his hands in the air. "And what of your family? Your responsibilities? You are a Charbonneau, Fabian. You cannot do as you please."

Fabian crossed his arms, immovable. In light of his brother's recent display of temper, it was quite brave of him to continue to defy the family's wishes.

Maxime growled something in French that made Fabian gulp. He remained immovable, however, and that seemed to antagonize Maxime more. If I didn't do something quickly, Chronos's fence might be entirely ruined.

"The tea is getting cold," I said lightly. "Come through to the parlor and let's have a nice, *quiet* talk."

Tea seemed to have a calming effect on the brothers. The moments it took me to pour and offer the biscuits allowed them to take a few deep breaths. Now all that remained was getting them to agree.

"I will not marry her," Fabian said again. "You cannot make me."

Maxime shook his head in disappointment. "The family will withhold your allowance. How will you live?"

Fabian shrugged. "I will find work."

"You are not qualified to work in any capacity."

"I can teach French. I am also a good dancer."

"French dancing instructors are all the rage among London's debutantes," I said, knowing nothing of the kind. "Fabian won't have any difficulty finding work. My husband's family will see to it."

Chronos smirked.

Maxime sipped his tea and nibbled on a biscuit. "You will abandon your family for this? Your friends?"

"I am not abandoning anyone," Fabian said. "I love you and our parents. I do not love the company or the American you wish me to marry."

"You might if you knew her."

"I will never love her more than I love magic." He indicated the stack of papers we'd been studying. "Is that fair to her? Or me?"

Maxime sighed. "You were always strange, even as a boy."

"Because I did not like money, as you and Father do? Because I love magic best?"

Maxime lifted his chin in a nod. "You are certain this is what you want, Fabian?"

"It is, but I do not want to lose you, Brother. I do not want to upset our family. Please, say you understand and forgive me, and we will part on good terms."

"I do not understand you." Maxime set down his cup and rose. "But I do forgive you."

Fabian stood and they embraced, kissing each other's cheeks. When they parted, Fabian was beaming, but Maxime's smile was less certain. I suspected he was worrying about how to tell his family of Fabian's decision and what to do about the betrothal.

"I will restart your allowance," Maxime said as he sat again. "There is only one thing I ask of you in return."

"Yes?"

"Do not give the key to that man, Coyle. I do not care if it angers him. Give him nothing."

Fabian laughed and nodded. "As you wish."

"He will expect you to owe him," Chronos warned.

"He always did," I said. "The key was merely a token. The real repayment will come in the form of a favor he'll call in one day."

"I will not bestow him with a favor that I do not wish to give," Fabian assured me.

His sentiment was admirable, and one I also held with regard to the favor I owed Coyle. But knowing Coyle, he wouldn't give us a choice.

* * *

FABIAN and I didn't resume our studies after Maxime departed. Neither of us was in the right frame of mind for sitting still and thinking. I suggested we pay a call together on someone else he ought to thank for his freedom.

"Bring the key," I said. "If you don't mind donating it, that is."

Mr. Delancey was home for luncheon, which had not yet been served when we arrived. He and his wife enthusiastically invited us to join them, but we declined.

"I wanted to offer you this token of my gratitude." Fabian opened his palm to reveal the crooked and bent key he'd fashioned from the sliver of the iron bar in his prison cell.

Mrs. Delancey gasped. Her husband reached for the key, his smile stretching from ear to ear. "Is this it? Is this the very key?" he asked.

"It is," Fabian said, somewhat bemused.

"Magnificent," Mrs. Delancey murmured. "It's lovely."

I pressed my lips together to hide my smile.

"India says you gave her important information that led to finding the killer," Fabian said. "I would not be free if not for you, Mr. Delancey. Thank you."

Mr. Delancey shook his hand. "A pleasure. I would do it again."

"I helped," Mrs. Delancey said. "He wasn't going to tell you anything, but I prompted him. I knew it was important."

Fabian took her hand and gave it a lingering kiss. "You are most generous and kind, Mrs. Delancey. Thank you from the bottom of my heart."

She blushed and giggled. "He's so French, isn't he, India? So exotic and *foreign*."

Her husband studied the key on his outstretched palm. "Where shall we put it, my dear?"

"Somewhere prominent. In a glass cabinet, of course, with a plaque."

"A silver plaque."

"Gold. Most definitely in gold. It is the best kind of metal, after all."

"But different magic," Fabian told her. "My magic is iron and metals that contain an amount of iron."

"Yes, however gold looks better."

We left them to their luncheon and returned to Chronos's house, but I didn't alight from the carriage along with Fabian. We said our goodbyes, and I returned home to eat sandwiches in the dining room.

The others had already eaten but joined me when I told them I'd experienced a most eventful morning. The tale of Maxime's temper elicited various responses. Willie thought it exciting, Duke and Cyclops less so, and Aunt Letitia turned her nose in the air.

"The French are all mad," she muttered.

Matt, however, remained silent. He merely sat beside me, idly stroking his top lip in thought, his eyes hooded.

"Maxime was in complete control," I assured him. "The iron rod would never have hit anything but its intended target. You needn't worry, Matt. Besides, he's leaving tomorrow, and you know Fabian is not like his brother. He doesn't have a temper at all."

He offered me a grim smile. "I wasn't thinking about the Charbonneau brothers. I was thinking about Coyle."

"Oh?"

"Do you remember what he said when we first told him about the murder? It was he who gave us the idea that someone had loaned money to McGuire and called it in, and he who suggested the killer might be desperate to stop McGuire revealing information that could ruin him."

"I remember," I said. "Talking to him helped us focus our efforts on Stanhope."

"Precisely. You could say that he *steered* us in that direction."

Willie swore, earning a glare from everyone in the room. She was too busy gawping at Matt to care. "You reckon he already knew Stanhope was the killer back then?"

"It's possible," Matt said.

"How could he know?" Duke asked.

Matt didn't have an answer for that. None of us did.

"Does it matter that he knew?" Aunt Letitia asked. "Stanhope turned out to be the killer, after all. The means justify the ends, surely."

"That's a bit Machiavellian," Cyclops said.

Willie screwed up her nose. "A bit what?"

"Why didn't he just tell you he knew it was Stanhope?" Duke asked.

"Because Coyle wanted us to draw the conclusion ourselves," I said. "Perhaps so we wouldn't find out he was the one to call in McGuire's debt, setting Stanhope on a path to murder."

"He manipulated you," Cyclops added with a shake of his head. "Or tried to. You worked it out anyway."

"I don't like being manipulated."

Matt's jaw firmed. "Nor do I, but we cannot confront him."

"Why not?" Willie asked. "My Colt'll make a strong statement."

"Keep your gun to yourself," Duke told her. "You can't threaten to shoot Coyle or he'll get you thrown in jail."

Willie crossed her arms and sank in the chair. "England's got too many laws."

Duke chuckled. "Don't say that to Brockwell. He lives and breathes laws."

"Why won't you confront Lord Coyle?" Aunt Letitia asked Matt.

"Because he's too dangerous," I said.

"Because a player never reveals his hand," Matt countered.

* * *

HOPE'S ARRIVAL in the mid-afternoon was welcome. It saved me from visiting her, where I would have to attempt to speak to her without Lord and Lady Rycroft noticing. One look at her face told me all I needed to know, however.

It wasn't good news.

"Charity won't say a word to our parents," she said to Matt and me in the drawing room.

The others had all gone out for the afternoon, which was probably just as well. Willie and Aunt Letitia could barely be in the same room as Hope without offering snide comments, and Duke was little better.

"Then you have a problem," I said. "Our agreement was that you would convince her to tell them the truth and I would convince Lord Coyle that he shouldn't marry you. I won't be doing my part until you do yours."

Her brow crumpled into a distressed frown. "Please, India, you have to help me. My parents are more set than ever that I should marry him, and he is very keen. He sends me messages every day and tokens of his love. This morning his footman delivered an amethyst necklace."

"Our agreement—"

"I know what our agreement is!" She rubbed her forehead. "Matt, will you speak to him for me, or to my parents?"

"Once Charity speaks to your parents about Cyclops, I will, but until then, no," he said.

"Please."

I folded my hands on my lap and didn't dare look at Matt. I wasn't immune to her plea. Far from it. My feelings about her situation were entirely sympathetic, despite everything she'd done to us in the past. Being married to Lord Coyle would be an unimaginable sentence for a girl like Hope.

But I wasn't going to tell her that.

"I'm sorry," I said. "You must go home and try again."

"My parents didn't believe me! Not when Charity is telling them the opposite."

I merely shrugged.

"She won't change her story. Not for me. She hates me. She

can't wait for me to marry that man and gloat at my misfortune."

"Try again," Matt said, standing.

She took the hint and left, her eyes filled with tears.

"Do you think she's truly that upset?" I asked him. "Or is it all for show?"

"It's hard to tell with her, although she is opposed to marrying Coyle."

"Vehemently opposed. I feel a little sorry for her. I wouldn't want to marry Coyle, either."

"Fortunately you don't have to." He touched my chin, tilting my face, and kissed me.

We were interrupted a few minutes later by the return of Willie and Aunt Letitia.

"Bristow told us that Hope was here," Aunt Letitia said. "What did she want?"

"To tell us that Charity won't give in and to ask us to plead her case with Coyle," I said.

Willie grunted. "I hope you told her you ain't saying nothing to Coyle until Cyclops is off the hook."

"We did."

"What shall we do if she doesn't succeed?" Aunt Letitia asked weakly. "Should we send Cyclops away, where he'll be safe?"

Matt sat down again with a heavy sigh. "I don't want to do that."

"Then the Home Secretary will deport him back to America."

"Rycroft will have him thrashed first," Willie added. "I know his kind, and I've seen their hatred for folk like Cyclops. Rycroft won't let him leave the country without getting the message across that he shouldn't have touched his daughter."

She was right, and we all knew it.

CHAPTER 17

Willie barreled into the dining room at breakfast the following morning, her eyes bright and her cheeks flushed. "I got it!" she cried.

"You just get in?" Duke asked, not even looking up from his plate of fried eggs.

"No, idiot. I got home hours ago." She stood with her hands on her hips, inviting us to ask questions.

"So what've you got? A disease?"

She scowled at him. "An idea. I know what to do to get Rycroft to leave Cyclops alone."

"Don't get involved," Cyclops said from the sideboard. "I can handle Rycroft's men."

"This ain't about Rycroft sending his thugs around. This is about getting him to leave you alone for good." She glanced at Matt and he nodded at her to go on. "He's been speaking to the Home Office to get you deported."

Cyclops set his plate down at the table with a thud and a glare for Matt. Matt held it, but there was sympathy in his eyes, not censure.

"Don't look at me like that," Cyclops muttered. "I hate it. I hate you all for bothering with my business. I can take care of myself."

I touched his hand. "We know you can, but the point is, you don't have to."

Cyclops didn't look convinced.

"You took care of me when I was ill," Matt said. "Now let me take care of you, if I can." He picked up his coffee cup, frowning. "The problem is, I'm out of ideas. Unless Hope can convince Charity to tell the truth…" He ended the sentence with a shrug.

"Ain't no one been listening to me?" Willie cried. "I've got an idea. And it's a good one."

"Let us be the judge of that," Duke said. "But go on. Take the stage."

She straightened and squared her shoulders. "No one saw what happened in the stables, ain't that so, Cyclops?"

"She waited until I was alone," he said.

"Aye, but she was so focused on you that she wouldn't have seen anyone else arrive and look in."

"Nobody did. There were no witnesses, Willie." Cyclops picked up his fork and stabbed a sausage.

"You're too honest, Cyclops, that's your problem. You got to think like a dishonest person. Like Charity. You got to lie."

Duke wagged his finger at her, his smile breaking free. "Someone will pretend they saw you and tell Rycroft that Charity advanced on him, not the other way round. Good thinking, Willie. But which one of us will he believe?"

"It can't be any of us," Matt said, sitting forward. "It has to be someone they don't know, someone impartial."

"Or someone they *think* is impartial," I said. "Someone who'll lie convincingly and, as you say, Matt, someone they don't know."

Willie's gaze connected with mine. "Catherine," we both said.

* * *

CYCLOPS HELD me back from stepping out of the carriage after Catherine. "I don't like involving her," he whispered.

"It doesn't matter," I whispered back. "Everyone else, including Catherine, thinks it's a marvelous idea." I took Matt's hand and allowed him to assist me down the step to the pavement.

"Don't let them see you," Matt said as he closed the door.

Cyclops had already melted into the shadows of the cabin.

Catherine clutched her reticule in both hands as we climbed the steps to the front door of the Rycrofts' townhouse. She showed the perfect amount of nervousness, not too much that it appeared false, but just enough to make her look as though she was in awe of the grand nobles she was about to meet.

"You're an excellent actress," I told her.

"I'm not acting. I'm terrified I'll ruin everything."

Matt had sent a message ahead to ensure both Lord and Lady Rycroft were at home when we called, so the butler showed us through to the drawing room upon our arrival. Tea was already waiting to be served. Lady Rycroft poured without so much as a greeting, although she did nod at both Matt and me first. She didn't give Catherine a moment's attention.

"Sit down and let's get this over with," Lord Rycroft said, checking his watch. "I have to get to my club."

"We asked for Charity to be here too," Matt said. "We'll wait for her."

Lord Rycroft sighed and sat.

"This is absurd," his wife muttered. "What can this girl possibly have to contribute to the situation?"

"We'll inform you as soon as Charity gets here," Matt said.

Lady Rycroft invited Matt and me to sit, but not Catherine. Like a dutiful maid addressing her so-called betters, she remained standing, her head bowed and hands clasped loosely in front of her. Matt refused to sit while she stood, but his uncle didn't seem to care.

Charity finally swanned in, humming out of tune, only to halt upon seeing us. "What is this? Why have you summoned me here?"

"That's what we'd like to know," Lord Rycroft said wryly.

"This is Catherine," Matt said. "She works as a maid for one of my neighbors. She has something to tell you about the day Charity met Cyclops in the stables."

Lord and Lady Rycroft exchanged glances.

"It's none of her business," Charity spat.

"I was there," Catherine said in a tremulous voice. "I witnessed what happened between you and the one-eyed giant."

Charity made a scoffing sound. "She couldn't have," she told her parents. "I saw no one."

"Let her finish," Matt said.

Catherine gulped. "I was delivering a message to our coachman in the stables next to Mr. Glass's. I was about to leave when I saw her approaching." She indicated Charity. "I could tell she was someone important so I didn't want to cross paths with her. I thought it best to let her go on her way. She seemed to know where she was going. So I stayed in the stables, out of sight."

"What happened then?" Matt asked.

"She went into your stables and approached the giant."

"Cyclops," Matt told her.

"Cyclops," she repeated. "The stables are close to my master's, and I heard every word." To Charity, she said, "You told Cyclops that you...liked him."

Lord Rycroft closed his eyes.

"This is absurd," Lady Rycroft muttered.

"I didn't say that," Charity said with a smug smile. "You weren't there. You're making it all up."

"Liked isn't the word you used," Catherine agreed. "But…I don't want to say what you said. It's not a word I've ever said in my life and I don't want to repeat it here. Please don't make me say it, Mr. Glass."

"You don't have to," he assured her. "Am I right in suggesting that the words Charity used implied she desired him?"

Catherine blushed. "In a way."

"Wanted him in a physical manner?"

"That's enough, Glass," Lord Rycroft snapped.

Catherine nodded. "It's true. She used a vulgar word."

"Another lie!" Charity cried, shooting to her feet. "You can't believe a thing she says!"

Her mother pinched her lips and her hand fluttered at her flushed throat.

"Sit down," Lord Rycroft barked. "I want to hear the rest."

"Then what happened?" Matt said to Catherine.

"I was going to walk back out of the lane but stopped outside your stables, sir, because I…I admit I was fascinated by what was happening inside. I saw the lady here trying to kiss Cyclops."

Charity shook her head. "All lies."

"He pushed her away and tried to walk off, but she blocked his exit. To get past her, he would have had to hurt her." That wasn't a line we'd rehearsed, but was a nice touch of Catherine's own invention. "Then she tried to kiss him again."

"You can't believe a word of this," Charity blurted out. "She's a filthy little sewer rat. She'll do anything for a few shillings, including lie."

"No, miss, I don't lie. My mistress is very strict about such things, and I wouldn't dare risk her anger. She didn't want me coming here at all today, but Mr. Glass insisted I had to speak up. My mistress told me I must speak the truth. And that's what this is, the whole truth of what I saw and heard that day.

You tried to kiss Cyclops, and told him you wanted more from him, and he tried to get away. He refused you and acted the gentleman the entire time."

It was precisely the words Matt had instructed her to say with just the right amount of deference. People like the Rycrofts believed in their absolute superiority over the domestic class, but they demanded honesty above all else from their staff. It was more important than efficiency, and certainly more important than being able to think for oneself. Indeed, they tended to believe maids were too stupid to form an opinion and, by extension, to lie convincingly.

"She's made it up!" Charity said, appealing to her parents.

"Be quiet," Lord Rycroft barked.

Charity flounced into the chair and folded her arms with a *humph*.

Lady Rycroft turned to Catherine. "Nothing you've said proves that you're telling us the truth. Why should we believe you?"

"Because there's one more thing," Catherine said, dipping her head to hide her blush. "Something I hoped I wouldn't have to say."

"What is it?" Matt asked. "You can tell us. Indeed, you must tell the entire truth. What else did Charity say?"

"It's not what she said, it's what she did next." Her gaze flicked to Charity then back down to the floor. "She jumped on him."

Charity's reaction gave her away. Instead of the brief second of stunned silence, she should have denied it. But she did not. She looked trapped.

Then the explosive denials spewed from her lips until her father ordered her to stop. "Enough! Charity, get out of my sight. I can't stand to look at you."

"But—"

"Go!"

Charity launched herself out of the chair and landed on

her knees in front of her mother. "Mama, please, you believe me, don't you? I'd never do such a thing. This girl is lying. She's an actress. She's doing it for money."

"Are you suggesting I'd pay someone to lie for me?" Matt asked, sounding both offended and regal at the same time.

"Mama!" Charity cried, reaching for her mother.

Lady Rycroft batted her daughter's hands away. "It's too late. You've been caught." She looked neither shocked nor repulsed by Catherine's story. Had she known all along that Charity was lying? Was her complicity in the lie her way of hurting Matt and me?

Charity sobbed. "No, no, no! You have to believe me. He—he hurt me. He wanted me. He still does."

Her father grabbed her by the arm and hauled her to her feet. He marched her to the door then pushed her through and shut it behind her. Her wails receded as she ran off.

"Why are you coming forward now, girl?" Lady Rycroft asked Catherine. "Why not earlier?"

"I didn't know there was a problem, ma'am. I don't like to meddle in the business of others. I keep myself to myself. But when our cook said she'd heard from Mr. Glass's cook that Cyclops was in trouble over the incident, I came forward and told Mrs. Glass the truth. It's not right that a good man should suffer."

Lady Rycroft put up her hand. "Spare me the sermon." To Matt, she said, "There will be no more discussion of this. Is that understood? If I hear even a whisper of it, I will see that your man is whipped."

"You won't touch him," Matt said darkly. "My wrath is far more dangerous than the law, and you won't know what form it will take. Is that clear?"

Lady Rycroft paled then nodded. Her husband blew out a measured breath.

"We agree that the incident should never be spoken about again," I said, rising. "By any of the parties."

"And Charity is not to go near Cyclops," Matt added. "If I were you, I'd keep a closer eye on her."

We saw ourselves out, only to be intercepted by Hope in the entrance hall. She rushed out of the shadows and glanced up the stairs. "I heard everything," she whispered. "What does this mean for our agreement, India?"

"I—"

"You failed to help us," Matt cut in. "The agreement is no longer valid."

"But I *intended* to help!" she said. "Is that not enough?"

"Cyclops intended to avoid your sister and look where that got him. Good day, Hope. And good luck."

She lunged at him. "Help me or I'll tell Patience you blackmailed Cox into marrying her."

My heart stopped. My scalp tingled. I tried to think of an answer that would dissuade her from the truth, but all clear thought fled.

"No one blackmailed him," Matt said, pushing past her.

"I know you did! I just don't know what leverage you used. But I will find out!"

Matt escorted me outside with Catherine a little behind, according to her so-called station as a maid. He did, however, hold the carriage door open for both of us and assisted us up the step.

"How did it go?" Cyclops asked as we drove off.

"Very well," Matt said. "You have nothing to worry about now."

Cyclops tilted his head back against the wall and closed his eyes. "Thank God."

Catherine took his hand between both of hers and smiled at him.

"You were wonderful," I told her. "You played your part perfectly."

Cyclops laid his other hand over hers. "Thank you, Catherine. I owe you so much."

"You owe me nothing," she said cheerfully. "I did it willingly and would do it again, if necessary."

He kissed her cheek and she blushed. Then they both turned away and stared out their respective windows. Their hands remained linked, however.

"What about Hope?" I asked Matt. "Are you really going to leave her to Coyle after what she just said?"

"She's bluffing. She must have guessed about the blackmail, but she'll never find out how you convinced Cox. Without that knowledge, she can't do or say anything." He gave me a reassuring smile. "We'll let her think we're doing nothing with regard to Coyle. Let her fret for a little."

"But you will talk to Coyle and try to convince him she wouldn't make a good wife, won't you?"

"We both will. I suspect he'll value your opinion above mine."

I only hoped he was right and she had no way of discovering the truth about Cox's past. If she did discover it, she wouldn't fret for long. She'd act, and there was no telling what damage she could do with the information.

* * *

LORD COYLE SENT a message the following morning inquiring if we could receive him later that day. So when Bristow announced a caller at precisely three o'clock, we thought it was his lordship.

It was, in fact, Oscar Barratt. "I'd like your permission to talk to Fabian Charbonneau," he announced as he settled into the drawing room with Matt and me.

"You don't need our permission," I said. "Fabian is a free man and can accept or refuse you himself."

"But I don't know where he is. You do."

"Why do you want to speak to him?"

"My editor wants me to write an article about Scotland

Yard's suspicion of his involvement in the murder of McGuire. There are some unanswered questions about his escape and other matters."

"He escaped by using magic," Matt said. "Are you going to write that?"

"Ah. I didn't realize. No, I can't mention magic. It's not that kind of article. However, I wouldn't mind speaking to him about it for my book."

"It's still going ahead?" I asked.

"Of course."

Bristow entered and announced Lord Coyle. His lordship hesitated in the doorway upon seeing Oscar. "Barratt," he said in greeting. "I wasn't aware you already had company, Glass."

"I was just leaving." Oscar rose, his gaze never wavering from Coyle.

Despite both being magic enthusiasts, their interests didn't align. Oscar wanted to share magic with the world, and Coyle wanted to keep it hidden for his own purposes. If Coyle found out that Oscar planned on writing a book, and Louisa was financing its printing, he'd go to great lengths to suppress it.

"There's one more thing I came here to tell you," Oscar said, puffing out his chest. "It's a personal matter, but I don't mind if Lord Coyle hears it too. It'll be in the papers very soon anyway."

"Not another article on magic," I said.

Oscar chuckled. "Not unless you consider that love is magical. I'm getting married."

"Congratulations," I said. "Do we know her?"

"Indeed you do. It's Lady Louisa Hollingbroke."

"Oh!"

He tilted his head to the side. "You no longer seem pleased."

"I'm just a little surprised," I said through my hard smile. "I didn't realize you'd become that well acquainted."

"It is sudden, but I find her intriguing. She has quite a unique perspective, and she knows her own mind, which I like."

"She's also worth a fortune," Coyle said. "Congratulations, Barratt. You're going to have your hands full with that one." He moved past Oscar.

Oscar's gaze tracked the earl's plodding progress. "I'm not marrying her for her money. I love her. We're very happy."

Lord Coyle lowered himself into a chair with a grunt.

I looked to Matt, hoping he would take the lead and tell Oscar what we knew about Louisa and her search for a magician husband. But he looked as stupefied by the news as me and remained silent.

Oscar said his goodbyes and saw himself out.

"I don't know which of them is the bigger fool," Lord Coyle said. "She only wants him for his magic, and he only wants her for her money."

"She has her charms," I said, not quite sure whether I was defending Oscar or Louisa. "She's intelligent and independent. I think he really might be in love with her. As to *her* motives…I'm quite sure you're right on that score."

Lord Coyle grunted again. "Speaking of marriage. That's why I've come to speak to you. Mrs. Glass, I wish to call in my favor."

My legs suddenly felt weak and I plopped down on the chair.

Matt stood beside me, his hand resting on my shoulder. "Go on," he said.

"I want you to encourage Hope to marry me."

I was prepared for something related to magic, something that would cross the line of morality I'd drawn for myself, or perhaps even something illegal. His request was… Well, I wasn't entirely sure what to make of it.

I certainly wasn't sure what I would do. Matt and I had agreed to use this meeting to convince Coyle that Hope wasn't a good match for him. We planned to list all her faults, the ways in which she'd manipulated us, and even tell him about her greedy parents. We wouldn't have to lie, simply show him what she was truly like.

But I forgot every word of our speech. The need to rid myself of the cloud hanging over my head in the form of Coyle's favor was strong. I could be free of him, of his influence, his menacing presence and the hold he had over me. All I had to do was say a few words to Hope.

I wouldn't be able to convince her to fall in love with Coyle, but I could try to convince her it was the right thing to do to marry him. That had been all he'd asked.

"India?" Matt prompted gently. "Do you need time to consider your answer?"

I nodded numbly.

He squeezed my shoulder. "She'll give you her answer in a week," he said to Coyle.

"Three days." Coyle hauled himself out of the chair. "No more."

* * *

"LET HER SUFFER," Willie declared. "She deserves to be married to that fat, old tyrant."

We sat in the drawing room after dinner with Willie, Cyclops, Duke and Aunt Letitia. Having told them the reason for Lord Coyle's visit, we'd been able to talk of nothing else. So far, I was the only one who couldn't decide what to do. Everyone else thought I should encourage Hope and wipe my slate clean with Lord Coyle. I wasn't sure I could do that to her. It was a decision I'd have to live with for the rest of my life.

"She won't suffer too much," Duke said. "He lives in a big house, has a big estate, mountains of money, and a title. She'd be Lady Coyle and can have parties every night if she wants."

"But he's an ogre," I said, accepting a glass of sherry from Matt.

"An ogre who can give her everything she desires," Aunt Letitia said. "Not only that, he's old and seems quite unhealthy. He'll probably only last a few more years then she can be a rich widow while still having her youth."

Willie pointed at her. "Good thinking, Letty. I reckon I could put up with him 'til then if I had to."

"They got along well at the dinner that night," Cyclops added. "She didn't hate his company."

I looked to Matt, but he simply shrugged. The only time he'd offered an opinion was when he noted that it would mean I no longer had to owe Coyle a favor, and that was all he cared about.

"Let's stop talking about them." Willie stood, glass of whiskey raised. "Let's celebrate Cyclops being finally free of Charity."

We all raised our glasses in a toast.

"And to Catherine for her help," Cyclops added.

"I hope you thanked her good and proper," Duke said with a smirk.

Willie snickered. "Or are you going around there later tonight to thank her?"

"Willemina!" Aunt Letitia cried. "Unlike you, Cyclops does not have the morals of a trollop."

Willie put her hand up in defense. "I've got morals on plenty of things. Like friendship and family, honor and truth. But when it comes to my body, I'm free of society's constraints."

Aunt Letitia pulled a face. "Don't mention that word in my presence. It's vulgar."

"Body is a bad word?"

"It is in polite society." Aunt Letitia indicated all of us. "Which this is."

"Ain't nothing polite about them two." She pointed at Cyclops and Duke.

"It's an English thing," I told her.

"Nope. It ain't. If it were, Brockwell wouldn't want to see my body and—"

"Don't!" Matt cried. "I don't want to hear it."

Duke downed the remaining contents of his glass and got up. "I need another to drown out the image."

Willie chuckled and held out her empty glass. "Me too, please."

* * *

TWO DAYS LATER, I still hadn't decided what to do about Hope. Every time I thought I'd made up my mind, I changed it again. Working on my watch and the black marble clock didn't help as I'd hoped. Everyone continued to advise me to do as Coyle asked and encourage Hope. Everyone except Matt. Since his one and only comment on the matter, he'd left the decision up to me. It was maddening.

"You look like you need some fresh air," Matt said, perching on the edge of the table in the library where I was working. He picked up a tiny cog and held it to the light coming through the window. "You've been tinkering with this clock most of the day."

"It's supposed to clear my mind and allow me to have a better insight into my problems. But this problem won't be easily resolved. My head is telling me to encourage Hope in Coyle's direction, but my heart is telling me I can't do that to a young woman. No matter what she has done to us, she ought to be free to make her own decision about who she spends her life with."

He put down the spring and touched my chin. A smile ghosted his lips and warmed his eyes. "That's one of the reasons I love you. Your heart is kind."

I stood and circled my arms around his neck. He settled his hands on my hips, a hopeful look replacing the warm one in his eyes. "Perhaps it'll help me think if you kiss me," I said.

His smile spread. "That's strange because my mind goes completely blank when we kiss. Well, not completely blank. It does become more aware of you."

"Are you being vulgar and talking about my body?" I teased.

He pressed his smile to mine. "There's nothing vulgar about it. I love every curve, every dimple."

The movement at the door had us springing apart. Bristow cleared his throat.

"A letter arrived for you, Mrs. Glass. It's marked as urgent."

I checked the sender's name and my heart thudded to a halt. "It's from Lord Cox." I looked up at Matt. "Patience's husband. What can he possibly want?"

He read over my shoulder. He was so close that I heard his breath hitch as he read, and felt the quickening of his pulse. It matched mine.

"Oh god," I whispered. "He's blaming me."

The scrawl was tight, small and barely legible. It seemed to have been written in haste. No doubt Lord Cox was terrified. His older half-brother, who should have inherited their father's title and estate, had written to him, demanding Cox relinquish what was rightfully his.

The last I'd heard, the half-brother knew nothing of his father, and certainly didn't know he should have inherited. His mother had been poor, but her marriage to the previous Lord Cox was legal, although conducted in secret. He'd committed bigamy to marry someone deemed more worthy, meaning the current Lord Cox was illegitimate.

"He thinks I told his brother," I said weakly.

"The question is, who did tell him?"

Had Hope found out and followed through with her

threat? She was clever and could have discovered the truth, but had there been enough time for her to inform the half-brother, and for him to then confront Cox, who then wrote to me? I didn't think so. That left only one possible suspect.

Coyle.

GET A FREE SHORT STORY

I wrote a short story for the Glass and Steele series that is set before THE WATCHMAKER'S DAUGHTER. Titled THE TRAITOR'S GAMBLE it features Matt and his friends in the Wild West town of Broken Creek. It contains spoilers from THE WATCHMAKER'S DAUGHTER, so you must read that first. The best part is, the short story is FREE, but only to my newsletter subscribers. So subscribe now via my website if you haven't already.

A MESSAGE FROM THE AUTHOR

I hope you enjoyed reading THE PRISONER'S KEY as much as I enjoyed writing it. As an independent author, getting the word out about my book is vital to its success, so if you liked this book please consider telling your friends and writing a review at the store where you purchased it. If you would like to be contacted when I release a new book, subscribe to my newsletter at http://cjarcher.com/contact-cj/newsletter/. You will only be contacted when I have a new book out.

ALSO BY C.J. ARCHER

SERIES WITH 2 OR MORE BOOKS

After The Rift

Glass and Steele

The Ministry of Curiosities Series

The Emily Chambers Spirit Medium Trilogy

The 1st Freak House Trilogy

The 2nd Freak House Trilogy

The 3rd Freak House Trilogy

The Assassins Guild Series

Lord Hawkesbury's Players Series

The Witchblade Chronicles

SINGLE TITLES NOT IN A SERIES

Courting His Countess

Surrender

Redemption

The Mercenary's Price

ABOUT THE AUTHOR

C.J. Archer has loved history and books for as long as she can remember and feels fortunate that she found a way to combine the two. She spent her early childhood in the dramatic beauty of outback Queensland, Australia, but now lives in suburban Melbourne with her husband, two children and a mischievous black & white cat named Coco.

Subscribe to C.J.'s newsletter through her website to be notified when she releases a new book, as well as get access to exclusive content and subscriber-only giveaways. Her website also contains up to date details on all her books: http://cjarcher.com She loves to hear from readers. You can contact her through email cj@cjarcher.com or follow her on social media to get the latest updates on her books: